THE OTHER WOMAN

BY JANE ISAAC

The DC Beth Chamberlain series

The Other Woman
For Better, For Worse

THE OTHER WOMAN

Jane Isaac

An Aria Book

This edition first published in the United Kingdom in 2020 by Aria, an imprint of Head of Zeus Ltd

A CIP catalogue record for this book is available from the British Library.

ISBN (P) 9781035905263
ISBN (E) 9781838933678

Cover design: Charlotte Abrams-Simpson

Typeset by Silicon Chips

Aria
c/o Head of Zeus
First Floor East
5–8 Hardwick Street
London EC1R 4RG

www.ariafiction.com

Printed and bound by CPI Group (UK) Ltd, Croydon, CR0 4YY

To Derek and Sarah

Prologue

The moments before death were not at all how she imagined them to be. No images, carved from the recesses of her memory, flashed before her. No celebrated successes or missed opportunities. Instead, an overwhelming fear beat a tune beneath her skin, faster and faster, picking up momentum, immobilising her organs, one by one.

Were they out there? She risked a fleeting glance at the window. She couldn't see them, hadn't heard the soft thrum of their engines in the distance, or felt their clandestine footfalls as they crept around the perimeter of the house. But there were children inside, they would be discreet.

She willed them to be out there. Trussed up in bulletproof vests. Semi-automatics clutched to their chests. Hell, they should have evacuated the neighbouring houses by now. Cordoned off the whole estate.

'Eeny, meeny, miny, mo.'

She turned back to the room, just in time to stare down the barrel of the Glock. And froze.

A tremor ran through the sofa as a knee juddered a staccato beat beside her.

Their captor repeated the rhyme, moving the gun down the line, from child to adult, child to adult. A cat playing with his prey. A pernicious smile tickling his lips.

Please be out there. Eventually they'd make some contact, attempt to negotiate a deal. Wouldn't they?

The knocking knee squirmed beside her, sending a trail of urine down its calf. She swallowed, the heat of the bodies squeezed beside her on the sofa failing to suppress the chill of raw ice in her chest. Two adults, two children. To kill an adult was gruesome enough. But a child? That was pure evil.

The urine crept forwards, a languid line on the polished flooring.

Wasn't this where self-preservation was supposed to kick in? That animal instinct, sewn into living genes from the dawn of time. They'd tried screaming, reasoning, pleading, even begging. To no avail. The face opposite was calm and still. And now the fight was fading from her bones, numbing the fear biting at every sensory receptor.

The breeze picked up, a sudden gust whistling through the trees out front. The sound cut her breaths. Even if the surrounding pavements weren't deserted, the house was set so far back from the road that nobody would have heard their screams, their pleading. This wasn't the movies. No one was out there. There would be no heroic rescue.

The Glock snapped as it was racked up. Her stomach curdled as she watched the face of death stretch and curve. Listened to the words drip from his mouth.

'Right. Let's begin, shall we?'

I

Seven days earlier

Residents of Collingtree Park were just taking their waking breaths when the roar of a motorbike broke their Sunday morning reverie.

At high speed, the rider took the bends effortlessly, radiating a cool calmness in dark leathers. He passed houses with curtains drawn tightly, manicured lawns, driveways adorned with estate cars and people-carriers screaming out for their weekend wash.

Exhaust fumes dispersed into an air thick from a sun already flexing its muscles, reigning supreme in the clear blue sky. Summer was in full swing, the recent heatwave showing no signs of abating. In a few hours, paddling pools would be refilled in back gardens, the sound of children's shrieks and laughter filling the area.

At precisely 7.05 a.m., Cameron Swift emerged from number sixteen Meadowbrook Close, pulling the door to a gentle close behind him.

The bike dropped a gear, rounded the lip of the close, and pulled up the incline.

Cameron was loading his golf bag into the boot of his Mercedes when the motorcyclist swerved and stopped a couple of yards from the end of his driveway. The rider tipped his head to attract Cameron's attention. An intimate gesture, as if this rendezvous was expected, had been arranged for weeks.

Cameron frowned, checked his watch, and looked back at the house. For a split second, he considered calling for Monika, but she wouldn't welcome the interruption to her early morning slumber, especially if it woke the baby. He sighed and started down the driveway, step by curious step, then paused at the kerb, angling his head to see the face through the tinted visor.

Their gazes locked. 'Can I help you?' he said.

The motorcyclist ignored the question, unzipped his jacket and reached inside.

At the sight of the gun, Cameron's eyes widened. He swallowed, shook his head. Opened his mouth and closed it again. Arms flailed out as he made to turn. Not quickly enough. His body jolted with each impact, sending sprays of red leaping into the air before he folded to the ground. Ribbons of blood curled and coiled on the tarmac.

The motorcyclist replaced the gun in his jacket and pulled out his mobile phone. He switched to camera, clicked three times, then slipped the phone back in his pocket, revved the engine and sped off down the street.

2

Beth was awoken by the incessant jangle of her mobile phone trilling an unfamiliar tune. She stirred slowly, took a deep breath, stared at the red digits winking at her from her alarm clock and jerked forwards.

'Damn!'

By the time she'd jumped out of bed and rushed along the landing into the room next door, Lily was sitting up in bed, rubbing the heels of her hands into her eyes. Beth stroked her niece's back gently. 'Time to wake up, darling. It's almost eight-thirty.'

The seven-year-old pushed a tangle of blonde hair out of her eyes and groaned. 'We're late.'

'No, we're not. We've still got fifteen minutes before your mum gets here.'

'But my swimming gala. I'm supposed to eat at least an hour before. Coach Walters said so!'

'Okay, you get yourself up and dressed, and I'll fix you some cornflakes. They'll have had plenty of time to go down before you get in the pool.'

Beth ignored the discordant gripes and groans that followed her along the landing. Back in her bedroom, she checked her phone and heaved a sigh. Lily had changed the ringtone and the missed call was from the control room – never a good omen on a Sunday morning.

She dialled back, tapping her foot with each ring.

'Inspector Tess Gleeson.'

'Morning, ma'am. It's DC Beth Chamberlain.' Beth balanced the phone between her chin and neck and tied back her dark hair into a half ponytail. 'I have a missed call.'

A second's pause. A paper rustled in the background. 'Ah, yes. Thanks for calling back, Beth. There's been a shooting in the western district. Collingtree Park. We're pulling in detectives for a homicide team. Need you here as soon as.'

'Okay, I could be with you in about forty-five minutes,' Beth said, padding across to her wardrobe, searching for something that looked vaguely ironed.

'Make it half an hour if you can. The DCI's already at the scene. He'll be on his way back shortly.'

The line cut. Beth switched her phone to radio, hoping to catch the news bulletin, and chucked it on the bed. A shooting would attract press attention quickly; it would be interesting to hear the early reports. But instead of a clipped newsreader, the voice of Robbie Williams filled the room, although she couldn't place the song. She grabbed a white, fitted shirt and a pair of black trousers, turning the scant information over in her mind as she breathed in to zip up her size twelves.

Northamptonshire was a sprawling county that expanded in the mid-1980s to attract London overspill and was now made up of several small towns, surrounded by rolling countryside and picturesque villages. Sandstone cottages, ancient churches, and country houses were dotted around the area, attracting a number of tourists in the summer months, but nothing to rival the likes of nearby Warwickshire or the Cotswolds. Situated in the heart of the Midlands, and only an hour from London, it was better known for its distribution centres and manufacturing plants. The crime figures were relatively low and mainly acquisitive – shoplifting, burglary, theft – with the odd murder which was usually domestic-related or a drugs feud. Shootings were rare. But it was the location that really caught her. The salubrious Collingtree Park estate was located close to junction fifteen of the motorway and encircled the private golf club nearby. She'd looked at houses there several years back, more in hope than expectation; there were few her police salary would stretch to. It was largely commuter land, filled with detached family homes arranged into closes and cul-de-sacs with immaculate gardens and sweeping driveways. Not the sort of place accustomed to a homicide on its doorstep.

The radio was still playing the same tune when she reached the kitchen. Lily was already at the table, concentrating hard as she poured herself a glass of orange juice under the watchful eye of Myrtle, Beth's grey tabby cat, curled beside her.

'You look nice,' she said as her aunt placed a bowl of cornflakes in front of her.

'Thank you,' Beth said, lifting the cat off the table and placing it on the floor. 'I have to go to work, I'm afraid. Mummy will take you to the gala.' Lily's face fell. 'But I'll get her to film your race, so we can watch it together afterwards.'

The child brightened at this prospect. 'You are coming to county finals, right?'

Beth encased her in a tight hug and kissed the top of her head. 'That's not for another week,' she scoffed. 'Of course I'll be there.'

'Cameron Swift. Forty-six years old.' The chatter in the conference room hushed. Detective Chief Inspector Lee Freeman wasn't a tall man, barely five feet seven, with thinning ginger hair and an overhanging girth. He'd worked homicide as a DC in the Nineties and kept the connections as he moved through the ranks, returning when he made DCI. That, coupled with the fact he knew practically everyone on the team by their first name and was always willing to listen to the views of others, irrespective of rank, meant they were in safe hands. Recently there'd been rumours of him applying for promotion in a neighbouring force and Beth was relieved he was still with them, at least for now.

'Shot at close range at approximately 7.10 a.m. outside his home at sixteen Meadowbrook Close on the Collingtree Park estate this morning.' Freeman tapped a board beside him twice as he continued. A collection of enlarged photos of the victim's body lying on the tarmac, taken at a variety of different angles, stuck out like cold sores on the pale surface. 'Immediate neighbours claim to have heard three shots. Some of them reported hearing the sound of an engine, one of them saw a green Kawasaki leave the close soon afterwards, although nobody, so far it seems, witnessed the actual event.' He tapped the board again, the hollow sound echoing around the room. 'Needless to say, tracing that motorcyclist is our top priority at the moment.'

'Do we know what route they took to and from Meadowbrook Close?' All eyes turned to the thick Northern Irish accent at the side of the room. Sergeant Nick Geary was leaning up against a radiator, a navy A4 notebook tucked underneath his arm. He pushed a lock of dark hair out of his eyes with his free hand. 'Might dredge up some other witnesses?'

'Not yet,' Freeman responded. 'It was early on a Sunday morning. Most people were tucked up in their beds. We have started uniform on house to house and asked them to collect any CCTV footage as they work through the estate. Lots of these houses have private cameras. Shouldn't be too difficult to put it together, work out the arrival and exit, which might give us an indication of which direction they were heading from and to.'

Freeman turned back to the main room. 'So far, we only have one witness sighting of the motorcyclist: black leathers, medium build. Nobody has come forward with a number plate or any other distinguishing features about either the bike or the rider. But it's early days. We'll draw up a press appeal for witnesses, see what that churns up.' He looked back at the sergeant, indicated for him to join him. 'Nick has done some background checks on our victim.'

Nick Geary strode to the front of the room. He was taller than Freeman and sported an athletic stance. With his dark features and tailored beard, in different circumstances the two of them stood next to each other like that would have been comical. He opened the notebook. 'The victim was an asset manager, a partner at Barclay Swift in Birmingham, and a member of the golf club near his home where he occasionally played on a Sunday. He's lived at Collingtree

Park for the past three months with his Polish partner, Monika, and their two sons, Oskar and Jakub. No criminal record. No intelligence on file about either the victim or the family. None of them are known to us.' He lowered his notes. 'That's all we have so far.'

Freeman thanked him and faced the room again. 'Okay, people. Priorities. I'd like a team to visit the nearby golf course. He was dressed in golf attire. The boot of his car was open and had a bag of clubs inside. We need to find out where he was due to play this morning and who he was due to meet.

'His mobile phone was found at the scene. Let's pull his phone records, speak to his friends and family and find out who he's been associating with, both privately and professionally.' He turned to Geary. 'Get those phone records fast-tracked, will you? I want to build up a picture of his last few weeks as soon as possible.

'We also need to interview his business partner. I want to know what he's been working on recently, whether he's upset anyone.

'A POLSA search team have been despatched to comb the surrounding area and look for the missing bullets and casings. The pathologist reckons three bullets entered, two in the chest and one in the head.' He pointed out the entry points on the photographs beside him. 'Only two exit wounds, so one of the bullets is still lodged inside. We were fortunate that PC Grover was first on the scene. For those of you who don't know him, he used to work in the armed unit. He reckons the weapon was likely a 9mm handgun. One of the casings was found nearby. We need to find the others and get them to ballistics for examination.'

He took a long breath, then exhaled as he continued. 'I'm in no doubt this was a planned attack. The killer knew where the victim lived and travelled out there, armed, with the sole purpose of confronting him. Maybe they even knew he'd planned a round of golf this morning.'

'It has the hallmarks of a professional job, does it not?' Geary said. 'Two bullets to the chest, one to the head. The killer must have been quite a marksman to be accurate with a handgun, even at close range, especially with a moving target.'

Silence pervaded the room for a moment. 'What bothers me is the location,' Freeman said. 'If it was an assassination, and they took the trouble to watch him, learn his movements, they could easily have found more private places. Killing him outside his own home on a residential housing estate on a Sunday morning, when people are generally at home, was a risk. Okay, thanks, everyone. Inspector Aston is still on sick leave, so Sergeant Geary will be organising the teams and allocating tasks. We'll meet back here at 4 p.m. for the next briefing.'

Beth scratched down the last of her notes, waited until the room thinned, and then approached the board at the front to examine the photos in more detail. The body was laid on its back, the right side of his face pressed into the tarmac, less than a yard from the kerb. She flicked to the later pictures, taken after it had been moved. In between the congealed blood, she could make out the messy wound to his head where his left eye had once been.

She peered in closer, tilting her head, forcing herself to examine the photos forensically. One of the pictures was taken at a distance. The edge of a hanging basket filled with coloured petunias sat in the background. Its cosy presence against the red-brick frontage of the house beyond gave her a pang. During her nine years in the force, she'd seen many shocking sights: flesh ripped apart by knives, glass wounds, severed limbs in road traffic collisions, victims beaten to a pulp to the extent that their faces were virtually unrecognisable. Some colleagues were able to numb themselves, the years inuring them to the grotesque effects of violence, but this was something she'd never quite mastered herself.

'You okay?' Beth turned to find Freeman's eyes on her. He'd moved away from the clutches of other detectives who'd also sauntered to the front and were now in deep conversation together.

'Was that his car?' Beth pointed at a Mercedes in the background of one of the photos.

'Yes. Looks like he was disturbed on his way out.'

'So he walked past the car and down to the end of the driveway to meet his killer?'

'That's the current thinking.'

Beth chewed the side of her mouth, turning over her thoughts. Why walk to the end of the driveway to meet somebody? Why not let them come to the door? Unless, of course, you knew them or were expecting them. 'Did someone call or text him before the incident?' she asked.

Freeman narrowed his eyes. 'The last message on his phone was a text to his partner yesterday. Nothing since. Why do you ask?'

Beth was about to answer when the door of the conference room thumped the wall as it flapped back on its hinges. All eyes followed the gait of Elsie Neale, the press officer, as she marched down the room, her face tight, closely followed by Superintendent Rose Hinchin, who was adjusting her scarf, no doubt in readiness for the upcoming press conference. They stopped beside Sergeant Geary and spoke in low voices, just out of earshot. The superintendent's face turned grim. She called out to Freeman, beckoned him to join them.

Freeman held up his hand in acknowledgement, hesitated a moment and then swivelled to face Beth. 'Meet me in my office in five minutes. There's something we need to discuss before you rejoin the others.'

3

Monika sat at the kitchen table wringing a tissue over and over in her hands until it slipped through her fingers and floated to the floor. Without thinking, she adjusted Jakub, her nine-month-old baby, into a more comfortable position on her lap. From the moment she'd been helped back into the house that morning and retrieved him, wailing, from his cot, he'd clung to her torso, refusing to let go, even when she went to the toilet. At least now he'd fallen into an exhausted slumber, he was quiet for a while.

'Are you sure there isn't anyone we can call to come and sit with you?' the detective said.

She looked up at his salt and pepper hair, the cowlick that framed his face, and shook her head. What was his name? She was sure he'd introduced himself when he'd arrived that morning and prised her from Cameron's lifeless body, allowing the paramedics through as he guided her trembling frame into the house. But she couldn't for the life of her remember his name. The mug of tea he'd made her still sat on the table between them, a dark, gelatinous skin wrinkling across the top.

The sound of footfalls traipsing across the floorboards above punctuated his words. Officers in white suits arrived in droves, even before the ambulance left, and moved into her house, searching the rooms, rifling through their belongings. The detective opposite had said they were looking for clues, for some indication of who might have done this and why. 'A necessary part of the investigation', he'd assured her, encouraging the family to sit with him in the kitchen while the search took place. The sound of a chair scraping laminate flooring made her flinch. The focus now appeared to be on the room above: Cameron's study. As if the pain of cradling her partner's dead body wasn't enough, they had to endure the humiliation of strangers rummaging through their cupboards, picking through their personal effects; an officer had even been in to collect the waste bin to check the contents.

Monika stroked the forearm of Oskar, her eldest son, sat on the chair beside her. His eyes were buried in the table; the screen of the games console clutched in his hands, blank. A flashback: Cameron's smiling face, teasing Oskar, telling him he was 'the man of the house' when he was away on business trips. At twelve years old, Oskar had laughed at his whimsical jibes. Now he looked like a boulder was balanced precariously on his shoulders, clearly torn between protecting his mother, looking after the family, and not quite knowing what to do or say. A situation that manifested itself in crippling silence.

The lump in Monika's throat expanded. Cameron had woken up early that morning, as he always did when he was home on a Sunday, ready for his round of golf. She'd felt him squeeze her buttock as he slid out of bed, but feigned sleep as he crept around the bedroom, snuggling under the warm duvet while he dressed. At any moment, the baby would wake, forcing the start to her day. Anything she could do to delay that on a Sunday morning and enjoy those few extra minutes in bed was precious.

She'd felt his hot breath tickle her face as he pecked her on the nose before he tiptoed downstairs for breakfast. Still, she hadn't opened her eyes. A single tear pricked her eyelid. She hadn't laid eyes on him that morning until... Monika closed her eyes, blanking out the image of Cameron's contorted body on the tarmac, his hair slick with blood. The last time she'd seen him properly was when she'd said goodnight the evening before, leaving him downstairs to watch the end of his beloved *Game of Thrones* before he turned in. He'd looked up at her, his eyes glistening, a dimple forming in his cheek as he told her to wait up for him. But she'd fallen asleep as soon as she'd crawled under the duvet.

The detective continued with yet more questions. 'Do you know of anyone who might want to hurt Cameron? Does he have any enemies?' She shook her head to each. The words merged together, until the sound eventually became a low hum in the background.

The events earlier that morning rolled out again and again in her mind. She'd just stepped out of the shower when three cracks pierced the air. Only a few months earlier they'd lived in Birmingham, where strange sounds, the hum of the traffic, the backfire of a lorry, were commonplace. But here, when the intermittent drone of the refuse van climbing the close on collection day chimed like a church bell, they sounded unusual. Wrong. By the time she'd dried off and moved to her bedroom window, the residents of Meadowbrook Close filled the road. Hands covered mouths; shocked, taut faces looked at one another.

The open boot of Cameron's car had caught her attention. She'd barely felt the steps as she ran down the stairs and yanked open the front door, grappling with the cords of her bathrobe. Wet clumps of hair bounced on her shoulders as she'd scooted around the Mercedes and down towards the huddle, the gravel picking at her bare feet.

She'd looked past the smudges of colour clogging the road, craned her neck, desperately scanning the road for Cameron's familiar golf jumper. He'd only left minutes earlier. Couldn't have gone far.

A line of blood had trickled out from between the shoes of the throng.

Heads turned. Voices blurred into the distance. Bodies parted to form a natural funnel, exposing the crumpled mass in the road.

She closed her eyes. Blocked out the images. When she'd watched television programmes where people lost loved ones, there had been doctors and sedation. Right now, she'd give anything for a pill to switch off the world, relieve her of the pain and raw anguish scouring her insides. But sedation wasn't an option for her. She was left with a family to care for: a baby who wouldn't let her out of his sight and a twelve-year-old who clung to her side. And nobody nearby to help. No, she had to bear the pain which, right now, was growing to insurmountable levels; pressing down, suffocating her breaths.

'Do you have any family locally?' The detective angled his head. 'What can you tell us about Cameron's friends or business associates?'

The detective's pen scratched the questions on his pad as he spoke. She willed him to finish, move out of her house and take his team of officers with him.

Cameron's broken body in the road out front slipped in and out of her mind. How could that happen? Outside their family home on a quiet Sunday morning. How could somebody do that to Cameron? To all of them?

Jakub wriggled on her lap. Thankfully she'd managed to shield Cameron's bloody body from her boys, although the sight of Oskar's face when she woke him and shared the news that his stepfather had been killed would be forever branded on her brain. At least their youngest had no idea his daddy was gone. For now. A doorbell rang, wrenching her thoughts from the depths of their melee. The detective left the room, closing the door behind him. Noise. Strangers clattering about outside, constantly coming and going, talking in low voices. Her thoughts were intersected by movements and footfalls above them. She didn't want this. Right now, she wanted to gather up her family and disappear into their bubble of grief. Alone.

4

Beth made her way along an empty corridor to Freeman's office. Phones were ringing in unison as she passed the incident room. The first thirty-six hours after any homicide were crucial, the excitement palpable in the chatter of her colleagues as they prepared to receive their allocated tasks.

Freeman's office was situated at the far end, just before the lifts, a pokey room dominated by a laminate pine-effect desk with an easy chair behind it. Slats of sunshine squeezed in through thin gaps in the venetian blind. Beth could see the red bricks of Wootton Hall Police Headquarters beyond the sports field in the distance. When she'd joined the homicide and major crime team, she'd been excited about being located at headquarters and based in such an ancient building, only to find they were actually ensconced in a temporary structure at the end of its driveway, beside the dual carriageway, which wouldn't matter apart from the fact that they couldn't open the windows at the front in summer due to traffic noise.

She lifted a plastic seat off the stack in the corner and dragged it across the floor, scanning the nest of papers and files that filled the desk. Edges of papers curled on the equally messy noticeboard on the far wall. A photo of four children on a beach, each sporting wide grins, sat at an angle on the far side of the desk, precariously close to the edge. Her gaze paused on a buff file resting on the top. It looked clean and new. Unmarked. The exchange in the conference room intrigued her. The tightness of the press officer's face suggested something important: a new development maybe. She looked at the buff file again and flicked it open. It was Freeman's notes from the case so far, the investigation policy file. She stole a glance behind her and listened a moment. All was quiet. Beth retrieved the file and worked through its contents. Myriad pictures of the victim faced her, taken at various angles; copies of those she'd seen earlier. There were various spidery notes on possible strategies. She leafed through them and ran her eyes over a piece that she realised was a brief for the earlier meeting. A draft of a press release followed.

The sound of a door slamming rang out. She closed the file, sat tight. But when it wasn't followed up with footsteps she relaxed, worked back through it to a map, and a list of addresses in Birmingham that she assumed belonged to the victim's business partner or colleagues. Her mind was starting to wander now, to the taut faces in the conference room, when she turned the next page. And gasped. It was an enlarged screenshot of a Twitter post. A blood-stained photograph of the victim, sprawled beside the kerb, filled the shot, and underneath it bore the message:

Who was #CameronSwift #bbcnews #c4news #itvnews

The squeak of a footstep behind her.

Beth froze. She hadn't heard anyone coming. It was too late to even try to fold the papers back into the file, let alone replace it on the desk. She turned, her veins flooding with relief when she came face to face with Sergeant Nick Geary. 'You made me jump.'

'Not as much as Freeman would have done.' He looked down at the papers on her lap. 'What do you think you're doing, Beth?'

She shook her head. 'I was just—'

'You were going through Freeman's desk.' The atmosphere in the room tightened a notch, until his face slackened into a lopsided smile. 'Let me give you a tip. If you're going to go through a senior officer's desk, make sure you don't get caught. Now put the damn papers back before Freeman gets here.'

Beth threw him a grateful look and did her best to arrange the papers back in the file as she'd found them. She paused at the Twitter message, holding it out. 'Have you seen this?'

Nick rolled his eyes in acknowledgement. 'I'm about to brief the team on it. That's why I was looking for you.'

'Is that what the kerfuffle in the conference room was about?'

He raised a brow, nodded. 'Bloody social media. It has a lot to answer for.'

Beth looked back at the message. 'I take it we think the killer took this shot?'

'That's the premise we're working on. Somebody else could have taken it, a neighbour even, but why would they share it?'

'The evidence so far points to a personal attack. The killer singled him out, followed his movements, and knew exactly where to find him on a Sunday morning.'

'We already know that.'

'Taking a photo and posting it on social media indicates they want to send out a message, let the world know.'

Nick rested his back against the wall and folded his arms across his chest.

Beth ignored his response, working it through in her mind. 'Everything about this shows an effort to gain maximum exposure: shooting in a public place, photographing the body and not only sharing on Twitter, but tagging in some of the main news channels too. They wanted attention. The question is why?'

'That's what we need to find out.'

She placed the file back on the desk. 'The wording's odd though, isn't it? "Who was Cameron Swift?" It's an invitation to look into his life. As if there's a secret there somewhere, they want us to unravel.'

'Everything okay?' Beth felt the heat in her face as Freeman's voice filled the room.

'Yes, we were just talking about social media,' Nick said, giving Beth a knowing look. 'I've brought Beth up to speed.'

'Good.' Freeman scooted around to the other side of the desk and gave Nick a sideways glance. 'Was there something else?'

'I wondered how long Beth would be. She's needed in the incident room.'

'I'd like to have a quick word with her first,' Freeman said. 'She'll be along in a minute.' He watched Nick retreat.

'Do we know how far it's been shared?' Beth asked.

'The Twitter message? Not yet. We were alerted by one of the news channels. Our techies are checking other media, shutting down the main message, and Twitter are working with us to delete the image on the basis it's liable to hamper a live murder investigation. We do know it had already started trending though. Not a good sign.'

'I take it the sender is untraceable?'

'It's too early to say. The account was set up three months ago and has amassed hundreds of followers. Previous tweets have been nondescript, impersonal. Sharing news articles, that sort of thing. We've got our experts working on it, but anyone, it seems, can set up a Twitter account. You only need an email address. They weren't even able to confirm the location of the sender, apart from somewhere in the UK.'

'There must be a reason why they wanted to make it so public?'

'That's what we need to find out. It's ramped up the stakes though. The superintendent's been asked to prepare a statement for national news. Nothing like a grisly photograph of a dead body to gain public attention.'

Beth sat forwards. 'That could work to our benefit, sir, in the appeal. The wider the better?'

'That's one way of looking at it. Unfortunately, not everyone sees it that way. The chief constable is complaining about bad PR, cancelling all leave. He wants extra officers drafted in to work around the clock.' He swiped a hand down the front of his face. 'We're playing it down at the press conference, taking the approach that we're working closely with Twitter and other social media outlets to prevent this kind of grotesque exposure. But I suspect the damage has already been done on this one.' He sniffed, eased back into his chair and loosened his tie.

'Anyway, how are things generally with you, Beth? How's your sister – and Lily?'

'They're all right, thanks. Lily's at a swimming gala this morning.'

'How did she do?'

'Don't know yet. I'm waiting to hear.'

'County finals?'

'No, that's next week.'

'Ah. Well, I'll keep my fingers crossed for her.' His expression relaxed for a second, as if he was recalling a distant memory, before his face turned grave again. He leaned his elbows on the desk and steepled his fingers. 'How are things between you and Chris?' he asked.

The reference, out of the blue as it was, threw her. 'No change.' Beth spoke slowly, suspicion pecking at her as she wondered where the conversation was leading. She pictured Chris's tall frame in her mind – her sister Eden's ex-husband and Lily's father, a fellow police officer. There had been a messy separation four months earlier. Soon after the breakup, he'd left his job as an intelligence officer at force headquarters and applied for a position as a Digital Media Investigator, based at one of the satellite offices in the north of the county. Their paths rarely crossed these days.

'I need to make you aware that Chris has been brought in to do the techie stuff and deal with the social media companies on this operation. He'll be based here at headquarters.'

Beth frowned. 'Where's Elaine Channing?'

'Sunning herself in Tenerife and, frankly, I haven't got time to find anyone else. I hope Chris being here won't be a problem?'

Beth shrugged off the question. While she didn't relish the awkwardness of bumping into him in the corridors, or having to share office space with him, the argument with Chris was her sister's, not hers. Chris was in a niche job. His skills were worth far more to the investigation than hers right now. So, unless she fancied being transferred to a desk job in cold case for the next couple of months, to free up a detective to replace her, she was in no position to cast opinion. 'Not at all.'

'Good.' He shifted some papers around on his desk and pulled out a sheet of A4. 'I notice you've done your family liaison officer training?'

'Yes.'

'Do you think you're up to putting it into practice?'

'You want me to be the family's point of contact on this case?'

'Why not? You have to start somewhere. We'll partner you with Warren Hill. He's been a liaison officer a few years, worked on several murders and kidnappings, although nothing on this level. It would only be temporary, until we can get Andrea Leary back from region, but it'll give you a chance to test out your skills at the beginning of an investigation. What do you think?'

The rush of excitement almost knocked her sideways. 'Sure.'

'This is a high-profile case, Beth. The media will be all over it. You'll need to steer them away from the family as much as possible, let us control the feed of information from here. It'll mean long hours too, certainly for the first few days, and lots of note-taking. Are you sure you can manage this? If you want me to find someone else, I need to know now.'

'It won't be a problem.'

'Excellent.' He sat back, satisfaction spreading across his face. 'Warren is already at the scene. Get over there and introduce yourself to the family. It's all about building up a rapport and establishing a victimology profile – working out the family set-up, who their friends are and who they associated with. You've got my mobile number.' He held up his phone. 'Keep in touch.'

Beth thanked him and turned to leave. She was at the door when his words called her back. 'Are you sure you're up to this?'

'Of course.' She gave him a reassuring smile. 'I won't let you down.'

'Right. Your first task is to inform them about the Twitter message. I want them told by us before they see or hear anything from elsewhere.'

5

DC Warren Hill greeted Beth at the door with a warm smile. 'Nice to see you again, Beth,' he said in a low voice. 'You're looking well.'

'Not as well as you.' He didn't look a day over forty, even though, a late joiner in the force, he was easily pushing fifty. All those hours spent training for triathlons clearly paid off. Beth pushed a stray strand of dark hair out of her face, feeling self-conscious; she couldn't remember when she'd last donned her running shoes.

'What time did you get here?' she asked, as he stood aside for her to enter.

'A few hours ago. I only live a mile or so away, in Hunsbury. Freeman sent me straight here. I've received updates on my phone since.'

Beth's heart warmed. She'd worked with Warren on an auto-crime operation several years back when she was still in CID, an appointment that caused great hilarity in the office as Warren had a reputation for bumping and scraping cars and was serving a ban from the station pool cars at the time. But he was so easy-going he didn't mind being the butt of the jokes. Driving aside, he was a solid detective with common sense, good instinct, and enthusiasm in abundance.

Not like some of the cynics she'd worked with back on shift in her early days.

'How's it going?' She slipped off her jacket, hung it over her arm. Sooner or later, she would need to fill him in on the morning briefing. But first they needed to establish their priorities, and obtaining as much information from the family, so the incident room team could build up a profile of their victim, was all important.

He gave her a knowing look. 'The partner and two sons are in the kitchen. They're like bunnies caught in headlights. All I've managed to get so far are a few friends' details and a couple of recent photos of the victim from her phone for the press release.'

Beth's shoes squeaked on the polished oak flooring as she followed him past a curved staircase and an oversized weeping fig plant, and into a spacious kitchen fitted with pine high and low-level cupboards. In the far corner, a dark-haired lady sat at a table with a child fast asleep on her lap. The woman's hair was pulled back into a messy bun, exposing an attractive heart-shaped face, despite the sallow complexion and dark smudges beneath the eyes. A boy with the same dark hair sprouting around his crown sat beside her. He eyed Beth warily as she approached.

Beth nodded at them and introduced herself. 'I see you've already met Warren.' She gestured to her colleague. 'We're going to be your family liaison officers. We will be spending time with you over the next few days, to update you on the investigation and support you as much as we can at this difficult time.' Two pairs of eyes stared back at her, their flat gazes a contrast to the baby sleeping peacefully on his mother's lap. During her nine-year career in the police,

Beth had dealt with death in all its murkiest elements and spending time with families in their darkest hours never served to numb the raw humanity of the situation.

She cast her eyes over Warren's sparse notes. He'd covered the basic questions: family, friends nearby, any concerns for her late husband's welfare, but there were bare lines beneath many of them. Either they weren't prepared to answer, or they couldn't, and she suspected it was the latter.

The social media message pressed on her mind, along with Freeman's request. She had to break the news to them soon but right now they'd suffered enough. The screen of the games console was blank. She could see no other devices within reach. Time was on her side, while they were kept in there. For now, anyway.

'It's Monika, isn't it?' Beth cocked her head in an effort to make eye contact. 'And Oskar?' she said to the young boy beside his mother.

Monika looked up. Hollow eyes hooked hers.

'Have you seen a doctor?' Beth asked. 'We can arrange for that if you think it would help?'

Monika closed her eyes and gave a single head shake.

'Okay. But please don't hesitate to ask if you need help. For the children too. That's what we're here for. Let's get you another tea.' Beth removed the mugs from the table and busied herself with washing them up, searching through the cupboards for teabags and making drinks. Heaping spoonfuls of sugar into each mug in an effort to alleviate the shock. She was just resting them down on the table when a thump came from above. The baby jumped and fidgeted a moment before he settled back down. 'I'm so sorry,' Beth said. 'Is there somebody you could stay with? You know, for a while? It might be easier for all of you.'

Monika shook her head.

'What about family?'

'They're back home.'

'Which is?'

'Olsztyn, northern Poland.'

'I see. That must be difficult.' She slid into a seat beside Warren. 'What about Cameron's family?'

Another head shake. 'Cameron doesn't have any family. Not that he is in touch with.'

Beth exchanged a quick glance with Warren. Cameron's family would be routinely looked into, a prerequisite of the investigation. The fact that he might have family members he was estranged from could be significant. Had he upset somebody? Enough to play a part in his murder?

'A neighbour maybe,' Beth persisted, 'or a friend. We'd be happy to—'

'No.'

Beth took a deep breath and decided to change tack. 'Has Cameron ever ridden a motorbike?' she asked gently.

'I don't think so.'

'Does he have any friends or associates with bikes? Perhaps someone that has visited him here before?'

'No.'

She chewed the side of her thumb and for the first time Beth noticed her nails, bitten to the quick. Every finger, even her thumbs like cigarette stubs. Her clothes – a loose T-shirt and jeans – were casual but bore the cut and logo of branded goods, and she looked like the kind of woman who usually took care of herself. Which made her nails incongruous with the rest of her.

Warren caught her eye, held it a moment. He'd seen them too.

A crash above was followed by a rumble of thuds and a tremor that rattled through the house. The baby pulled his head back this time and let out a huge wail.

Beth scowled at the ceiling. 'Excuse me,' she said.

6

Beth closed the kitchen door behind her, exchanged pleasantries with the detective carrying a PC tower down the stairs and stood aside for him to pass. The staircase twisted as she rose, opening out onto a wide landing at the top. Cream linen drapes hung over two opposing windows at the front and the back of the house, giving it a light and airy feel.

She paused beside the study entrance. 'Who's making all the racket then?' she said.

A red-faced Brian, from the homicide team, responded with a sheepish grin. A broth of a man at six feet six, he was crouched on the carpet lifting manila files and papers back into a drawer that appeared to have fallen out of the cabinet beside him – the source of the bang. Brian was known as 'leave it' back at the station. He couldn't be gentle if he tried.

She recognised another colleague, Pete, sat at a Georgian-style desk, carefully recording a line of evidence bags and their contents into a book. 'How's it going, Beth?' he said. 'Are you on this one too?'

'I think everyone's on it. I'm doing the family liaison stuff, working with Warren.'

'Lucky you.' Pete's latex gloves squeaked against the shiny surface as he pushed an evidence bag to the side.

'Anything of interest?'

'Difficult to say as yet. It's all papers, disks, and memory sticks. It'll take us a while to work through this lot.'

'What about the rest of the house?'

'We're pretty much done there. Nothing of any immediate significance.'

She looked past him out of a window that overlooked a long garden, laid mostly to lawn. An oversized trampoline sat in the far corner. Beside it was a generous block paved patio dotted with colourful pot plants. The manicured grass of the golf course stretched out beyond. 'Okay. Well, keep the noise down, will you? It's disturbing the baby.'

They both nodded and turned back to their work.

Doors hung open to the other rooms upstairs. She peered into a room painted purple with posters of Gothic bands on the walls. A drum kit was set up in the corner, an acoustic guitar resting against the wall beside. Sunlight streamed into the next couple of rooms which looked unnaturally tidy, as if they'd been prepared for a magazine shoot. A cot, with a baby mobile of stars hanging above and a blanket folded back, was visible on the other side of the landing. She paused outside a large bedroom at the front. The curtains were hanging free from their tie-backs and flapping in the light breeze.

Beth wandered into the room and approached the window. It looked out onto the driveway and the street beyond. One of the wardrobe doors was open, exposing a line of men's shirts, suits, ties, and a messy rack of shoes at the bottom. She imagined Cameron waking that morning, creeping around to get ready for his early round of golf, closing the front door gently behind him so as not to disturb his sleeping family. The boot door of the Mercedes still sat vertical on the drive, a wide-open mouth, decorated by a cluster of coloured forensic markers.

Across the road, the eyes of a family were glued to the screens erected around the crime scene as an officer guided them past, the parents protectively cradling the shoulders of their little ones. The body was gone, already in the morgue, but splashes of blood still coloured the surrounding road. They needed to wait until the CSIs finished before they could sluice down the area. The family moved on, smudges of colour in the distance now. The people of Meadowbrook Close would have to walk their children down a controlled route, over the front gardens opposite, and shuffle through the media frenzy outside the cordon at the bottom: reporters with microphones, jostling shoulders with their photographers, keen to grab a quote or a picture, anything that would give them an original angle for a news piece.

As she reached the bottom of the stairs, Beth could hear Warren's West Country lilt seep through the gaps around the closed door to the kitchen. Part of her felt inclined to join him. They were chasing the clock; Freeman was relying on them to help build up the family profile of the victim. Although, by the state of the family, she suspected they weren't going to get much out of them that morning, or for the rest of the day for that matter.

Instead, she felt the need to get to know the family better so she turned on her heel. The doors to most of the rooms downstairs sat ajar. She glanced into a downstairs washroom, the gold fittings dazzling in the midday sunshine; a playroom, filled with a colourful array of soft toys, games, and building blocks stacked neatly beside each other; a dining room that looked barely used. The front room, directly beneath the master bedroom, contained two large sofas with bright cushions squished into the backs, arranged around a wood burner. The screen of the television wouldn't have been out of place in a small arena. She sauntered in and paused beside a latticed bay window that overlooked the road. The view of the operation out front was greater here, like a scene from a crime drama on television. Officers in white coveralls crawled around nearby gardens doing a fingertip search. Others swept metal detectors over the ground, searching for the remaining bullets and shells. A white and blue police tent had been erected, just inside the screens, over the area where the victim's body once lay: the signs of death lingering in abundance and she was thankful Warren had taken the family into the kitchen at the back of the house, away from these stark reminders.

She tried to work through the evidence so far. They didn't yet know the route the attacker had taken into the estate. Meadowbrook Close was a cul-de-sac. One way in, one way out. A risky move for any attacker, increasing the chance of being cornered if something went wrong. The incident indicated the killer knew where Cameron lived and his movements, suggesting someone close to him. But their determination to attack in such a public place, and share news of it so widely, was perplexing. She tried to ponder the killer's mindset, put herself in their shoes. They weren't content with killing him, they wanted to soil his lasting memory. But why?

A school photograph of Oskar sat above the fireplace alongside several baby photos of Jakub, taken at various stages of growth. She bent down and peered at the family portrait on the sideboard. The fixed wide grins, arms hooked around each other, indicated a close-knit family. Her eyes lingered on Cameron. He was a handsome man, with a square jaw, a wide smile. A smile they'd never see again.

She was stuck, freeze-framed, the question marks over the killer's actions taunting her until the buzz of her mobile pulled her from her thoughts. 'Freeman' flashed up on the screen as she dragged it out of her pocket.

'Sir?'

'How is it going there, Beth?'

'Okay. The family is in deep shock. Naturally. Warren's got a list of immediate friends, but we've not been able to build up much in terms of a family network yet. Monika said her family are in northern Poland; there's nobody nearby. According to her, Cameron wasn't in touch with his side. Might be significant?'

'All right, thanks. See if you can press her further. And get that list of friends and associates sent over as soon as possible. Can you persuade her to leave the house?'

'It's not looking good. I've already suggested it. She's digging her heels in at the moment.'

'Try again, will you?'

'Do you think they are at risk?'

'It doesn't look that way at the moment, but of course we can't be completely sure. If nothing else, it'll be easier to complete the searches without them there. See if you can get them out. As soon as possible.'

★

Beth pocketed her phone, stepped out of the front room, and almost collided with Oskar in the hallway. He gave her a look that made her feel a bit like a naughty schoolgirl, snooping around their home, and pointed to the washroom. She moved aside for him to pass.

Back in the kitchen, Monika was cradling the baby, feeding him a bottle of juice.

'Somebody's thirsty,' Beth said.

The baby coughed slightly and Monika rubbed his back. His eyes widened as he jolted and belched. Beth smiled. 'How old is he?' she asked, even though she already knew. She'd studied the names and ages of the family before leaving the station.

'Nearly nine months.' Monika's voice was barely a whisper.

'My niece was really windy until she was two,' Beth said.

Monika jerked her head back, as if she couldn't imagine the detective around children, and placed the bottle back in the baby's mouth. Warren's phone rang and he stepped into the garden, shutting the door behind him.

'There is something I need to talk to you about,' Beth said, glancing towards the hallway door, 'before your son comes back.'

Monika looked up, her eyes suddenly alight with expectation. 'You've got some news?'

The optimism in her face pinched at Beth. This wasn't good news, and sharing these sordid details meant shovelling more grief onto a pile that was already brimming. 'No, not yet. But...' she hesitated a moment, not quite sure of how to word it. 'There is an image of your husband online, taken after the attack.'

'What are you saying? Did somebody film what happened?'

'Not exactly. A photograph was taken and uploaded onto Twitter.'

Monika's mouth fell open as she gasped.

'We shut it down as soon as we were alerted to it,' Beth assured. 'But it had already been shared a number of times. Our technical team are working to remove all shares of the image online, but it is still possible you or your son—'

'Oh my God.' A mixture of disbelief and confusion coloured Monika's face. 'Who would do something like that?'

'We don't know at the moment. But we are doing everything in our power to find out who is responsible.' Monika was still for a moment. She looked like she was about to faint. The baby finished the juice, pushed the teat out of his mouth and started playing with the button on his mother's cardigan, oblivious. 'I'm so sorry.' The words were inadequate, and Beth knew it. Monika had lost her partner, her soulmate, the father of her baby, in the worst possible circumstances. A murder investigation allowed little room for privacy, but pictures of the victim's body were usually the one exception. Now even that sacred area had been violated.

For a minute, the sound of the footsteps trampling around above them filled the room. 'I can talk to Oskar myself if you want?' Beth continued.

Monika's face twisted as she struggled to take it all in. 'No. I'll speak with him.' She was breathless, the words almost too unbearable to utter.

'We'll need your consent to examine your social media, if that's okay?'

'I only have Facebook. To keep in touch with my family back home.'

'What about Cameron?'

'He didn't do social media. He said it gave out mixed messages. He didn't believe in it.'

'What about for his work?'

'No. He avoided it at all costs. Wouldn't even have his photograph posted on the company web page.'

The sound of a door handle snapping back on itself crashed into their conversation. Beth lowered her voice. 'What about your son, Oskar?'

'I'll have to talk to him. He's only twelve. He doesn't have a Twitter or Facebook account. I don't know about the others.' At that moment Oskar walked back into the room and eyed them all, as if he knew they'd been talking about him.

'Could you write down the details for me?'

Monika scratched the login details for her Facebook account on the piece of paper Beth passed to her, slid it back across the table and stood. 'Is my bedroom clear?' she asked.

'The room upstairs at the front?' Beth checked.

Monika nodded.

'Yes.'

'I need to change the baby.' She placed the bottle on the table and left the room with Oskar on her tail.

7

It was late evening when Monika and Oskar reappeared. The low sun smeared the sky with crimson and coral dashes, presenting a dazzling display through the kitchen window. Monika's hair hung loose and clumped on her shoulders. They looked like they'd fallen asleep in the bedroom together.

Beth snapped her laptop shut as they entered. After feeding back the social media details to the station earlier, she had written up her notes and then switched to Facebook and viewed Monika's account, noting down associations, looking for anything untoward. The history would be scrutinised in detail by experts, but she was hoping for references to Cameron. Some indication of their recent movements, family days out perhaps. Instead she was greeted with 'before and after' photos of the house redecoration, comments about the weather, and pictures of the baby. At least she'd found no trace of the macabre image shared of Cameron's corpse on Monika's timeline.

Monika looked around the room suspiciously.

'Warren's left for the evening,' Beth said, guessing her thoughts. 'But I can stay here for as long as you need me to.' What she didn't add was that he was attending the evening briefing. One of them needed to be there and since he'd missed out that morning, it seemed only fair Warren made this one. She expected her inbox to ping with a lengthy email later. Warren might not be very adept behind a wheel, but if past experience was anything to go by, his reports were nothing if not detailed.

Jakub chewed his fist. 'I need to give him his bedtime bottle,' Monika said.

'Of course.' Beth stood aside. 'Why don't I make you something to eat? I saw some cheese in the fridge.' Monika looked at Oskar who shrugged a single shoulder.

Beth busied herself with making sandwiches from the bread she'd found in the breadbin earlier then placed them on the table along with fresh drinks. The weight of Freeman's request for more information on the family sat on her mind. The first twenty-four hours of any investigation were tense; it was a race to identify and eliminate associations, narrow down potential suspects. And that included everyone known to the victim. The tricky part was to balance the needs of loved ones with the demands of the case. She needed to keep it light, extract information without distressing the family unduly. Go in too heavy and they shut down.

'Would it be okay to ask some more questions?' she asked casually as she settled herself into the chair opposite.

Oskar grabbed a sandwich and tucked in. Monika rocked the baby, who was clearly more interested in looking around him than feeding from his bottle. When Beth opened her notebook, Monika eyed her warily.

'Don't worry about the notes,' Beth said in her most reassuring voice. 'It helps us to keep a record and ensures we address all your questions.' She clicked the end of her pen. 'What can you tell me about Cameron's family?'

'Not much.' A weary husk coated Monika's voice. 'His parents died before I met him. He talked about a brother a few times. I think his name is David. He lives in Canada.'

'Do you have an address for him?'

'No. They weren't in contact anymore. I never met him.'

'Oh. Do you know why?'

Monika shook her head, placed the bottle on the table and bounced the baby on her knee. He squeaked in delight, clearly more enamoured with playing games than settling down for the evening. 'No. Cameron didn't like to talk about it.'

Oskar, who'd now eaten two sandwiches, wiped his mouth with the back of his hand and asked if he could go to his bedroom. After a tentative glance at Beth, his mother agreed. His footsteps on the stairs were soon replaced by the gentle thud of music, drowning out the scraping above.

'How has Cameron been recently?' Beth asked.

Monika looked slightly taken aback by the question. 'Okay. Same as normal.'

'What about yesterday?'

'Fine. He didn't get back until late afternoon. He travelled a lot with his work.'

'What did you do yesterday evening?'

'We ate dinner together. He put Jakub to bed, then played on the Xbox with Oskar. Later we watched television. The usual family stuff.'

'Does he often work on a Saturday?'

'Sometimes. His work involves lots of social events: golf, dinners, that sort of thing. He travels all over the UK.'

'And where was he travelling back from yesterday?'

She lifted her shoulder, let it drop. 'I'm not sure, somewhere in Yorkshire I believe. His work would probably be able to tell you.'

Beth narrowed her eyes. 'You don't know exactly?'

'He didn't talk about his work, said he came home to relax. On odd occasions, if he had to work at home, he used the study upstairs.'

'When was Cameron last at home, before Saturday?'

'Err, Tuesday evening. But I spoke to him on the phone daily. He always called in the evenings to check on the children when he was away.'

'And before that?' Monika stared at her, unspeaking. 'We need to build up a profile of Cameron, his movements over the last few weeks,' Beth explained. 'Anything you can tell us will help.' Monika stood and retrieved a calendar from the wall nearby and they worked back through the dates that Cameron had been home. Beth jotted down the details as they went along. 'You mentioned social events,' Beth said as they finished up. 'Did you ever go to any of them?'

'I went to a dinner once, with his colleagues. It was when we were living in Birmingham, before Jakub was born.' She wrinkled her nose. 'They were nice enough, but all they did was talk about finance and investments. It wasn't my scene.'

'What about his clients?'

'I never met them.'

'Did Cameron talk about any of them?'

'He moaned occasionally, if someone was getting on his nerves or he'd lost a client. He never mentioned names though.'

Beth reached down and retrieved her iPad from her case.

'What about work colleagues, friends, people he played golf with?' she asked as she logged in. Monika closed her eyes and pressed a hand to her brow. She was beginning to wane. 'Look, I know this is difficult,' Beth continued. 'But any assistance you can give us now will help to speed up the investigation.'

'I gave some names to the detective this morning.'

The effects of shock often caused gaps in people's memories. It was common practice to track back and check information to ensure they weren't missing anything. Beth gave her most encouraging smile. 'You did, and we're very grateful. I'm just wondering if there was anyone you might have missed, especially anyone who Cameron might have been in contact with over the last month or so?'

Monika gave a resigned sigh and started to list names. She paused a few times, searching for the right combinations, expanded only when Beth asked for more information. The baby reached out and fingered some of the sandwich crumbs on the table. At the mention of Oskar's father, Beth raised her eyes.

'Does Oskar see him often?' she asked.

'Not really. He moved back to Poland about five years ago. He was an engineer in Poland, but because his English wasn't good, he had to do agency work when we first came here. He struggled to learn the language to a sufficient standard, got disillusioned, and in the end decided to go home. He phones occasionally, generally around birthdays and Christmas. I send school photos.' She reeled off the address.

'Does he visit?'

'He visited once after he left, when we were living in

Birmingham. Cameron, Oskar, and him played on the Xbox. I've talked to Oskar about going over there, but he doesn't seem interested.'

'So it was an amicable split then?'

She gave a single nod. 'We weren't married. He still pays maintenance for Oskar.'

Beth added a quick message, clicked a couple of keys and emailed the details to Freeman. When she looked up, the woman before her appeared to shrink, a deflated balloon. 'Is there anything else I can do to help?' Beth said softly.

The baby squirmed restlessly on his mother's lap. 'The television in the front room.' She choked out the ailing words. 'He watches it before he goes to bed. It soothes him.'

A rerun of the family being guided down the close earlier flew into Beth's mind. Alarmed faces drawn to the police operation. She hesitated a split second, and then led the way out of the kitchen, feeling the heat of Monika's eyes on her as they reached the front room and she closed the curtains, even though it was still light outside.

'How much longer are they going to be out there?' Monika asked.

'The searches will take a while, I'm afraid. We need to be thorough. Are you sure there isn't someone you could stay with until they are over? Might be easier for the children,' Beth said, sitting on the sofa beside her.

'Jakub is happier at home.'

'We would feel more comfortable if you moved out. It wouldn't be for long. We could arrange a hotel room.'

Monika switched on the television, selected a children's channel and placed the baby at her feet. The sound of the coloured creatures that filled the screen, chatting to each other in high-pitched voices, grabbed his attention. 'Are we in danger here?' she said turning to face Beth.

'We have no reason to think that. But the manner in which Cameron died does give us cause for concern. There is a possibility his attacker may return or be looking for something. We would feel much easier if you'd all stay elsewhere, until we are aware of what we are dealing with. We could help to make the move as smooth as possible. It would only be temporary.' Monika was still for a moment, eyes fixed in a trance-like state. Beth took a deep breath, keen to press on, to take advantage of the momentum she'd built, but just then the baby turned to his mother, grunted, and pointed at a wooden rocking horse in the corner.

His mother's face softened. She carried him across the room and placed him on the rocking horse, gently supporting his back as it swayed back and forth. He looked up at his mother, gave her a watery smile. Nobody spoke for several minutes until she lifted him off and he nuzzled into her chest.

She jutted up her chin. 'We're not going anywhere,' she said. 'Jakub needs his routine. He needs his toys around him.'

'I'm sure we could—'

'No. What we need are for the strangers clattering about upstairs to leave.' She pulled back the curtain a moment. When she turned to Beth, her eyes were hard. 'No one's coming back here with all those officers outside.'

'Would you like me to stay over?' Beth asked.

'There's no need. I'm going to put Jakub to bed. When I come down, I want those officers upstairs out of my house, for tonight at least.'

8

Monika scooped up the baby and left the room before the burgeoning tears escaped and spilled down her face. She couldn't inflict a strange hotel room on her boys, especially after everything that had happened. She wouldn't. They'd just lost their father. Home was their one sense of normality, their one connection with his memory.

At the top of the stairs an officer waited for her to pass. An array of plastic bags curled over the top of the cardboard box he was carrying, although he was much taller than her and it was impossible to see what was inside them. Her stomach flipped. She quickened her step. The beat of Oskar's music thudded louder as she opened his bedroom door. He was spread-eagled across his bed, staring at the ceiling. He sat up and pressed a button on the iPad beside him. The volume sank to a whisper. When she bid him goodnight, he asked if she was all right, her nod signalling him to rest back against his pillows. Should she take him into her bedroom? Probably not. He was almost a teenager. They'd spent all day together, and Oskar was the last person who'd want to be coddled by his mother. He'd always been an independent child, preferring to work things out for himself. He needed time alone with his music. Time to piece together his thoughts.

As Monika closed the door to her own room, a voice outside pulled her to the window. An officer stood on the pavement, mobile phone pressed to his ear. She focused on him awhile, tried to listen in, but couldn't decipher the conversation. Her eyes wandered. This was the first time she'd gained a clear view of the close since the incident that morning. The car was gone from their driveway, a forensic tent erected in the road out front. Over the top of the screens, she could see the neighbours opposite watching television, the soft glow of a lamp illuminating their front room. The hanging baskets of the house beside them were dripping, having recently been watered. In spite of a horrific murder which left the quiet corner of their lives overrun by police, people took solace in continuing their daily routines, craving the restoration of some kind of normality. Somehow, she'd expected it to be different, for them to be different, as scarred by the earlier episode as she was.

She recalled the detective's earlier comments, encouraging her to move out until they knew what they were dealing with. Was her stubbornness and insistence to stay in the house putting her children at risk? But she'd also said there was no reason to think they were in danger. Her mind whirled. Her eyes followed the officer outside who'd finished his call and was now speaking to a female officer, while beckoning another from down the road. Nobody would risk coming back with all this police presence nearby. No. They were safe here. For now, at least.

The thought of Cameron's bloody corpse being shared on the Internet sickened her. Who would do something like that? Violate their lives in such a grim manner. And why? The idea that the lasting image friends, neighbours, and family might see of Cameron would be of him crumpled on the ground, soaked in a pool of his own blood made her recoil. Mercifully, Oskar was on school holidays and wouldn't have to face his fellow students for a while.

Monika sat on the edge of the bed. Time stood still. Jakub relaxed in her arms and she placed him against her shoulder, patting his back. Her eyes rested on a bathrobe pooled on the chair in the corner. She used to moan at Cameron for leaving it there instead of hanging it on the hooks in the en-suite. Now she wished there were piles of them scattered around the bedroom. Cameron was gone. He'd never walk through the front door again with that gleam in his eye, throw his young son up and down in the air until he chuckled. They'd never sit in the garden and enjoy a glass of wine together… This was their new life. 'A new start,' Cameron had called it, 'for all of them. Everybody deserved that, didn't they?' A raw anguish rose in her chest, the spear of pain almost doubling her over. The squeak of Oskar's bed springs filtered through as he shifted and turned in the room next door. She held the baby close, a hand pressed to the back of his head as a shower of grief rained down on her. And she bent over and wept.

Sara Swift felt the heat rise in her head as she twirled around the dancefloor. The pulsating beat was sinking to a finish, only to be replaced by something slower. She recognised Abba but couldn't place the tune. Was that down to her poor memory or the amount of wine she'd drunk? In fact, she'd lost count of how many glasses of wine she'd ordered. But that was the whole idea of an all-inclusive holiday, wasn't it?

She tapped the shoulder of one of the bodies bopping nearby and indicated she was going back to the table. Her friend nodded and carried on dancing, edging forwards to fill the gap Sara left behind.

Sara glanced at her daughters as she inched back towards their table, wiggling her hips to the music as she did so. They were sitting on the floor at the far side of the room with a group of friends, sandals scattered to one side, eating crisps and playing a game of snakes and ladders. At this late hour. She'd never allow them to do that back home. But they were on holiday right now and, after having suffered her family for the past couple of weeks, they needed a little respite.

She'd reached their table now, and eased into a chair, simultaneously knocking her cardigan off the back. As she leaned down to pick it up her bag tipped over. Coins, a hairbrush, lipstick, and her phone rattled as they hit the floor. It took her a while to gather together the items. When she picked up the mobile, the screen lit, exposing a message. She flicked down automatically. It was a text from Yvonne, their friend and neighbour back home.

Call me as soon as you get this.

Sara stood gingerly, the thick Indian heat causing a moment of dizziness, and worked through the time difference in her mind. It would be late afternoon in England. The message had been sent five hours earlier. She considered calling back, but Yvonne hadn't said it was urgent. It was probably the rabbits. God, Yvonne was such a whinger. Next time she'd find someone else to look after those damn rabbits.

'Want a top up?' Her friend sauntered over from the dance floor and held a bottle of prosecco over her glass.

Sara looked across at her girls. 'I shouldn't really, it's way past their bedtime.'

'Oh, go on. You're on holiday. It's not often you get to treat yourself.'

She wrinkled her nose. 'Well, okay, one more then.'

She slipped the phone back into her bag as Elise topped up her wine. They raised their glasses and clinked them together. There'd be plenty of time to call Yvonne back tomorrow.

9

Beth stepped outside and pulled the door of 16 Meadowbrook Close closed behind her. The family had turned in, exhausted from the day's events, although she doubted they'd sleep soundly tonight, or in the upcoming days, weeks, and months for that matter.

Evening had fallen, veiling the surroundings in a khaki dusk. The road was quiet, the fading light temporarily putting paid to the search. The tent still stood like a beacon out front, a haunting reminder of murder.

The police tape fluttered in a wind that was picking up and gathering momentum, injecting a freshness to the night air and buffeting Beth down the close. She paused to chat with the officer guarding the outer cordon at the bottom, gave a sympathetic nod when he told her he was beginning a twelve-hour shift, and was relieved to find that, apart from a white saloon parked further up from her Mini, the road at the bottom was empty. The knot of local press that had greeted her with such vigour that morning had finally given up for the night.

She pulled out her phone as she reached her car, discovered a missed call from her sister and dialled back.

'Hello.' Eden's voice was muffled by a gabble of conversation in the background.

'It's me,' Beth said checking the clock on the dashboard. It was just after 9 p.m. 'Sorry, did I disturb you?'

'No, it's only the television.' A yawn reached down the phone. 'How's your day been?'

'Busy. I'm on my way home now.'

'Oh. Are you on that shooting? I've been watching it on the news.' The weariness in Eden's voice was replaced with a faint buoyancy. 'It's dreadful.'

'Yes. I think everyone's on it.'

'I can't believe they shared a photograph of the dead body online.'

'Everything okay there?' Beth said, keen to change the subject.

'The usual. Sunday dinner, and homework for Lily.'

Beth pictured them sitting around the table together, Lily picking through her vegetables. The sweet aroma of roasting meat filtering through their home. The heat of the oven reddening their cheeks. Her stomach kicked out, reminding her she'd barely eaten all day. 'I have a missed call from you.'

'Oh, Lily wanted to say goodnight, that's all.'

'I'm sorry. I was tied up.'

'That's what I said. She wanted me to try anyway.'

'Do you need any help tomorrow?'

'No. It's Chris's evening. He's picking her up from school.' Beth shifted in her seat at the mention of Chris's name. He would have arrived at the incident room earlier, bagged himself a desk. Perhaps it would have been better if she'd been there on his first day, to deal with any initial awkwardness. She decided not to mention his presence on the investigation to Eden.

'How did the gala go?' she asked.

'Good. Lily came second in her race. She was a bit disappointed, but her coach was pleased with her times. I've emailed you the footage.'

Beth's heart swelled with pride. Swimming had been her own passion until her late teens. There was something about gliding up and down a pool, the water lapping the sides, the warm, clean smell of chlorine tickling her senses that made her feel vital, alive. It was heart-warming to watch her niece embrace the sport. 'Okay, thanks. I'll see you tomorrow.'

Branches of established oaks lining the kerb swayed in the wind, casting intermittent shadows on the main road out of the estate. She noticed the headlights of a white car behind her on the dual carriageway. It followed as she turned off and drove through Moulton village. She paused at the roundabout and was surprised to find it still there as she turned off for the A43. The white saloon car parked up the road in Collingtree Park entered her mind. Surely this wasn't the same one.

Another check of the rear-view mirror. The number plate wasn't familiar. She remembered the lack of press presence as she'd left the scene that evening. Surely these weren't media boys, trailing her for the hint of a story, a quote to elaborate on, harbouring the naïve assumption that if they followed her home, she'd give them something. She checked again. The car was on her tail as she passed the rundown Red House pub. It followed her to the next roundabout.

By the time she'd reached the next turn, she'd memorised the number plate. Someone was going to pay for this. She took a left at the roundabout and suddenly the road was an empty well of darkness behind her. Beth checked several times, and then let out a deep breath. It had been a long day. She'd barely eaten. Maybe the night shadows were playing tricks with her mind.

She turned into Mawsley Village and steered off into a side road, out of view from the main drag. Her eyelids grew heavy as the headlights highlighted the curtain of Virginia creeper shrouding the front of her terraced cottage.

Beth was out of the car, fiddling with her keys beside her front door when another car pulled into the lane. She turned, just in time to see a white Audi saloon extinguish its lights. Her eyes dropped to the number plate, immediately recognising the car tailgating her earlier. She hadn't lost them after all.

10

Beth gritted her teeth and marched towards the car, surprised when a familiar figure climbed out sporting a toothy grin. 'Hello, stranger.'

She switched a perplexed gaze between Sergeant Nick Geary and the Audi and pulled a face. 'You gave me a start. Where's your Spider?'

'In the garage, having the brake pads done.'

Beth rolled her eyes. He'd 'invested' a fortune in that vintage Alfa Romeo, yet it spent more time in the garage than it did on the road.

He snaked his arms around her waist as he spoke and moved to plant a kiss on her cheek, but she ducked away and glanced around. For the past couple of months, they'd kept their liaisons under wraps, away from the prying eyes of the team and the public display of affection made her nervous.

Beth freed herself from his grasp, doubled back to the door and worked the keys through her fingers until she found the right one. 'I'm tired, Nick. Not really in the mood for a social.'

'One coffee and I'm out of here. Promise.' He gave a cheeky wink and followed her into the house, pushing the door to a gentle close behind him.

'Okay, well it's going to have to be decaf. It's all I've got left.' She pressed the light, illuminating the narrow passage with the dull hue of a low energy light bulb and hung her jacket on an old-fashioned coat rack beside the door. 'I'm surprised to see you outside the office actually,' she added.

Nick held up his phone. 'On call. We've implemented a shift rota to man the phones. Tomorrow's duties are already allocated and—' another cheeky grin '—I've got to sleep some time.'

Beth moved through to the kitchen and switched on the kettle. 'How's it going back at the office?' she said, searching through the cupboards for a couple of clean mugs.

He leaned against the side and crossed one foot over the other. 'We're waiting on forensics reports, working through phone records, and bank schedules. The autopsy didn't tell us anything more than we already knew: three wounds, one bullet lodged inside. The search teams have found three shells but are still searching for the other two bullets. There are a few leads from the public appeal, but nothing that looks meaty at the moment.'

'What about the door to door nearby, or his work?' Beth asked as she carried two steaming mugs through into the lounge, indicating for him to follow. Nick was the statement reader of the team, a pivotal role which meant he coordinated all the evidence. With their inspector on long-term sick leave, he reported directly to Freeman, the next link in the chain of command, allocating tasks as required. Nothing went on in the investigation without going through him in some way.

'We've retrieved lots of camera footage to work through. So far nobody appears to have actually seen the motorcyclist, or anything else untoward. The family are fairly new to the estate, only lived there a few months. He joined the golf club soon after, but they've not really been there long enough to put down roots. A couple of the neighbours got to know him a bit, said he was a chatty and sociable sort. She was more reserved. It seems a lot of people knew him, but nobody knew him particularly well. Or so they say.'

'Nothing from his work?'

'Ah. That's challenging to say the least. We're building up a list of his clients and trying to work out who he's visited over the past few weeks. But he wasn't exactly good at feeding back his movements or his files to the office. He wasn't in the office much, worked pretty independently.'

Beth sat down on the sofa, tucked her feet beneath her, and cradled the warm mug.

'They did find something interesting when they stripped down his car though. A hidden compartment behind the glovebox, looks like he'd had it put in specially.'

'And?'

He took a sip of coffee before he answered, 'It contained a memory stick and a mobile phone. They're both encrypted, unfortunately. Our techies are trying to get into them at the moment.'

'That's interesting. They already found a phone on him. He must have had two.'

'What was more interesting was that this phone was sealed in a Faraday bag.'

The information took a moment to click into place. 'What, like the ones we use when we seize phones?'

'Different to ours, it looked more like a black case. You

can buy them online, I believe, but does the same job by shielding it from Wi-Fi, Bluetooth, tracking, etc.'

'Why would you use a Faraday bag to protect a phone, if you didn't have something to hide?'

'Exactly.' He took another sip and rested his elbow on the arm of the sofa.

The room quietened. 'Did you see Chris today?' she asked.

Nick looked up at her over his mug. 'He arrived late this morning. I've not really spoken to him; his head's been stuck in the computer most of the day, trying to trace the source of the Twitter message.'

'Feels weird, him working in the same office.'

'You're not in the office. Well, not much.' He placed his mug down and sidled up beside her.

She ducked back as he nibbled her earlobe, made a play of placing her coffee on the floor. His lips brushed her cheek and found hers as she sat up. Beth felt a shiver of excitement skitter down her spine.

He kissed her slowly at first, sensually, licking her lips with his own, then slipped his tongue in and grew hungrier. He moved off the sofa and knelt beside her, his fingers working furiously to unbutton her shirt, before reaching inside and snaking his hands beneath her bra, kissing her neck. Beth murmured in delight, pulled him back onto the sofa and lost herself in him.

Beth woke later to find Nick's body sprawled across her. She crawled out from beneath him, pulling a throw from the back of the sofa and covering him with it. He shifted, sniffed as the soft wool connected with his skin, then turned towards the back of the sofa and slipped back into his slumber.

By the time she'd gathered up her clothes, showered and was back downstairs in her bathrobe, he was snoring loudly.

She entered the kitchen, poured herself a large bowl of cornflakes, all she could face making at this late hour, and opened her laptop. The cold milk sharpened her senses. She clicked on an email from Warren and was faced with a summary of the afternoon's briefing notes. It pretty much concurred with what Nick had told her earlier. The focus was on victimology, building up a picture board of Cameron's friends, family, acquaintances, and working out his movements and connections over the past week. Not easy with the issues relating to his work diary.

She recalled her discussions with Monika that day, cross-referencing them for consistency, noting her body language, searching for signs of any latent guilt, any little nuggets of information that would take the investigation in a new direction. But, apart from Cameron's movements, his estranged brother and the list of contacts she'd emailed the office earlier, she had very little to offer.

The sound of a cat meowing lifted her head. Myrtle was at the door, hustling to be let in. Beth leapt up and opened it. 'You are a lazy girl,' she said as Myrtle slunk in past the cat flap in the door and wound her tail around Beth's ankles. She filled the cat's bowl, flinching as she caught her finger on the chip at the side, and was reminded of Monika's ragged gnawed fingernails. Some of those injuries were dry and old, the skin tough where it had repaired itself and been picked at once again. Something had been on Monika's mind to worry her for a while.

Beth sat back at the table, read through her notes, and pressed save. Her gaze wandered, eventually landing on a photograph on the fridge door: her late mother wearing her work coveralls, the green accentuating the colour in her eyes. Wisps of dark curls, escaped from the ponytail, hung around her face. They were so similar. They'd plucked the same strings. Thoughts of her mother's sense of adventure lifted the corners of Beth's mouth. Her mother worked as a paramedic and was full of exciting tales when she and her sister were young, of racing through traffic at high speed with lights and sirens blaring, on a quest to save a life.

After ambling through jobs in admin, retail, and waitressing, it was her mother that drew her attention to an advertisement for Northamptonshire Police. 'You should apply,' she'd said. 'It would really suit you.' The article talked about the excitement of no two days being the same, of giving something back.

Beth took in a lungful of air and yawned. Her colleagues back at the incident room would be taking phone calls, jotting down details; searching through bank records; visiting witnesses and taking statements. For the past eighteen months, since she'd joined the homicide squad from CID, she had been engaged in similar tasks.

After months of grafting in the background, this was the first time she'd gained a key position. Statistics indicated most people were killed by someone close to them, someone they knew. Which made her role with the family all the more crucial. She needed to find a way to get Monika to open up, and soon.

11

Sara Swift sat up, sinking her toes into the sand, shading her eyes from the stark sunshine as she searched the waves for her two daughters. It didn't take long to locate their squeals as they rushed in and out of the surf. She smiled and held her head back, soaking up a few more healing rays. It had been a good decision to come to India and finish the school holidays with a few weeks of guaranteed sunshine, even if a last-minute turn of events meant they travelled alone. In fact, she was quite enjoying being out here on her own. No man breathing down her neck, expecting her to unpack his suitcase, iron his shirts before they went out in the evening. No, she didn't miss that at all.

The hotel was resourceful; she'd chosen well. Three restaurants, a children's club, and evening entertainment meant they didn't really have to go far. Last night, the girls enjoyed pre-teen karaoke while she polished off several bottles of prosecco with her newfound friends.

A plane passed overhead. She reached a lazy hand inside her bag and retrieved her phone, more in habit than expectation, and was surprised to find a string of texts from her friend, Yvonne. The message yesterday evening flashed up in her mind. She hadn't called her back. God, she hoped something hadn't happened to the rabbits. She opened the messages, shaded the screen with her free hand and read:

Call me as soon as you get this.

Sara, have you seen the news? Are you all okay?

Worried about you. Call me back when you get this message.

The messages were sent at intervals throughout the night. Not the rabbits then. Sara squinted to reread them. She clicked onto the Internet. Her phone whirled around a moment but didn't connect. Not surprising since she was on a beach in Goa and had refused the exorbitant Internet roaming fees. She paged back to the message, pressed call. Nothing. Her phone was out of signal. A good job really. It would cost a fortune to call home, and it was probably an aeroplane strike or a terrorist threat at the airport. Not something she could do anything about. She didn't want to uproot the girls, they were having such a lovely time, skipping about in the shallows now, throwing around a colourful beach ball with their friends.

Sara chucked the phone back in her bag, lay back and nestled into her towel. The sand shifted beneath her, moulding around her body. She closed her eyes. The heat on her face was soft, inviting, easing the dull ache, the aftermath of last night's prosecco. Minutes hummed past. She opened her eyes, idly watched a paraglider circle the bay. But something about the text messages bothered her. She sat up and called to the Dutch family, only a few metres away, that they'd spent the last two evenings with. 'Would you watch Amy and Zoe for me, Elise?' she said. 'I need to pop back up to the hotel to make a call.' She held up her phone.

'Of course. Take your time.' The Dutch woman gave a nod and turned back to drying off her toddler.

Sara gave one more cursory glance at her girls, half-wondering if she should let them know, but they were so engrossed in their game. No sense in disturbing them. And she'd be back before they missed her.

By the time she'd climbed the stone steps up to the hotel a wavering bar showed on her mobile. She clicked on Yvonne's latest message, pressed dial and waited outside the entrance. It crackled a few times. She heard the edge of a dialling tone before a broken voicemail kicked in. Sara cursed and punched out a text asking her to ring back.

In her room there were two bars of signal. She called again. Still no answer. Frustration was starting to pummel her. She checked her watch. It was almost eleven. It would be early morning in the UK right now. Yvonne must be up – she'd sent the last message over an hour ago. She tried her landline and was greeted with an incessant ringtone.

Sara switched on the television, grabbed the bottle of water from her bedside table and took a swig as she flicked through the channels. The only news channel in English here was CNN and she watched a while, reading the newsfeed across the bottom of the screen. No mention of a terrorist attack or a plane hijack there. She reached back and scratched the back of her neck as a rivulet of sweat trickled down. The heat of the day was kicking in now. She ought to go back down to the beach and urge the girls to put more sunscreen on. Just as she was considering this, she noticed the edge of her iPad, poking out of her bag in the corner of the room. She'd brought it for the girls to play games on. Yvonne's message had mentioned the news.

Maybe she could log on to the BBC website. It wouldn't take long. The girls would be okay for a few more minutes.

She reached for her iPad and took another swig from her bottle as it sprang into action, selecting current news on the BBC. A headline about world leaders ran along the screen; another announcing the death of an elderly actor. A box flashed up below – the shooting of a man in Northamptonshire.

She scrolled down, about to switch it off, when something caught her eye. A photograph. She peered in closer and froze. Surely it wasn't? The tagline beneath read 'Northamptonshire family shocked by shooting'. The link took her to a news report and a much larger photo with a caption underneath that read:

Asset Manager Cameron Swift shot dead outside his family home in Northampton.

Sara gasped. A rush of blood to the head forced her to the bathroom. She splashed cold water on her face. Her heart was pounding her chest. No, surely not her Cameron?

The tinkle of her phone drew her back to the main room. 'Yvonne' flashed up on the screen.

'Hello.'

Yvonne's voice was desperate. 'Sara, I've been trying to reach you. Have you seen the news?'

Sara opened her mouth to speak and closed it again.

'Sara, are you there? You need to come home, love. Cameron's dead.'

12

Early morning fog curled around the rooftops, making for a grey and bleak start as Beth drove through the Collingtree Park estate. She arrived at Meadowbrook Close to find crowds of reporters scurrying in the road, moving backwards to allow one of the residents to pass through in a Range Rover. It was almost 7.30 a.m. and, after leaving early the evening before, the news teams were now back in abundance. She'd noticed the logos of national news channels on vans parked down the street and thought again of the Twitter message. The killer had gone out of their way to attract public attention and she couldn't help but wonder why.

Guessing she was police, they approached her as soon as she climbed out of her car. A blonde journalist with hair fastened into a bun and far too much makeup for that time in the morning, shoved a microphone in Beth's face. 'How are the family doing?' she asked. 'Any leads on the investigation?' shouted another voice from behind.

'I have nothing to say.' Beth ducked away, raising her hand to cover her face from the camera flashes and waded through the sea of press. She took her time signing into the crime scene log and climbed the incline of the close. Many of the driveways were empty that morning, their inhabitants already having left for work, and, away from the crowds, a stillness descended, broken only by the breeze swishing through the trees of the nearby golf course, as if whispering secrets just out of earshot. Relieved to see the downstairs curtains of number sixteen open, she tapped lightly on the door, avoiding the bell, not wishing to disturb a family member who might still be sleeping.

The low murmur of the television inside was masked by a series of footsteps, growing louder, until the door pulled open. Monika was dressed in a long denim shirt and dark leggings. Untamed hair hung loose on her shoulders. Her young son straddled her waistline.

'Morning,' Beth said. 'I hope I'm not too early.'

Monika didn't answer. She tightened her hold on the baby, now wriggling on her hip, and cast a furtive glance past Beth and down the road. 'Are you alone?'

'Yes.' Beth looked down the close. 'Is everything all right?'

'The phone keeps ringing. They said they're outside.'

'Who did?'

'The papers. The news channels. They want an interview.'

'It might be a good idea not to answer the phone,' Beth advised as she stepped inside and closed the door behind her. 'Let the machine take it. We'll go through the messages for you.'

Monika nodded. Her shoulders lowered slightly, although her face still looked like she wanted to cry. 'Where's the other one?' she said.

'Warren's gone to the morning briefing.' Beth gave her a reassuring smile. 'I thought I'd come straight here.' She hadn't been sorry when Warren phoned her first thing with some tale about taking his son to the dentist. He could attend the morning briefing, he'd be in town anyway, if she didn't mind? Of course she didn't mind. The house was less intense without both of them there.

'Is there any news?' Monika's voice was choked with emotion.

'Nothing new at the moment. Let's see what today brings.'

'You've not caught them yet?'

'It's early days,' Beth reassured. 'We're following up lots of leads.' She chanced a smile at the baby in an effort to dissolve a fraction of the tension tightening the air. 'Someone looks spritely this morning.'

Jakub hid his face in his mother's shoulder. 'He was awake at 5.30 a.m.'

'Youngsters don't respect mornings, especially this time of year when it's light early,' Beth said kindly.

'I was awake anyway. I didn't want him to wake Oskar. He's worn out.'

'You look tired too.' Beth dropped her briefcase on the floor and slipped off her jacket, hanging it on the pegs beside the door. She followed Monika into the front room and watched her sink into the sofa. 'Can I get you a coffee?'

Monika shook her head and placed the baby on the floor beside her, next to a tower of coloured bricks he promptly knocked over. 'I needed to phone my mother anyway,' she said. 'Poland is an hour ahead of us. She works in a supermarket in the daytime, I wanted to catch her before she left.'

'How was she?'

'Upset. Worried. She wants to come over.'

'That would be nice.'

'It would. I'm not sure she's well enough though. She suffers with asthma and has panic attacks at the thought of travelling long distances.' Monika rested her head back, the pained expression still crumpling her forehead. 'Are you sure there isn't any news, Officer?' The words croaked in her throat.

'Call me Beth, please.' Beth moved to the armchair beside her. 'I'll let you know as soon as I hear anything.'

Beth leaned down and piled a few of the bricks on top of each other. The baby edged closer to his mother. 'It's difficult when they're young, isn't it?' she said. She recalled Lily at that age, always hiding her face in her mother's shoulder when a stranger spoke to her.

Monika ruffled Jakub's dark curls. 'It's inevitable really. His dad's away a lot. Was.' She fastened a forlorn gaze on the family portrait on the hearth.

'He's lucky to have an older brother around,' Beth said encouragingly.

A faint smile eased up the corners of Monika's mouth. She tore her eyes away from the photo. 'You don't have any children of your own?'

'Just a niece. Lily. She's seven.'

'I'd have loved a girl.'

'She suffered from separation anxiety for her first two years. It was tough for her mum.'

'Was her dad away a lot?'

'He's a detective. Worked long hours, changeable shifts.'

'Cameron was a great father,' Monika said with a brief sprinkle of pride. 'Happy to feed, change nappies. It's not his fault he wasn't around much.'

'He travelled around the country for his work, didn't he?'

Monika's chin trembled as she nodded.

'It must have been difficult for you. To run the house and look after the family on your own.'

She lifted a shoulder, shrugged it off. 'Cameron wanted me to enjoy Jakub. He paid the bills and gave me an allowance, so I could give up my job and be a full-time mum.' She stared longingly at her son. 'I only had the first few months off with Oskar, then went straight back into nursing. Oskar's father and I needed the money at the time. It's only later when you realise how much you've missed.'

'You were a nurse when you met Cameron?'

'Yes, I worked on the Accident and Emergency Department at City Western, Birmingham. He came into A&E with a suspected whiplash injury after somebody drove into the back of his Mercedes. I was the nurse who attended him. He was cheeky, asked me to have dinner with him. I turned him down.' Her jawline twitched at the memory. The flicker of a sunbeam passed over her face, bringing with it a radiance to her complexion that betrayed the hidden beauty of happiness, now buried deep. 'He visited the hospital every day afterwards, even when I wasn't on shift, until I agreed.'

'How long had you and Cameron been together?'

'Almost two years. I'd only known him a few months when I fell pregnant. I thought he'd run off as soon as I told him, but he was over the moon.' She twisted an engagement ring up to her knuckle, exposing a narrow dent in the skin beneath.

'You were engaged?'

'Cameron was keen to show his commitment. We moved in together when he found out I was pregnant, and he proposed when Jakub was born.'

'You moved in together in Birmingham?'

'Yes. Cameron rented a flat on St Vincent Street, overlooking the canal.' Her eyes widened. 'It was very exclusive. Long glass windows, modern furniture. Everything, even the heating, was remotely controlled. His flat-screen TV covered practically the whole of the main wall in his lounge. Oskar loved it.'

'It's good they got along so well.'

'They shared a love of computer games, often played together. Cameron became really fond of him.'

The sound of footsteps filtered through from outside. A voice called out a greeting, another responded. The officers were arriving, ready to resume their search.

'Why did you decide to move to Northamptonshire?'

Beth almost missed the shadow that flitted across Monika's face. 'The flat wasn't baby-friendly,' Monika said, straightening her back. 'There were steps everywhere. Cameron grew up on the edge of Duston in Northampton. His parents lived there until they died eight years ago. He'd always hankered to come back. The countryside is so beautiful around here.'

The jangle of the doorbell sounded.

As Beth stood to answer it, the landline also rang. It seemed the world had decided to wake up all at once. 'Leave it for the machine,' Beth said, nodding at the phone. 'I'll deal with it in a moment.'

13

As soon as Warren crossed the threshold, the air in the household cooled. He strode into the front room, wasting no time in retrieving his notepad and clicky pen from his bag. Beth sighed inwardly. Having deliberately left her briefcase in the hallway earlier, it felt as though she'd left behind the police investigation with it and, for a short time, they were two women, simply chatting. Finally, Monika was starting to open up. But Warren's arrival reinstated their roles, wedging the case between them. She was keen to press Monika about her time in Birmingham, but Monika's face had already darkened, the shutters behind her eyes firmly closed.

Warren was a man on a mission that morning. There was none of the usual easiness to his mannerisms. 'Freeman wants to speak with you,' he announced.

Beth settled them in the front room, checked the landline's voicemail – the caller had rung off without leaving a message – moved out to the hallway and pressed her mobile to her ear. The call rang out several times then switched to voicemail. She slipped her phone into her pocket and crossed to the kitchen. She needed to find a way to calm Monika and restore some of their earlier informality.

By the time she'd made tea and wandered back through, Warren was busy scribbling notes in his notebook.

'Did Cameron ever talk about any other family?' he asked Monika.

'Yes, a brother. I told you yesterday. Have you found him?'

'Not yet. We're working with the Canadian authorities, trying to track him down.' He turned a page. 'What about any other family, here in the UK? Other children maybe?'

'I don't know what you mean.'

Warren looked up. The pen between his fingers wobbled as he sat forwards. 'Monika, we've been contacted by a woman who claims to be the mother of Cameron's children, two young girls. They live in Cheshire.'

Monika gasped. Her gaze switched to Beth. She looked like she'd been duped. Beth shook her head, dumbfounded. Was this what Freeman wanted to talk to her about?

'Has Cameron ever talked about Cheshire?' Warren pressed on.

'No, never.'

'Has he visited there?'

'Not that I'm aware of. But he does travel with his job.' She pressed her hand to her chest, swallowed.

Beth's phone buzzed, but she ignored it, staring directly at Warren. What the hell had happened?

'Has he ever mentioned the name Sara Swift?'

Monika's mouth dropped. 'No.'

The ringtone of Beth's phone filled the room. Warren shot her an irritated glance. 'Are you going to get that?' he said.

Beth slipped out into the hallway and clicked answer, surprised to hear Nick's voice on the line. 'Beth, it's good to reach you.' He sounded out of breath, as if he'd been running.

'Do you want to tell me what went on at briefing this morning?' Beth cut in, 'Warren is asking some really interesting questions of the family.'

'He hasn't updated you?'

'There's been no opportunity. I was with Monika when he arrived.'

'Have you checked your inbox?'

'Not yet. Why?'

'Can you talk freely?'

Beth looked around the hallway. Warren's voice seeped out of the gap where the door to the front room sat ajar. She moved into the kitchen, closed the door behind her and checked the window. Only when she was sure she couldn't be overheard, did she respond. 'Okay. What is it?'

'We received a call early this morning from a woman who claims to be connected to Cameron. Has Monika ever mentioned that Cameron might have other children?'

'Warren's just asked her. Not apart from Oskar and Jakub. Why?'

'What about a Sara Swift? Has she mentioned her?'

'No. I thought the victim hadn't been married?'

'We've checked. He wasn't.'

'What's going on, Nick?'

'We had a call from a woman in Goa who claimed to be Cameron Swift's partner, the mother of his two girls.'

'In Goa?' Beth scoffed. The phone lines of a murder incident room always attracted a stream of crank calls. 'How did she find out?'

'She's on holiday there. She actually lives in Cheshire. Her friend got in contact with her when they saw the incident on the national news.'

Beth pressed the phone to her ear, tucking her free hand beneath the elbow of the other. 'Maybe it was an old relationship, an ex-partner.'

'That's what we thought initially. But we made some enquiries. The address she gave us in Cheshire is owned by Cameron Swift.'

'So, he set her up in a house there.'

'She claims she's his next of kin, and he lives with her. Made a real fuss about us not getting in touch to let her know about the shooting.'

'How does she explain the newspaper reports that say he was killed outside his family home here in Northamptonshire?'

'Cameron's late parents lived in Northamptonshire. She seems to think he was shot outside their family home. Apparently, he'd told her he was renting it out. She's quite adamant.'

'Are you sure she's not a nut, Nick? Or somebody keen to get their mitts on his inheritance?' She rested her hand on the granite kitchen work surface – certainly not a flat-pack job from the local DIY. 'He must be worth a fair bit.'

A sigh winged down the phone line. 'Nothing's sure at the moment. But we'll find out soon enough. She's flying home tonight. Freeman wants you in for a briefing right away, to see how we can take this forward.'

The blind rattled against the window in the light breeze which did nothing to alleviate the stickiness in Freeman's office. The fog had long since lifted, giving way to humid sunshine. Beth fanned herself with an empty file.

'Sara Swift. Lives at twelve Knighton Lane, Alderley Edge, Cheshire,' Freeman said. 'No previous convictions. We've been in touch with Cheshire police who claim they've no intelligence on her. Mother of two children: Zoe, six, and Amy, four.'

'They're definitely Cameron's children?'

Freeman nodded. 'So she says. We're currently checking with Births, Death and Marriages to see whose names appear on the birth certificates. Obviously, if she was in Goa on Sunday, she wasn't the killer. But that doesn't mean to say she's not involved in some way.'

'Any news on the motorcyclist?' Beth asked, keen to check on the wider investigation. She might be in a specialist role, but she wasn't going to allow herself to be sidelined.

'We've pulled some images from private camera footage taken from residents on the estate, but can't identify the rider,' Nick interjected. 'The plates were matched to a Kawasaki stolen from Coventry last month. We haven't been able to trace it since.'

'What about tracking the route, in and out of the estate?'

Nick shook his head. 'Private residential cameras pick up the bike at various stages of Windingbrook Lane, coming in and out of the Collingtree Park estate. But there's nothing on the A45 cameras. We tried other possible routes and it seems to disappear between the golf club and the dual carriageway. They either live nearby or had another vehicle, a van or something similar, to drive the bike inside and continue their journey.'

'And work colleagues?'

Freeman exhaled a laboured sigh. 'His business partner gave us very little. It's like they barely know each other, even though they've shared a business for the past twelve years. They didn't socialise much. We've got a team in Birmingham going through his caseload. They'll be interviewing his other colleagues today.'

'Sara Swift sounds like the scorned other woman to me,' Nick chipped in, moving the meeting back on course. 'Perhaps she discovered his family in Northamptonshire, sought revenge. Might explain the assassination type manner in which he was killed.'

'Why share it on social media though?' Beth said. 'If she arranged it herself, surely she'd want to keep a low profile.'

'I don't know.' There was a hint of irritation in Freeman's voice. 'So far, all we've had is a brief phone call with her which mainly consisted of her screaming obscenities.'

'Do we know who the beneficiary is in the victim's will?' Beth asked. 'Might have a bearing here?'

'Not yet,' Freeman said, 'but we're working on it.' He laced his fingers together and rolled his thumbs. 'Her flight is due in at 11.30 a.m. tomorrow. I want you to be at the airport to meet her, Beth. Introduce yourself, call it a welfare visit to update her on the investigation. God knows, she's made a real fuss about the lack of police contact so far.'

Beth's shoulders sagged. 'Are you sure you want me to go, sir? Only I think I might be more useful here.' She relayed her conversation with Monika. 'I feel I'm starting to get through, build the beginnings of a rapport. I'd like to pursue the family angle in Birmingham, especially as we know so little about the victim.'

'Thanks, Beth. I've got detectives looking into the victim's life in Birmingham. I'll get them to do some digging into her background there too. Warren can continue where you left off for the next few days.'

'But I really think—'

Freeman interrupted her, 'See if you can establish their relationship status. When did he last visit their home? When did they last speak? Look for anything in the house that proves an association or recent contact.' He scratched a patch of scalp, the wispy hairs sticking upwards in protest. 'Maybe she found out about his family in Northamptonshire, instigated all of this. Maybe they found out about her. Maybe none of them are involved. But, if half of what she claims is true, it opens up a whole new line of enquiry we cannot afford to ignore.'

The phone trilled on Freeman's desk. 'I can't spare anyone to go with you, I'm afraid, so take it easy and book a hotel for the night on expenses if it turns out to be a long day.' He tipped his head for them to go and grabbed the receiver.

'Better organise you a pool car for tomorrow then,' Nick said with a wink as they made their way up the corridor towards the incident room. 'I'll give you her mobile number and the flight details.'

Beth didn't answer, her insides smarting at being taken away from Monika and the family, just when she felt she was getting somewhere.

'Hey,' Nick grabbed her arm, pulling her to a halt. 'What's with you?'

She pulled it free, nudged her head back towards Freeman's office. 'Is this because I couldn't get Monika to move out of their home?'

'What?'

'Look, I know somebody has to go up to Cheshire. I don't see why it should be me though. He's not giving me a chance.'

'Well, he can hardly send Warren up there, can he?' The edges of Nick's mouth curved into a smile.

'Why not?'

'With his driving record?' Nick raised a brow. 'He's lucky to still have a licence.'

Beth couldn't resist the chuckle that escaped.

He guided her along as he continued, 'You imagine the look on Freeman's face if he had another prang.'

They were both laughing when they reached the door to the main office. Beth pulled it too vigorously and it shot open to reveal Chris standing on the other side. He was taller than she remembered, his skin tanned from the recent hot weather.

Nick pushed past and strode into the room, ignoring Chris, but for some reason Beth's feet were rooted to the ground. 'Hello, Beth,' Chris said. His face coloured slightly and eased into a half-smile. For a moment she was reminded of how close they once were, only a bloodline between brother and sister. The incident room hushed around them. 'You're looking well.'

Beth's stomach lurched. Seeing him there like that, she was swamped by a wave of protectiveness for her younger sister. After what he'd put Eden through these past few months, he deserved nothing more than a good punch in the gut. But this wasn't the time or the place.

'Thanks. You're not looking so bad yourself,' she said, reeling from the sarcasm that laced her words. She stepped around him, moved across to her desk and made a play of rummaging through the top drawer, although she had no idea what she was searching for.

She felt the eyes of the room on her. The police were well versed in relationships both between staff and within their families, and always keen to follow the drama. She was aware of the door flapping closed. Later, another flap, followed by Chris's wide gait striding past her to speak to the analysts at the side of the room. He didn't look back at her. Heads turned away. She grabbed some papers out of the drawer, stuffed them in her briefcase, settled into her chair, and worked through her emails.

14

Freeman's decision played on Beth's mind as she turned off the dual carriageway and into Collingtree Park later that afternoon. While she was grateful for the opportunity to put the skills she'd learned into practice, it was only temporary. Family liaison officers worked in pairs. Andrea Leary was experienced in the role, a senior liaison officer, and would soon return and work with Warren, which gave her little time to assimilate herself and really make a difference. Moving her away from the family at this crucial time certainly wouldn't help.

She rounded the lip of Meadowbrook Close and was greeted by a stream of cars, vans, and trucks. The press had taken advantage of the earlier removal of the cordons and moved in closer, clogging the area with their presence. It was difficult to find somewhere to park and she had to cruise to the top, turn around, and squeeze into a space several houses down from number sixteen.

Reporters flew to her side, moths to a night lamp, the minute she emerged from the car. Beth waded through, ignoring the questions touted from all angles; the footsteps shuffling around her, trailing her as she walked up the road. Freeman had made it clear he wanted to monitor the feed of media information himself and she didn't want to do or say anything that might jeopardise his stance.

But as she walked up the road, the voices in her ear and the elbow nudges were starting to grind. This wasn't the first time she'd been plagued by the press in a major enquiry. As a rookie, she'd guarded a cordon to a road traffic collision with multiple vehicles and fatalities. The experience taught her early on that while the police and the media worked closely together, their agendas were different: the police used them as a tool to feed updates to the public, appeal for information, and only shared what was absolutely necessary to drive an investigation forward. Members of the press, however, were in constant competition with each other, always looking for a scoop, a unique angle to make their story original and attract more readers, and they were tenacious in their approach.

As soon as the house came into view, she noticed the curtains were closed, both upstairs and downstairs, even though it was early afternoon. The sight made her inwardly recoil. Monika had asked for the family to be kept out of the press, as much as possible, for the sake of the children, and here they were tucked away behind shades, desperately trying to avoid the camera flashes.

Beth recognised the overly made-up blonde from earlier that day, speaking into a microphone in front of a camera, the house positioned carefully in her background. She was standing in the driveway.

'Excuse me,' Beth said.

The blonde ignored her, angling her head to the camera, continuing her speech.

'Excuse me.' Beth raised her voice a decibel, cutting through the journalist's words. The blonde turned and pinned Beth with a hard stare. The cameraman lowered his lens.

'We'll have to take that again,' he said.

Beth ignored him, focusing on the woman. She didn't want to alienate the press, but she wasn't about to let them take liberties. Not on her watch. 'Can you move back please?'

The reporter's expression changed. Her eyes lit up as she recognised Beth from earlier that morning. She stretched her face into a sweet smile, edged closer, and gave a swift nod to the photographer. 'Ah, detective. Can you tell us—'

Beth placed a flat hand over the lens. 'You're on private property.' She flicked her eyes to the gravel as she spoke. 'I need to ask you to move off the driveway.'

The reporter retreated a few steps. 'Oh, sorry. If you could—'

'Please keep off the driveway,' Beth interrupted, and turned on her heel towards the house.

Warren was at the door before she reached it. He opened up enough for her to scoot through and closed it again.

'How long have they been there?' Beth asked, as he turned the key in the lock.

'About an hour.' Warren's eyes turned skyward. 'They moved in as soon as the cordons were taken down. One of them even had the nerve to knock on the door.'

'Have you rung Freeman?'

'I've tried, but he seems permanently engaged. I've just emailed.'

'How's Monika dealing with it all?' As she acclimatised herself to the new surroundings, the house felt inordinately quiet. No chortling baby, no television babbling in the background.

'She's upstairs with the kids. I think they're trying to get some rest.'

They wandered into the kitchen. Warren's laptop was open on the table. He slid into the chair in front of it.

'How was Monika after you'd told her the news that Cameron might have other children?' Beth asked, resting her briefcase on the table.

'Not good. She claims she had no idea. Went straight upstairs afterwards.'

Beth passed on the information about Sara and the children from her discussions with Freeman. 'I have to go up there tomorrow, meet her at the airport.'

'That should be interesting.'

'Hm. Maybe.' Beth remained standing. Something bothered her. She wasn't sure if it was Cameron's connection with Sara Swift or the fact that Monika had been banished to her bedroom. 'I think I'll go and check on the family.'

The tinny beat of music, barely audible, fed from under the door of Oskar's room. Beth suspected he was wearing headphones so as not to disturb the baby. She hesitated a moment, wondering if she should leave Monika to rest, but something inside – a silent need to check – tugged on her. She knocked on the other bedroom door as gently as she could.

It was a moment before she heard Monika's voice call, 'Come in!'

Beth blinked twice as she entered the room. The mixture

of bright sunlight, seeping in through the swathes of curtain material, and the artificial light was initially blinding. Monika was languishing on the bed with Jakub beside her, a colourful array of soft toys scattered around them. 'Is there some news?'

'Not yet. I wanted to let you know I'm back,' Beth said. 'Are you okay?'

'Are they still out there?' She shot a glance at the window.

It was deplorable that Monika felt she had to hide away in the bedroom, after all they'd been through these past two days. The press could be so intrusive sometimes. 'They are. But we have been speaking to our DCI to see if he can have a word. I'm sure things will get easier soon.'

Monika pulled a face and looked away, tugging Jakub closer to her, a clear display of zero confidence.

'Can I get you anything?' Beth asked.

'No.' She closed her eyes, lowered her head and sniffed the baby's hair, indicating an end to the conversation.

Beth's heart wrenched as she descended the stairs. The press weren't causing an obstruction and weren't on private property which meant they had no legal power to move them. She tried Freeman again. When the engaged tone filled her ear, she called off and tried Nick. He answered on the second ring.

'Hi, Beth. You okay?'

She didn't waste time with pleasantries, instead launching into a description of the situation in Meadowbrook Close and the problems with the press camped outside. By the time she'd finished, Nick could be in no doubt of the strength of her opinion.

'Leave it with me. I know the DCI received Warren's

email. We've been distracted by another line of enquiry. I'll go and speak with him right away, see if we can't put an informal request out to the news editors, ask them to scale it down and respect the family's privacy at this time.'

'Thanks. We're not going to get anything out of Monika in this state. What's the other line of enquiry?'

'We've traced the brother, David Swift. He doesn't live in Canada at all. He flew back from Newfoundland about six years ago and is based in Scotland now. The Shetland Islands to be precise.'

Beth hovered at the bottom of the stairs, resting her hand on the banister. 'Have you tracked his movements for Sunday?'

'Yes. He has an alibi, claims he hasn't spoken to his brother for six years, and wouldn't discuss why he fell out with Cameron, not on the telephone anyway. We're sending an officer up there tomorrow to interview him.'

'Why hasn't he been in touch?' It seemed odd he wouldn't have spoken to the police after all the national news coverage.

'That's what we need to find out. And, Beth?'

'Yes?'

'Speak with Monika if you can. See if she has any recollection of Cameron's brother ever living in Scotland or the Shetland Islands, and also if Cameron has been up there recently.'

That evening, Beth wandered into her own kitchen, dragged the tie out of her hair, wrapped it around her wrist and combed her fingers through her unruly curls. She flicked the switch on the kettle, absentmindedly, and leaned against the side.

The frustrations of the afternoon itched away at her. Colleagues at the station were struggling to break into the memory stick and phone found in the victim's car. Freeman had clearly spoken to the news editors because there were only two reporters loitering when she left the house that evening, the throng that caused the earlier pandemonium now dissipated. But even without the hounding from the press, Monika hadn't said much. She'd only come downstairs briefly to make some tea for Oskar and her, and then retreated to her room. Beth tried to grab the opportunity to ask her some questions about Cameron's possible presence in Scotland, but Monika had simply shaken her head, and Beth wasn't sure whether she didn't know or wasn't prepared to answer.

Tomorrow, she would meet Sara Swift at the airport. There was no police record and no intelligence on her. All she knew was Sara had lived at Alderley Edge in Cheshire for around seven years and claimed to be the mother of Cameron's two girls, Zoe and Amy. Births, Deaths, and Marriages confirmed both Sara's and Cameron's names appeared on the girls' birth certificates.

Ignoring the kettle, wheezing in the background, she grabbed her laptop off the table and flicked open the lid. The kettle switched itself off as she entered Sara Swift into a Google search and scrolled down. A few LinkedIn results came first: an Australian professor, followed by a Sara Swift working in project management on LinkedIn, and a doctor of neurology in Nevada. A row of images appeared next, half a dozen of which could be about the right age group;

there was no way of knowing if any of them was Cameron's alleged partner. She switched back to the top of the search, found a link to Facebook profiles, and pressed enter. It always surprised her how people spread their lives across social media. Few people kept their Facebook accounts private, it seemed.

A list of Sara Swifts came up. The top entries were based in Australia and the US. She changed the search to the UK and only five entries filled the screen. The first profile picture was of a poodle puppy. She clicked on the profile and found a fifty-year-old grandmother in Newcastle. The second entry was a teenager, still in school. The third was based in Scotland. The next image was of a black and white cat. Beth clicked on the profile. Her introduction claimed she was from Alderley Edge, Cheshire. It looked promising.

The main photo showed two young girls with buckets and spades; white sand, set against an azure backdrop, filled the background. Surely there couldn't be more than one Sara Swift in Alderley Edge? The timeline showed a photograph of a beach at sunset. The next post was a picture of a group of women and children sat around a table at dinner. A joke about parents' relief at their children going back to school followed. There were photos of several puppies further down. She dipped into the previous year and a bunch of flowers with the words 'Thank you, Yvonne' came up.

She selected 'About', clicked on relationships and bit her lip. Sara recorded herself as 'married'. Cameron had never been married. Yet if this was the right Sara Swift, she'd taken his name. Why? There was little in the other categories, so she tried the photos. There was one of a couple of glasses of wine. Several of two young girls, in various outfits. No mention or images of Cameron though.

The names and rough ages of the children fitted, but there was no picture of Sara Swift on there, no indication of what she looked like. Beth shut down her computer and sighed, not a step closer to knowing who she was meeting in the morning.

15

Monika jolted awake to find herself propped up in bed with Jakub glued to her chest. Vague memories of him wailing in the early hours floated into her mind. This was the second night in a row she'd been forced to jump up and hush him before he woke Oskar.

She lay perfectly still in the darkness, staring at the ceiling. If she concentrated hard enough, she could hear the vague swish of cars passing on the nearby dual carriageway through the open window. There were times in Birmingham, living in the hub of the city, when she'd craved solitude. Although now, lying here, she realised she despised loneliness more. She couldn't go back to Birmingham. She wouldn't. But she couldn't help but wonder what was to become of them now. A single tear escaped as she pushed the duvet down, moved the child into the middle of the bed and laid him gently on his back. He wriggled around awhile and wrestled his arms out to the side. Another tear dropped off the end of her nose, spotting the duvet as she stroked the pillow beside her, all plumped and ready for use.

Careful not to wake the baby, Monika eased out of bed, approached the window and parted the curtains. It was a heavy night, the sky a murky grey, devoid of stars.

She sucked in a lungful of fresh night air. An owl called to its mate in the distance. The officer in the police car out front gave a short wave and she nodded her head back. Thankfully, the rest of the close was empty, quiet. No more watchful journalists.

Meadowbrook Close was a modern layout with open-plan front gardens, lacking the barriers of hedges or walls. Monika had loved this style when she first viewed the house. It made her feel closer to their neighbours, part of an obvious community. But its accessibility also gave members of the press a clear view of the house from the road and there was nowhere to hide.

Thoughts of earlier that day sent a shiver down her spine. The reporters had arrived as soon as the cordon was removed. Gathered at the end of the driveway with their microphones and cameras, beady eyes fixed on the house. It wasn't enough they had to bear the pain of losing Cameron in such grisly circumstances, that his murder would change their lives irrevocably. Now they were to be badgered by journalists, hidden behind drawn curtains, prisoners in their own home. With the police presence in the close reduced, she'd been told a patrol car would be placed outside tonight. 'To give you peace of mind,' Warren had said. She couldn't work out whether he meant peace of mind that she was safe from the killer, or peace of mind she was protected from the press. Two long days had passed. The detectives completed their searches, asked endless questions, and took copious notes. They constantly talked about 'leads' and 'lines of enquiry', yet the killer still roamed free.

A fingernail picked at the side of her brain. The police had plagued her for details about Cameron's friends and associates. Only today they'd asked more questions about his family, which made her think it might be somebody Cameron knew. Somebody close by. She shuddered.

Cameron's secretive nature about his job was understandable to a degree. He'd managed investment portfolios for wealthy high-flyers. People that wouldn't appreciate their personal details being discussed, even between man and wife. When they first started living together, it had niggled her how he refused to answer even the minutest questions about the general aspects of his job: vague enquiries about how his day had been, how his business trip went, or whether an investment had been successful. He'd simply answer with, 'Monika, my phone is always ringing when I'm away. I need to wind down, relax. Leave work behind.' In time, she acquiesced to his wishes and they lived their fragmented existence. In many ways it suited her. They had his full attention when he was with them. But the constant string of questions now only served to remind her how little she knew of his life outside home.

The notion he might have other children living in another part of the country, children he hadn't mentioned, was like swallowing a wasp and feeling the barb of its sting score her insides as it passed through. Sara Swift. The name reverberated around her head. When they'd talked about other relationships, he'd admitted to previous girlfriends, several of them over the years, but always said there was never anyone special.

How did somebody do that? Have children they never mentioned. She'd given up her job, her friends and her life in Birmingham to make a new life out here with Cameron.

After investing almost half his working life building his company and concentrating on his career, he wanted to move back to his roots in Northamptonshire, the county of spires and squires as he called it, to raise a family in the country. They'd spent endless evenings on the balcony of their flat in Birmingham, drinking wine, discussing what they both longed for in their dream family home. Cameron wanted a quiet location with a long garden and the promise of peace and tranquillity. Monika dreamed of a home with a view of the countryside, near other families, where her children would make friends and play outside safely, something they couldn't do in the centre of bustling Birmingham.

Sourcing their 'forever home', as Cameron called it, became his new project and he'd treated it with military precision, spending days and weeks, driving back and forth, talking to estate agents, seeking out the most suitable property in the right location. They viewed numerous houses together, many of which she would have been happy with, but nothing struck a chord with Cameron until they laid eyes on number sixteen Meadowbrook Close. She couldn't deny he had exceptional taste. It was a dank dour day, heavy clouds hovering in the sky, thick with the promise of rain when she first viewed it. Yet she could imagine herself tending the garden, planting colourful annuals and perennials; playing with Jakub on the lawn out back. She'd never contemplated living in a house so beautiful and, as Cameron showed her around, it filled her with pride as they discussed ideas for colour schemes, curtains, and soft furnishings. All those little extra touches that would transform their new house into a forever home.

But she was wrong. Cameron had done this before.

Was he separated from this other family, estranged like he was from his brother? The woman had taken his surname. Had they been married? She turned her engagement ring around on her finger. How could he have married somebody, made vows with them, and not told her? Another thought needled her. The detective mentioned two children. One could be forgiven, a mistake he didn't know about, but two...

What else didn't she know about him?

She surveyed the soft grey walls, the photo of Oskar and Jakub on the bedside table. Everything they had here, everything they'd worked for this past couple of years, everything that formed the bricks and mortar of their relationship was based on a lie. And right now, the foundations were crumbling before her eyes.

16

Beth cast a frustrated glance at the arrivals board. Sara's plane had landed three quarters of an hour ago. She pulled up Sara Swift's Facebook profile, took another look. A deluge of families, couples, and business people had waded through the arrivals gate, yet nobody with children that resembled those in this picture. Surely she hadn't missed them?

She was starting to scan the airport for a member of staff, with a view to checking the flight listing, when an Asian woman rounded the corner and came into view. She wore a white linen shirt with the sleeves rolled up and skinny black jeans clinging to her long legs. Her hair was pulled into a high ponytail accentuating razor-sharp cheekbones. From a distance she looked like she'd just stepped out of a *Vogue* shoot. It wasn't until she grew nearer that Beth spotted the weariness in her face, the dark shadows beneath her eyes. Two young girls in shorts and bright T-shirts, with slightly paler skin than their mother but the same bone structure, shuffled beside a trolley piled high with suitcases and bags. They looked very similar to the Facebook photo.

Beth pocketed her phone. 'Sara Swift?'

The woman, who'd almost walked past her, halted and looked Beth up and down, as if she wasn't quite what she'd expected, before she nodded.

Beth discreetly produced her badge. 'DC Beth Chamberlain.' Sara shook her extended hand warily. 'I'm sorry for your loss.' Beth released her grasp and smiled kindly at the two children. 'You must be Zoe, and Amy,' she said looking from one to another. Two pairs of eyes stared back at her.

'Sorry we're late,' Sara said curtly. A husk coated her voice. 'We had a toilet incident back there.' The smallest of the girls dipped her head sheepishly.

'No problem. I have a car outside. Let's get you all home, shall we?'

The half-hour journey to Alderley Edge from Manchester Airport felt four times as long, with the prolonged silence punctuated by stilted questions. There was none of the overt hostility that Freeman's feedback suggested, more a listless atmosphere in the car. Every time Beth checked her rear-view mirror, she could see Sara sandwiched in between her two girls in the back of the car.

Beth did her best to keep the conversation light, asking general questions about their welfare and their holiday, but steered clear of any specific questions while the children were present. If Sara Swift was already riled by police contact in the initial stages, she didn't want to provoke her further by questioning her in front of her grieving children. The girls remained quiet, in an almost trance-like state, while their mother gave short sharp answers to Beth's questions. By the time they reached Alderley Edge, Beth had gleaned the basics: they'd been away in India for nearly three weeks, a visit to Sara's family in Amritsar in the Punjab region, and finished off with a week's beach holiday in Goa, before the girls returned to school. They'd taken the holiday alone and she couldn't help wondering if that was significant.

It was almost 1 p.m. when they passed through the decorative wrought iron gates that marked the entrance to number twelve Knighton Lane. The youngest of the girls had fallen asleep, her head gently bobbing with the ebb and flow of the engine. The house was set back from the road, the view obscured by a tall hawthorn hedge. Gravel crunched beneath them as they swept up a driveway flanked by a finely manicured lawn, itself encased within deep borders stocked with established shrubs and colourful flowers.

Sara woke her daughter and they started gathering their things together. As soon as Beth cut the engine the front door swung open and an older woman in a long denim dress, her white-grey hair pulled back into a bun, appeared.

'Yvonne!' screamed the elder of the girls, her face brightening as she scrabbled to open the door.

Beth switched from the woman on the drive to Sara in the rear-view mirror. There'd been no mention that someone would be meeting them back at the house. 'Who's Yvonne?'

'A family friend,' Sara said. 'She's been looking after the house for us.'

The two children had now rushed down the driveway and wrapped themselves around Yvonne who was kissing their heads, holding them close.

Beth took her time at the car, watching them all furtively as she retrieved their cases from the boot. As soon as Sara reached Yvonne, the two women hugged tightly. Yvonne, who was virtually a head size smaller than Sara, reached up and stroked her friend's cheek affectionately. It was a touching gesture, suggesting an established friendship of some time in the making.

Sara sent the girls back to help Beth with the cases and followed Yvonne into the house. They were talking in low voices at the end of the hallway by the time Beth and the children entered, dragging the suitcases behind them, the wheels rattling against the chequered tiled flooring.

Beth introduced herself to Yvonne and showed her badge. A shadow fell on Yvonne's face as she shook her hand. 'And you are?' Beth asked.

'Yvonne Newman. I live around the corner, at 7 Templar Road.' A series of footsteps, gathering momentum as they slapped against the tiles, was followed by a shriek. The girls' energy levels had picked up the minute they'd crossed the threshold, the earlier sombre mood fading as the excitement of being home took over, and they were rushing in and out of the rooms downstairs, shrieking at each other as they did so.

'Oh dear,' Sara said to Yvonne. 'They've been cooped up for far too long.'

Yvonne swept a hand down Sara's arm. 'I'll take them upstairs to unpack.' She cast a glance at Beth, her face guarded. 'Leave you two to talk.'

17

Monika awoke to voices in the hallway. For a moment she was disorientated, taking in the familiarity of the photos that littered her mantel. Her gaze eventually fell on Jakub's chubby legs laid across her lap, the empty bottle tossed to his side. The clock read 1.15 p.m. She'd nodded off with him, not surprising really after the restless night's sleep yesterday had brought. She was still grappling with the notion of Cameron having other children. She'd pressed the detective for more information that morning, but all he said was their enquiries were ongoing and he'd feedback more details as soon as he could. The other detective was conspicuous by her absence today. Why couldn't anybody tell her anything?

A jaunty song accompanied the credits of a children's programme on the television. Before yesterday she'd had strict rules about the television with Jakub, only allowing him a short viewing in the mornings, an hour to wind down before he went to bed at night. She'd been trying to wean him off his bottle to a cup, but he was so much happier with his bottle it seemed easier to indulge him right now. The bizarre events of the last twenty-four hours had tipped the balance of her world, as if she was looking at everything askew. Her body was drained to the point that every word, every movement, was laboured. She wanted to shout, scream, and holler. Readjust the equilibrium. Disappear into a dark room, fold into herself and force a permanent sleep. Anything to lessen the pain and make the loss easier to bear. But life was cruel. Jakub needed her. The television kept him content. But it still saddened her, a recurring reminder as to how much their lives had changed.

The voices came again in low whispers. She switched off the television, picked out Warren's West Country inflection along with another female voice, and lifted her head, craning her neck to see out of the window. A pigeon sat atop a bird table in the front garden opposite, twitching its head with hers as she moved, almost mocking her. She looked past it, around the close and it struck her how empty it appeared to be. No reporters out there today. Did that mean their attention was diverted elsewhere, or were they continuing to heed the police appeal to respect the family's privacy? The voices in the hallway raised a notch. She strained her ears. There was something about the tone of the female, a soft lilt. It sounded vaguely familiar.

Jakub's head lolled against her neck as she rested him on her shoulder. She sniffed his wispy curls and winced at the combination of milk and carrot where he'd placed his sticky hands in his hair through lunch. None of the baby freshness of pear shampoo that he usually smelt of. He needed a bath. She mustn't neglect him. She wouldn't.

In the hallway, Warren was standing at the door with his back to her, talking to a woman who Monika now recognised as her next-door neighbour. Jakub murmured and nuzzled into her. Warren shifted to one side and turned, and she could see he was holding a tray with a white enamel casserole dish placed on top, covered with foil.

'Ah, you're awake,' he said. 'Mrs James—'

'Amanda,' the woman corrected him. She was a large woman, dressed in a colourful gathered skirt and loose white top. Fair hair was tied neatly away from a face that had once been pretty but sagged with age. She either wasn't aware of her size or didn't see it as a barrier to squeezing through small gaps. Within seconds, she was through the doorway and past Warren, enveloping a surprised Monika and Jakub in a light hug, kissing her on the cheek and stroking the baby's hair as she did so. Monika gave an embarrassed cough as the embrace broke and looked down at Jakub who was now awake and staring at their neighbour, bewildered.

'How are you, darling?' Amanda asked. A multitude of concerned crease lines formed around her eyes. The words, intimate and affectionate as they were, felt out of place between two women who barely knew each other, but with her last twenty-four hours filled with faceless police officers, detectives, and crime scene investigators traipsing through her home, even the brief comfort of a relatively recent acquaintance was enough to insert a fresh lump in Monika's throat.

Amanda brushed her arm. 'I've brought you a lasagne.' She pointed at the casserole dish Warren was still clutching to his chest. 'Pop it in the oven for forty minutes at one hundred and eighty degrees.'

'Thank you.' Monika's eyes swelled with fresh tears at the touching gesture.

Amanda stepped back and looked her up and down.

'Well, at least you look better than you did on Sunday. We've all been so worried about you.'

Monika's mind swirled. Her memory of Sunday was of myriad faces merging together in a blur of colour in the street, before being led into the house where she was babysat for the rest of the day by the two detectives. She neither recalled speaking to Amanda, nor seeing her. In fact, the last time she actually remembered them meeting was in Amanda's garden, almost four weeks earlier, when they'd been invited to a BBQ. If she closed her eyes, she could almost see them there. It was an overcast day; she'd had to wear a cardigan. Cameron had admired Amanda's husband's vintage Porsche, in a state of partial restoration, and spent ages talking through the various areas that needed work. Monika remembered feeling a little awkward as she stood eating steak sandwiches on their freshly cut lawn, with Jakub fastened to her hip and Oskar clinging to her side. It was only the second time they'd met; the first was when Amanda brought round cupcakes in a Tupperware dish, a week after they'd moved in, as a welcome present. Amanda had cooed over the baby during the BBQ, sharing that her only son was away, travelling around New Zealand, and had offered her services to babysit if they ever fancied an evening out. An offer they'd never had the chance to take advantage of.

'I'm sorry. Please, come in.' Monika looked at Warren as she spoke, although she couldn't understand why she felt the need to check whether she was able to invite guests into her own home at this juncture. It was her house, after all.

'That would be lovely. As long as I'm not interrupting anything.'

Monika led her through to the front room, leaving Warren to take the lasagne through to the kitchen.

'How is Oskar coping?' Amanda asked when they'd settled themselves into the sofas.

Monika placed the baby in his bouncer and dabbed a tissue to her eyes. She was worried about Oskar. Apart from brief respites to eat or check on her, he'd spent most of the day in his room, picking at his guitar. Not unusual for him but given the circumstances it still left her uneasy. Oskar had never been much of a talker. 'He's okay. It's difficult with...' She grimaced, pointing her forehead towards the kitchen. 'He's a shy lad.'

'How long will they be here?' Amanda said following her eyeline.

'I don't know. I suppose it depends upon...' The words trailed off. She didn't want to talk about the case. Not here. Not now.

'How are you doing?'

Monika's head moved from side to side, almost of its own volition. 'I have no idea.'

'I'm so sorry. We all are. If there's anything you need, anything at all, please ask.'

'Thank you.'

Amanda smoothed the creases in her skirt. 'I take it they haven't made an arrest yet?'

'I don't think so.'

'Poor love.' Silence fell upon them. The baby bounced in his seat nearby, his face full of smiles, oblivious to the gloominess around him.

'Is he crawling yet?' Amanda asked, eyeing the child.

Monika shook her head, barely comprehending her

words. She could hear Warren on the phone in the hallway but couldn't make out what he was saying. A wave of nausea hit her. The moment summed up her experience of the last few days. Officers slipping in and out of her house, talking in low whispers, leaving the room to take calls. She'd lost her partner. Yet, despite her questions, she had no idea how the investigation was progressing, or whether they were even close to catching his killer. She looked across at Amanda, about to tell her how she felt distinctly out of the loop when a thought nudged her. Cameron had got to know their neighbours better than her. He'd spent many an hour in their garage tweaking the engine of Amanda's husband's Porsche. Maybe they'd chatted. Perhaps he'd mentioned something about his other children.

'They're interviewing other family members,' she said, fishing.

'Oh, does he have other family nearby?' Amanda said. 'At least that will give you some relief.'

'No, he doesn't have adult family. Well, not in the UK. Other children.'

'Oh,' Amanda said. 'I didn't realise.' Her face was blank, empty. She didn't know. These were people that Cameron regarded as friends, people he spent time with. How many fragmented lives could somebody lead? She was beginning to wonder if he was completely truthful with anybody. 'Are they nearby?'

Monika's chest tightened. Her inner self fought a battle over sadness at Amanda's ignorance, and relief that she wasn't the only one kept in the dark. 'No. They're in Cheshire. I didn't know about them.'

'What a shock for you.'

Monika surprised herself by launching into the tale of her conversation with the detective yesterday and the details he'd shared about Cameron's estranged family members. Were they estranged? She didn't really know.

It wasn't like her to open up and share with someone she'd only met a couple of times, a virtual stranger. There were other friends she could have spoken to, but she deliberately hadn't looked at her mobile phone, especially after the detective's revelations about the photograph on Twitter, and hadn't used the landline, apart from to call home. This wasn't something she could share with her mother, not with her asthma. The intermittent flap of the letter box rattled through the house these past few days as cards landed on the mat, only to be placed on the hallway table, unopened. Warren had taken messages from friends and acquaintances in Birmingham sending their love, but this wasn't something she wanted to discuss down a phone line. It needed presence; she needed comfort. This was the closest she'd come to someone outside of the investigation and right now the desperate need for some relief overtook her usual reticent nature.

Amanda didn't utter a word as Monika's words gushed through the floodgates. When they dried up, she held her close.

'Can I get anyone a drink?'

Monika finally opened her eyes to view Warren's frame filling the doorway. Her voice was mute, weary from all the tears. Were they to have no privacy?

18

Beth followed Sara into a sitting room. It was a large space, flooded with light courtesy of an oversized bay window that looked out into the front garden. The window was framed with navy and cream shades, tied loosely back and decorated with swags and tails. Matching cushions adorned three sofas, arranged into an arc around a wood burner.

'You've had quite a journey,' Beth said. 'Can I get you a tea or coffee?'

If Sara was surprised by being offered a drink by a relative stranger in her own home, she didn't let it show. 'No, thank you. We ate on the plane.'

Yvonne's voice filtered through from the hall. 'Come on, girls. Calm down. We can only take up one case at a time.'

'How are they coping?' Beth asked, resting her briefcase on the arm of one of the sofas.

'After being told in a hotel room that we had to fly straight home, cutting short their holiday, because their daddy was dead?' The pithiness in Sara's voice rose with every word. She'd kept her temper deftly at bay in front of her children, but now they were away from the others her tone hardened. 'What do you think?' She pushed the door closed. 'Now, I want to know exactly what happened.'

'Cameron was shot outside—'

'Outside a house in Northampton,' Sara interrupted. 'I know that. I read the press reports online. I'm asking you what happened. What do you know so far?'

'Why don't we sit down?' Beth said.

The soft leather of the sofa squeaked beneath Beth as she shifted about, retrieving her notebook and pen. Sara reluctantly sat and tucked her hands in her lap, drawing an audible breath. Her sleek frame looked almost demure, like a model posed for a painting, but her face was tight.

She barely made a sound as Beth relayed the details of the shooting, a little over forty-eight hours earlier, in as much detail as she could without releasing any details that weren't already in the public domain. When she mentioned the picture shared on social media, Sara pressed her eyelids together, fidgeted but remained silent. *She's already seen it*, Beth thought to herself. 'We believe this was a targeted attack,' Beth continued, as gently as she could muster. 'Somebody knew Cameron's movements, where to find him. We are looking into all his associations at present, building up a picture of his life. If you feel up to answering some questions—'

Sara folded her arms firmly across her chest. 'So, you haven't found the person responsible?'

'Not yet, but we are doing everything we can.'

Sara released her arms, ignoring the last sentence. 'When can I see Cameron?'

'I'm not sure that's a good idea at the moment. He took a wound to the head. I'm so sorry.'

'How can you even be sure it's him?'

'He was identified by—'

'His partner. Yes, I read that in the papers too.' Her knack of interrupting was starting to grate. 'Rob Barclay doesn't really know Cameron well. He might have worked with him for the best part of twelve years, but Cameron is on the road so much, he barely saw him from one month to another. And if he was disfigured...' She swallowed, a pained expression spreading across her face like a stain. 'Well, he could have made a mistake.'

She doesn't know about Monika and the children. Beth had scoured the press reports online before she'd left that morning. They reported Cameron's body had been identified by his partner. That he left a girlfriend and two children behind. Monika had asked for their names to be kept out of the press, for the sake of her children, for as long as possible. If Sara assumed Cameron's work partner identified his body, did she also assume the girlfriend and two children referred to in the press might be her?

'There's no mistake,' Beth said.

'How do you know that?'

'There are other ways.' Beth didn't elaborate, not wishing to discuss the intimate details of DNA and dental records. Now didn't seem the time, or the place. 'We're absolutely sure.'

Sara sank back into the sofa and covered her face. Tears bled through her fingers, spotting her shirt. A tiny sob escaped.

'I'm sorry.' Beth retrieved a tissue from her case, passed it over and gave her a moment. Her eyes scoured the room, taking in the photos of the girls at various stages of growth, adorning the walls. On the dresser was a pewter statue of a man carrying a shotgun with a Labrador at his feet. Beside it was a family portrait: Cameron, Sara, Zoe, and Amy, with fixed smiles. From the look of the girls, it had been taken fairly recently, in the last twelve months or so. Her gaze rested on two gilded frames, one either side of the fireplace, that contained snapshots of Cameron and Sara. In the first, she wore a strapless, purple ballgown. He wore a black suit with a matching bow tie. They sat at a dinner table in the second, heads resting against each other, raising their glasses to the camera. 'Do you know of anyone who might want to hurt Cameron?' she asked, when Sara's tears eased.

Sara wiped the soggy tissue beneath each eye. 'No.'

'Anyone he might have upset recently?'

A sniff was accompanied by a brief headshake.

'Anything you can tell us might help,' Beth pressed. 'When did you last speak with him?'

'He phoned on Tuesday evening. Goa is four and a half hours ahead, so it would have been the afternoon here.'

Beth mentally worked through Monika's recollection of when Cameron was home. He was in Northampton that evening. She imagined him driving down the motorway, calling up one family while on his way to visit another. Not unusual in itself. What was unusual was that they didn't appear to know about each other. 'He phoned you in Goa? You didn't talk over the Internet, or FaceTime?'

'No, we always kept in contact by phone. Cameron didn't do FaceTime. He didn't do anything online.'

At least that concurred with Monika's description of Cameron's dislike of social media, Beth thought. But what made him so private? Was he concerned about his secret families discovering each other, or was there another reason?

'How did he seem?'

'What?'

'When you spoke with him on Tuesday.'

'Good. He asked what the girls and I had been up to.'

'Why didn't he come on holiday with you, or join you out there later?'

'He was supposed to be coming, even booked a seat on the flight. But I wasn't surprised when he changed his mind. Cameron's not a holiday person. Work always takes priority.'

'You must have been disappointed.'

'For the girls, maybe.' Sara's eyes rose to the ceiling. 'It wasn't the first time.'

'Do you know where he was, or what he was working on when you spoke with him on Tuesday?'

'I think he said he was in Wales somewhere. I might be wrong though. He travelled all over, I didn't pay attention. We didn't talk about his work.'

'Never?' Beth was finding this perplexing. Monika had said the same thing on Sunday. Sharing the highs and lows of her day with someone was one of the things she missed most about living alone, but these two women were unabashed, as if it were normal.

'No. Not at all.'

'Did he come back here while you were away?'

'I'm not sure. He came and went as he pleased, to fit in with his work. You could ask Yvonne. She might have seen him. She was feeding our rabbits. Or Aggy, our cleaner. She comes in twice a week. She'd probably know.'

Beth jotted down their names and made a note to get their details later. 'What can you tell me about his family and friends?'

'Cameron doesn't have any family, not that we are in contact with anyway. His parents died before I met him.' She paused, squinting slightly. 'There's a brother in Canada. Newfoundland, I think, but they haven't spoken in years.'

Beth kept her face impassive, careful not to give anything away here. She wondered how the interview with David Swift in the Shetland Islands was going this morning. It seemed odd neither woman knew he'd moved back to the UK. Another piece of the jigsaw puzzle of Cameron's life that had been tucked away, detached. 'Do you know why they haven't spoken?'

'Not really. Something about their parents' will, I think. He didn't like to talk about it. I never met his brother; I don't think they ever really got on.'

'What about your family? Are you close?'

'Not particularly. They live in India. We visit them once a year. Yvonne is more like family to us.'

Beth gave a rueful smile. 'I'll need to take details of all your friends here, so we can eliminate them from our enquiries. You've lived here a long time, you said?'

'Seven years. Although Cameron wasn't here that much. And when he was, he wanted us to himself. He met our friends and neighbours occasionally, at birthdays and celebrations, but not regularly. He said the men were boring and the women affected. He was quite vocal about it.' She looked across to the window. 'Cameron didn't believe in keeping his views to himself.'

'How often did you see him?'

'What do you mean, "see him"? He lived here.' Her face tensed, as if something had snapped inside. 'Look, detective, what I want to know is, why wasn't I contacted before you released the details to the press?' She hissed the final word out through gritted teeth. 'Do you know what it's like to find out about your partner's death from a newspaper report on the Internet? My girls could have seen it, for Christ's sake! And that image...' She placed a hand over her eyes, circled her palm on her forehead.

'I'm sorry,' Beth said. 'I realise it must have been very disturbing for you. We are working with all the social media outlets to take down the image. I understand you've made a complaint and it will be fully investigated.'

They were interrupted by a scuffle outside. Yvonne entered, looking flustered. 'Those cases are heavier than they look,' she said, almost to herself. The bland comment melted some of the tension in the room.

Sara stared at her. 'Are the children okay?'

'They're fine. I've got them unpacking.' She patted Sara's knee as she sat beside her. 'Might take their minds off things for a while.'

'How many days a week was Cameron home, roughly?' Beth asked, keen to press on.

'During the week, two or three days, maybe. Sometimes none.' Sara shrugged a single shoulder. 'It depended where he was working. I could always reach him on his mobile though, leave messages and he'd call me back.'

'Did he ever work from here?' She didn't use the word 'home' because it didn't feel right somehow. At the moment, she wasn't sure where Cameron called home.

'He used to, in the early days, when the girls were babies.

When we first moved here, the room upstairs at the back of the house was converted into a study so he could work partly from home. Although—' she grimaced '—as the years passed, he spent more and more time in there. The girls would get restless, waiting for him to finish something so we could go out together. At times, it felt like I was a single parent; it was hard enough when he was away. I moaned about him working away, then coming home and working again here. A few months ago, he shut down his home office, moved his paperwork back to their main office in Birmingham, and made it into a spare room.' She flicked her eyes to the ceiling. 'Not that we needed another room. But it meant when he was at home, he was with us. He spent more time at the office in Birmingham, used his laptop in an emergency. I thought it would mean we saw more of him and the girls would have more time with their dad, but inevitably we saw him less. He still had the same amount of work to do.'

Just about the time Cameron and Monika moved to Northampton, Beth thought. 'What about weekends?'

Yvonne sat forwards. 'I don't think this is relevant.'

'We believe Cameron's killer had been watching him for some time, was aware of his movements. There may have been witnesses who've seen them and not even realised it.'

Sara pressed a hand to her chest. 'You think they came here?'

'We have no reason to suggest that at the moment. But we would advise you to be extra vigilant.' Beth looked out at the front garden. 'I see you have gates at the end of the driveway.'

'Yes, they were Cameron's baby. He insisted on having

them installed when we came here, but we've only used them a few times. They're electronically controlled by intercom from the hallway.'

'I would suggest you keep them closed for a while. I don't want to alarm you, but there's nothing wrong with caution.'

Sara nodded her head, wide-eyed, as Beth continued, 'Building up a picture of Cameron's life, his routine, movements and associations will help us track down whoever was responsible. So, what about weekends?'

'Weekends were difficult,' Sara said. She let her hand fall back into her lap, but her face was still pinched with concern. 'The travelling ate into them. Plus, his job required socials: golf games, networking, that sort of thing. He was usually here one day of the weekend, at least.' She paused a moment and viewed the eucalyptus tree out front. 'When you're with an ambitious man you get used to the absences, make allowances.' She turned back to the room and swallowed, her eyes brimming once more. Her hand danced in the air, a sweeping gesture. 'It provided us with all of this.'

Yvonne snaked an arm around her shoulder, pulled her close.

Beth decided to change tack. 'When did you get married?' she asked, although she already knew the answer to that question. Enquiries into Cameron's background showed he was unmarried, but she was curious why Sara had taken his name.

'We weren't officially married. We talked about it when Zoe was born and decided to wait to make it official, until she was old enough to be a bridesmaid. I changed my name to make things easier for all of us. Then Amy came along and, well—' she stretched out her hand, glanced down at her empty wedding finger '—it was always intended, always there in the background. We just never got around to setting a date.'

'You said his work required a lot of social gatherings. Did you spend time with his work colleagues?' Beth asked.

'I met his partner a couple of times, when we first got together. He visited with his wife when Zoe was born. They bought us a lovely Moses basket. I haven't seen them in years though.'

'You didn't attend social events with him, or speak with anyone at Barclay Swift on the phone?'

'I used to phone there, when we were first together. I got fed up, constantly leaving messages he didn't return. Cameron preferred his mobile. He was on the road so much, it was the best way to reach him. I never met his clients. He kept his work separate from his home. Like I said, he was insistent.'

Beth looked down at her notes. Sara's answers mirrored Monika's almost completely. If both women were to be believed, he was spending part of the week with one, and part with another.

A tear meandered down Sara's cheek. She turned to Yvonne. 'How are we going to manage without him?'

Beth watched her bury her face in Yvonne's shoulder. 'Why don't I make us some drinks?' she said.

19

The job required patience; people rarely opened up to the police right away. But, as she rummaged through Sara's cupboards searching for mugs, tea, and sugar, the relationship status of Cameron and Sara played on Beth's mind. The photos in the front room and her conversation with Sara hinted at a close family unit, still very much together. Was this true, or was she a manipulative ex-partner, creating a scenario, putting out photographs, looking to plant her stake for a portion of his estate? Did she play a part in his death?

Her mind wandered to her colleagues back at the station. Had they cracked the encryption on the memory stick and phone kept in Cameron's car? The victim had been careful to hide them away. Was there something on there that might implicate Sara, or Monika even?

The kitchen was fitted with cream, cottage-style cupboards with a workstation in the middle and a breakfast bar at the side. An archway led into a dining room beyond, located directly behind the lounge. There was a cat flap fitted into the back door, a food and drinking bowl beside it. No sign of a cat though. Beth retrieved the milk she'd bought on the way up, presuming the fridge might be empty if they'd been away on holiday, and continued to work her way through the cupboards, finding what she needed. She was stirring a heaped spoonful of sugar into one of the mugs when a grating sound at the front of the house caught her attention. She moved out into the hallway and hovered outside the sitting room. Sara's sobs had subsided slightly, and she could hear the crisp timbre of Yvonne's voice through the closed door. Another scratch. Followed by a squeak. Beth walked up the hallway to the bottom of the stairs where she found a disgruntled Amy tugging at the last and largest of the three suitcases. It scraped at the polished floor as she pulled.

'Are you all right?' Beth asked.

The young girl jumped, eyes wide.

'Did you want to take that upstairs?'

Amy nodded warily.

'I can do it for you, if you like? I'm sure that would help your mum.'

The girl's face brightened slightly. Beth hauled it to her side. 'Why don't you show me where you want it?'

They climbed the staircase to the first floor. Sunlight streamed in through an oval stained-glass window facing frontwards, inviting a rainbow of colour across the light landing carpet.

'Where would you like it?' Beth asked again.

Amy pushed open a door to one of the rooms at the back of the house and Beth followed her inside. It was a large room with a four-poster bed of the size Beth had only ever seen in a hotel room, while on holiday in Majorca.

'Is this your mum and dad's bedroom?' Beth asked.

The girl stared back at her blankly, her lips tight.

'I'll leave it on the bed there then,' Beth said, catching her reflection in the mirrored front of the wardrobes opposite. If only she could take a look inside… but Amy was at the door, waiting for her. The room looked like a show home, the bed dressed and ready, and nothing out of place. In fact, nothing out at all, apart from a pair of ornate lamps on each of the bedside tables. She saw another door on the far wall, sat slightly ajar, and her eyes narrowed.

'Do you want me to open the case for you?' she said, trying her best to look as though she wasn't prying.

The girl shook her head. 'Thank you.' The soft, high-pitched voice took Beth by surprise. 'For carrying it upstairs.'

Beth smiled at her. 'You're welcome.' She followed her back towards the landing, nudging open the door that sat ajar with her elbow as she passed. It swung back to reveal a Jacuzzi bath in the corner, a sink facing her. There was only one toothbrush in the holder above the sink. Did that belong to Cameron, or Sara? Since Sara hadn't had time to unpack yet, she couldn't be sure. Amy was talking to her sister on the landing now. Beth pushed the door wider. She spotted a bottle on the glass shelf above the sink – CK One, a unisex cologne. No help there then. As she left the room, she checked the back of the main door and clocked a charcoal towelling bathrobe. Sara's, Cameron's or someone else's? It was difficult to say.

Amy had disappeared into one of the other rooms by the time Beth reached the landing. She stood for a moment counting the doors in her head, six all together, when a door downstairs snapped open. She made for the stairs, descending quickly. Yvonne's inquisitive stare met her at the bottom. She reminded Beth of a schoolmistress.

'What are you doing?' Yvonne asked.

'Amy wanted to take the last suitcase upstairs, to help her mother,' Beth said lightly. 'I carried it up for her.' She walked past her, back into the kitchen. 'The tea is almost made.'

The soft lavender aroma of Yvonne's perfume filled the kitchen. Out of the corner of her eye, Beth noticed the cut of her denim dress. She didn't need a label to tell her it was high-end, the sort of thing she might purchase for a special dinner with friends or a night out, not a regular weekday when all you were doing was housesitting for a friend.

'How is Sara doing?' Beth asked, tapping the spoon on the side of one of the mugs.

Yvonne was quiet a moment. 'She's worn out with the flight and shock of it all. She needs to rest.'

'She said you've known each other a long time.'

'Must be...' Yvonne paused, patting her fingers on her chin. She spoke slowly, clearly, and with the faint hint of a Yorkshire accent. 'Around seven years. Shortly after she moved here.'

'Did you know Cameron well?'

'Not really. I'm mostly here when he's away.'

Did you see him at the house while Sara and the children were in Goa?'

'No.'

'When did you last see him?'

'Oh, it must be a few weeks ago.'

Beth placed the last mug on the tray and turned to ask another question, only to find Yvonne had disappeared. She carried the tray into the lounge and found her with Sara. As she handed out the drinks, a voice called down the stairs. 'Mum!'

Sara made to stand, but Yvonne held up a flat hand and rose. 'I'll go. You drink your tea. God knows, you need it.'

'It's good to see you have support,' Beth said, watching her go.

'Yvonne's brilliant,' Sara said woefully, taking a sip of the tea.

'How did you meet?'

'When Cameron and I first moved here, we took a short-term rent around the corner until the house was ready. Yvonne was our neighbour.' A weak smile curled her lip. 'I was pregnant back then, suffering from morning sickness. Yvonne has three grown-up children, all left home. She couldn't do enough to help. When we moved in here and the girls were born, we became even closer. She introduced me to the neighbourhood, helped me find the right schools for the girls. I don't know what I would have done without her.'

They sipped their drinks a moment. Yvonne eventually reappeared. 'Amy couldn't find her washbag. She's okay now.' She settled herself back onto the sofa beside Sara. 'They're doing well, all things considered.'

Beth placed her mug down on the coffee table beside her. 'I need to ask for a list of your friends, especially those known to Cameron, and any associations Cameron might have had here.'

'I think we can manage that,' Yvonne said, snapping back to Beth.

'Thank you.' She opened her iPad and took down the details, emailing them back to the office when they'd finished. 'There is another thing I need to ask you,' Beth said easing back into her seat and addressing Sara. 'I'm afraid it's rather sensitive.'

Sara's brows knitted together, but it was Yvonne that spoke. 'What is it?'

Beth ignored the other woman. 'Are you aware of any other family Cameron may have in the UK?' She stared directly at Sara as she spoke.

'No, I already told you, he only has a brother—'

'What about children?'

Sara's eyes widened at the interruption. When she spoke, her voice was tight. 'Not apart from his girls upstairs, no.'

Beth took a moment. 'Has he ever spoken about a home in Northamptonshire?'

'Yes, his parents' home. That's where he grew up.'

'Another home he had in Northamptonshire?'

Sara looked at Yvonne, and back to Beth. 'I don't know what you are talking about.'

Beth paused to choose the right words, aware that the news she was about to deliver could inflict a spear of pain that would drive deep. 'I have to tell you this, because this is a high-profile case and sooner or later you may hear something in the media. Cameron was shot outside his family home in Northamptonshire.'

'Yes, outside his parents'—'

'I'm afraid not. His parents lived in Duston, West Northants. Cameron was shot outside his family home in Collingtree Park.'

'I don't understand.'

'His family home. Where he lives with his partner, Monika, and their two sons, Oskar and Jakub.'

Sara's hand flew to her throat, aghast. The soft tinkling of the eucalyptus tree leaves out front filled the room.

'Are you saying he has other children, from a previous

relationship?' Yvonne's voice splintered as she spoke. For the first time since they'd arrived that day, she looked genuinely shocked.

Beth ignored her and watched Sara carefully. 'Did you know anything about Cameron's family in Northamptonshire?'

Sara swallowed. She looked like she was going to be sick. 'No.'

'What about any other children?'

She gave a single head shake. Her chin trembled.

'Are you sure?' Yvonne asked. 'I mean, are you sure they are his? That this isn't some woman claiming to be attached to him? He was worth quite a lot of money you know.'

'The house is registered in his name.'

Sara closed her eyes, pressed a hand to her forehead.

'That doesn't prove anything,' Yvonne remarked, defiant. 'How long do they claim to have lived there?'

'Three months.'

Yvonne sneered. 'They could be distant relatives, or a family he's been helping out.'

'They lived together in Birmingham beforehand. On the wharf. We've checked.'

'Were they married?'

Beth hesitated before she answered, holding back the body blow as long as possible. 'I'm told they were engaged.'

The air in the room thickened.

'How old?' Sara interjected. Her voice was barely a whisper.

'What?'

'How old are the children?'

'Oskar, his stepson, is twelve,' Beth said. 'Jakub is almost nine months.'

Sara closed her eyes, wincing as the sting of the youngest child's age penetrated deep. Her lip quivered. 'I don't believe you.'

'I'm sorry,' Beth said. 'I realise this must be difficult. That's why we hadn't reached you. Cameron was identified by his girlfriend in Northamptonshire. We had no idea he had other family, other children.'

Sara blinked, pulled up her knees and hugged them protectively. She pressed her head to her thighs and a sob escaped.

'I think you'd better go,' Yvonne said.

Beth ignored her, angling her head at Sara. 'It's better you know now.'

'Better! For who? You, the police? It's certainly not better for us,' Yvonne said cradling her friend.

'It may be mentioned in the media.'

'Wouldn't be a first for you guys to withhold information from the family,' she chided. 'Didn't you check with his work colleagues, his friends?'

'We did. They didn't mention Sara.'

An animal-like cry filled the room. Yvonne rubbed her friend's back. 'What did you say your role was?' she snapped.

'Family liaison officer. I support victims' families, update them on any developments.'

'Is that what you were doing upstairs? Helping out?'

Sara raised her head. Her face clouded.

'I was helping Amy with a suitcase,' Beth said. 'I'm here to help and support you all.'

'Help. All you've done is shower yet more sadness on a grieving widow. How does that help? This other family could be something and nothing. Have you considered that? This was Cameron's family. Right here. His family of seven years!'

Sara was rocking, backwards and forwards, catching her breaths as the cries rattled around her chest.

'I think you should go,' Yvonne said.

'I'm here for Sara, and the family.'

'They don't want you here, do you, darling?' She stroked Sara's hair.

Sara was quiet a moment, lost in the rhythm of her movements. When she looked up, her eyes darkened in glassy defiance. 'I don't need the police,' she said. 'And I don't want you near my children.'

Beth placed her notebook in her case and drew out a card, leaving it on the coffee table beside Sara. 'My contact details are there. If you think of anything else, or just want to talk, don't hesitate to call.'

20

Beth's mobile phone crackled as she overtook a lorry and crossed the Leicestershire border on her way back from Cheshire. 'She wasn't impressed by my meeting her at the airport, even though it had been arranged, and got rid of me as soon as she could.' She adjusted the phone earpiece and went on to recap the details of her meeting with Sara Swift to Chief Inspector Freeman. 'She doesn't want officers in and out of her house, and flatly refused the presence of a family liaison officer. Ran just short of calling me a snoop.'

'We've traced his will. She was certainly a beneficiary,' Freeman said with a sigh. 'Both Monika and she are mentioned, plus a few trust funds for the kids. Not that there'll be much of a payout if his bank accounts are anything to go by. He was in debt up to his eyeballs.'

'Well, he was providing for two families.'

'Hm. There's a lot more work to do, but the finances don't add up at the moment.' Freeman was quiet a moment. 'I think we'll instigate a search on the house in Cheshire.'

'It's worth a try. I'm not sure we'll find anything though. They've had a friend looking after the house while they've been away.' She gave him the rundown on Yvonne Newman. 'If Sara is guilty or connected to Cameron's death in any way, and there were any clues, they'll have likely already removed them.'

Freeman paused before he answered. 'I think we'll search it anyway. I don't want to antagonise her further, especially with the live complaint outstanding, but there is always the possibility her hostility is a front to put us off. I've got the press clogging up the phone lines, and the chief constable breathing down my neck. We need to make sure we cover every eventuality.'

'Do you want me to call to let her know?'

The line was quiet a moment. 'No, I'll phone her myself. I want her to know this directive is coming from the top.'

Beth pressed her foot on the brake as the traffic slowed in front. 'I don't know. There's something about her, an edge. She resented my presence.' She wiped a film of sweat from her forehead. The heat of the day was really kicking in now. 'Do we know any more about her?'

'She's been registered for council tax at Knighton Lane for the last seven years, since before her first child was born. Before that she was a teaching assistant at Steeples Primary in Manchester. We've spoken to the school who said her record was clean, attendance good. She worked there for almost a year.'

Disappointment clutched at Beth. First, she hadn't been able to persuade Monika to leave her house, now Sara had refused to have her visit. Some liaison officer she was turning out to be.

Freeman seemed to guess her mood. 'Don't take it to heart. She won't be the first family to refuse the services of an FLO. It's a difficult time. People react differently to grief.'

Beth edged forwards. Even the traffic was thwarting her today. 'Any news on Monika's background?'

A paper rustled in the background. Freeman gave a short cough before he answered. 'She moved to the UK in October 2008. Joined City Western Hospital in Birmingham soon afterwards. Met Cameron in 2015, and in 2016 Jakub was born. We've spoken with Oskar's dad in Poland via Skype. He appears to have genuinely liked Cameron and was shocked by his death. There's nothing in his background, or any of Cameron's details to suggest recent contact or any animosity.'

That concluded another line of enquiry. 'Any news from the brother?'

'Not yet. I've sent DC Latham up there. He had to take two flights, one to Edinburgh and another to the Shetlands. It's costing a bloody fortune.'

Beth grunted inwardly at his remarks. Senior investigating officers were always panicking about their budgets. At least he'd sent somebody decent. Latham was a grounded detective with almost twenty years' investigative experience behind him. If there was something amiss, Latham would spot it.

'Oh, one other thing about Monika,' Freeman added. 'The hospital said she took a period of extended sick leave in her early pregnancy and confirmed she resigned shortly afterwards.'

It seemed odd to resign before a child was born. Usually mothers, especially those in public service and with local authorities, took advantage of the maternity provisions and made their decision either to stay or leave a job after the child was born.

'The victim was a strange character, don't you think?' she said.

'Why, because he managed two families? Christ, most men struggle to keep one happy these days.' A throaty laugh filled the phone line.

'No. It's more the women he chose.'

'What do you mean?'

'Women that don't have any family nearby, no support network. He set them up in a nice house, financed a good lifestyle. Took them away from their friends.'

'He was controlling.'

'That's exactly it. He controlled them. Both houses were in his name. He paid the bills, gave them allowances. They were almost beholden to him.'

21

Later that evening, Beth sauntered into the kitchen of her cottage and opened the back door. Balmy evening air stretched in, carrying with it the sweet aroma of honeysuckle and phlox. She poured herself a generous glass of Zinfandel Rosé and stepped outside, listening to the birds twitter and flutter about in the willow tree next door.

The glass clinked as she placed it on the metal patio table. She closed her eyes, enjoying the flurry of fresh air filling her lungs, allowing the day's events to wash over her. While she'd been expecting some hostility from Sara Swift, she hadn't been prepared for the level of resistance she faced, even considering the sensitive news she'd had to deliver. Was her hostility a genuine combination of shock and anger at not being advised of her partner's death, or was it a tactic to keep the police from her door? She couldn't help but wonder how much her friend, Yvonne Newman, influenced her decision too. She made a mental note to check up on Yvonne's status with the office.

Both Monika's and Sara's accounts of Cameron's habits mirrored each other. Two grieving partners in different parts of the country. Did they really know nothing about each other, or were they good actors, colluding together, or with another, to kill off their joint partner?

She grabbed her phone, pulled up her emails and selected Warren's daily report. Apart from a short visit from a neighbour, Monika had been quiet and detached all day. Warren attended the evening briefing and talked about the trace of the brother – they were still awaiting Latham's contact. But there was no further news on the memory stick or the phone.

She closed the email and rested her phone on the table. She was beginning to understand why the victim had been so private with his work diary. He wasn't travelling so much as dividing his life between two families. How he'd kept up the pretence and lived a life of secrecy for so long, she'd never know. The Twitter message tripped into her mind. The techies still hadn't been able to trace the sender. She couldn't help but wonder what other secrets they were set to unfold before this investigation was over.

Myrtle slunk up beside her and she dropped a hand to stroke the cat's smoky-grey head. She wasn't sure how long she sat there, the peace of her surroundings slowing her thoughts to a calm pace. A pair of crows cawed at each other, rose into the air, and swooped overhead. She watched them a moment until she caught something. The distant sound of a voice. Beth glanced up at the spare room she kept for when her niece, Lily, came for sleepovers, an automatic gesture. The curtains were undrawn. Of course they were. She was with Eden tonight. She dropped her eyes as the wisp of a shadow enlarged and a face appeared at the back door.

Beth jerked back, knocking the table. Droplets of wine spilled out of the glass as it rocked and steadied itself.

Nick Geary entered the garden grinning.

'You could have called out,' Beth said, steadying the glass.

'You were the one who gave me a key,' he said as she wiped the wine from her trousers.

'I gave you a key to drop off some papers over a month ago. And you didn't return it.' The edge in her tone was mixed with a soft smile.

He smirked back at her. Nick lived on the county border, almost an hour's drive from headquarters. She'd told him to hold onto the key and use it to call in, rest there sometimes when they had a case pressing that didn't allow time for the long journey home. Truth be known, she enjoyed the impromptu company but still, she couldn't resist the opportunity to tease him.

He raised a brow. 'Bad time?'

'No, it's fine. I'm just taking a few minutes.'

He nodded at the glass of Zinfandel sitting in front of her. 'So I see.'

'You want one?'

He pulled a face. 'I'd love to, but I'm needed at the office. Only popped back to get a couple of hours' kip. Okay if I crash here?'

'Sure.'

He sunk his hands into his pockets and stared at the sky. 'We got an anonymous tip, a caller through the incident room. They said we need to look at Nigel Sherwood.'

Nigel Sherwood was the owner of Barton's snooker hall and Ruby's casino in the centre of Northampton town.

Intelligence suggested he had fingers in lots of pies, from drug trafficking to prostitution. The local organised crime unit had been trailing him for years and spent a small fortune on surveillance on several occasions, although he was far too clever to have been caught anywhere near anything sinister. 'Why?'

'We're not sure at the moment. They simply said, "Look at Nigel Sherwood in connection with the Collingtree Park murder," and rung off.'

'How odd. I suppose it could be a crank, of course, or someone with a vendetta against Sherwood. I imagine he's upset plenty of people over the years. Could we trace the caller?'

'No. It came from a mobile, pay as you go. Unregistered. We've nothing else to link Sherwood to Cameron. Sherwood was out of town this weekend, at his sister's wedding at some posh hotel in Norfolk. There will be cameras, no doubt.'

'It's unlikely he'd have done this himself though, even if he was responsible.'

'Quite. Freeman wants to play it close. You know what Sherwood's like. We'd need something pretty concrete before we pull him in. He sent the source handlers out to talk to their contacts, but nobody has come up with anything yet. It was a cryptic message. A man in Sherwood's position has got a lot of enemies, there'll be people lining up to take his place. Perhaps Cameron was gambling, using his casino. It might go some way to explain his wayward accounting. For a man who specialises in finance, he certainly didn't manage his own well. Unless there's some offshore bank account or investment we don't know about, it's hard to see how he's kept everything going.'

Myrtle looped around her ankles. Beth checked her watch. It was almost six. She began to think about something to eat. 'How did Latham get on with David Swift today?' she asked.

'Not great. David claimed he hadn't seen his brother in six years. He had no idea Cameron had family.'

'He doesn't know about the children?' Beth checked back the dates in her mind. That would have been around the time Zoe was born. It seemed strange that Cameron wouldn't have mentioned Sara or the new baby to his brother.

'He said not. He thought his brother was the perennial bachelor.'

'I can't understand why David Swift hasn't been in touch with us. His brother's murder has been all over the news.'

'He reckoned he'd only just found out about the murder when we called him. He lives alone, works for a local farmer and rents a cottage on their land. He doesn't do the Internet – doesn't even have a television. It was the farmer who saw it on the news; they noticed the connection with the name and asked him, or so he says. We'll check, obviously, but he claims he hasn't left the Shetlands in years.'

'Did he fall out with his brother?'

'Apparently so. An investment Cameron made for them both with some of the legacy from their parents' estate didn't work out. Cameron told him it was low risk; he lost a lot of money. He hasn't spoken to him since.'

'That must have made him pretty angry.'

'Possibly. But Latham said he was nonchalant. Invited us to look into his affairs, said we'd find nothing. He blamed himself for trusting his younger brother with the money.'

'Where does that leave us?'

'Barking up the wrong tree. Latham took a statement but doesn't think there's anything more in it. Freeman wants his bank records checked, in case there's been a recent exchange of cash. I think he's on a hiding to nothing, to be honest.'

'Or trying to recover some of that plane fare.'

Nick grinned. 'Yes. That's going to take some explaining. It's sent the budget into overdrive.'

Beth rolled her eyes. She reached out for the wine glass when her mobile trilled. 'Eden' flashed up on the screen.

'She won't stop crying.' The young voice spoke without preamble.

Beth lowered the glass. 'Lily, is that you?'

'Yes. I don't know what to do. She won't stop crying.' There was a crisp urgency in her voice.

'Where are you?'

'At home, on Mummy's phone.'

A car engine revved nearby. Beth pressed her free hand over her other ear. 'And where is Mummy?'

'Lying on the sofa.'

'Is she hurt?'

'I don't know. I don't think so. She just keeps crying. I don't know what to do.'

'Stay where you are. I'll be there in a few minutes.'

She cut the call and turned to Nick. 'I'm sorry, I have to go out.'

'What's going on?'

'I'm not sure. There's a problem with my sister. I need to get over there.'

'I'll come with you.'

Beth grimaced. 'I don't think that's a good idea.'

'Then I'll wait until you come back.'

'No, you get some sleep.' She stood and planted a kiss on his cheek. 'I'll see you later.'

22

The broad sound of cattle lowing filtered into the car as Beth turned into Chancery Court that evening. Almost immediately, she faced a black BMW heading out. The driver was approaching in the centre of the road at speed, holding a mobile phone to his ear. Beth slammed on the brakes, pulled down hard on the steering wheel, and missed him by inches. She turned to catch his number plate, but he was too fast. She caught the digits '42' before the wheels of the BMW screeched and rounded the corner, a wave of dry dust skipping up in its wake. Beth cursed under her breath. For a split second she was torn between chasing the driver down and giving him a warning, and parking outside her sister's. But the silhouette of a child in the front room window of number four settled matters for her.

Lily was at the front door before she was out of the car. It was clear from her distracted face she hadn't seen the near collision. 'She's stopped crying, but I don't think she's well.' She grabbed hold of her aunt's hand and led her through to the front room where Eden sat on the sofa.

Beth gave Lily a reassuring shoulder squeeze and crouched beside her sister. 'Eden?'

Eden's red-rimmed eyes were glassy, vacant. Mascara stains trailed her cheeks. Beth turned to her niece. 'Sweetheart, could you get Mummy a glass of water please?'

The child nodded and disappeared. 'Has something happened?' she asked, stroking her sister's hair.

Eden didn't answer, her eyes fixed in space.

The child re-entered the room, slowly putting one foot in front of another, both hands wrapped around the glass.

Eden lifted her hand and took the glass, her rising cuff exposing the edge of a star tattoo on her wrist. 'Thank you, darling,' she said to Lily. 'You are kind.' Her breaths cut. 'I've got a bit of a headache, that's all.'

Lily's worried glance passed between them.

'Oh, I almost forgot,' Beth said to her niece, injecting a light tone to her voice in an effort to disperse the cloud hanging in the room. 'I've got something for you in the car.'

'What is it?' The child's eyes were like bowls.

Beth pulled her car keys out of her pocket. They tinkled against each other as she held them up. 'Why don't you go and see?'

Lily looked at her mother, bit her lip. 'Go on,' Beth continued. 'I'll sit with Mummy.' A nod from Eden set her feet into motion.

'It's in the boot,' Beth called after her. The door slammed shut.

'You spoil her,' Eden said.

'It's only a school bag. I meant to give it to her on Sunday. The strap was frayed on her old one.' She looked at the watery stains on the cushion her sister still hugged. 'Are you going to tell me what's happened?'

Eden held out the glass at an angle, so as not to spill the contents, and tucked her feet beneath her. She swallowed a mouthful of the water. 'I'm numb, empty.'

Beth inhaled and paused a moment, recalling the antidepressants Eden had been prescribed after the separation. 'Have you been taking your medication?'

She gave a frail nod, swallowed down the rest of the drink, and placed the empty glass on the floor.

'Perhaps you need to go back to the doctor, get the dosage reviewed.'

Eden ignored the statement, grabbed a tissue and blew her nose. The buzz of Beth's phone filled the room. It was a text from Nick.

Call me when you get this.

She looked up to see Eden's eyes glued to her and cast the phone aside.

A wave of cool air was followed by the sound of the front door slamming. Lily ran into the room holding the princess bag high in front of her mother. 'Oh, that's lovely,' Eden said. She scraped the ailing words out. 'It'll be great for the new school year. Why don't you see if your new pens and pencils fit into the pockets?'

Lily beamed. 'Thank you, Auntie Beth,' she said and dashed out. Her feet pumped the stairs, the noise inordinately loud for her small frame.

Beth's phone buzzed again. She ignored it.

'I got this,' Eden said. She reached into her pocket, pulled out a folded square of paper and handed it to Beth, who opened it slowly. An embossed company address decorated the paper in blue at the top. Underneath it read 'Member of the Family Mediation Association'. Her sister's eyes filled again. 'He wants to take her away from me.'

The letter invited Eden to an appointment with Chris and a family mediator to formally agree the details of their separation, and listed issues like their home, pensions, savings and custody of Lily. 'I'm sure this is a standard part of the separation process,' Beth said gently. 'He wants to make it official. There's nothing here to suggest he wants Lily to live with him.'

'It says custody. Not access. It's specific.'

Beth surveyed her a moment. Lily had moved freely between Eden and Chris since the separation, an informal agreement which appeared to suit the child. 'It's probably the way they word things. I think you're overreacting.'

'You have no idea.'

Eden's response surprised her. 'Have you spoken to him? Or has Lily mentioned something?'

'No.'

Beth folded the letter back into its square. 'I don't think it's anything to worry about,' she said in her most reassuring voice. But seeing her sister's forlorn face, she added, 'Do you want me to speak with him, to set your mind at rest?'

'No. Promise me you won't? You do enough for us already.'

She nodded, opened her mouth to probe her sister more, but closed it again when Lily dashed back into the room. The new bag was now packed to the brim and rattling with pencils and pens and she went to great lengths explaining which fitted into the different compartments.

'Have you guys eaten?' Beth asked as Lily quietened.

They shook their heads.

'Why don't we get a takeaway together?'

Lily stood and did a little dance. 'Yay!'

It was after nine when Beth left. Her stomach was full to bursting with the aromatic crispy duck they'd ordered from the Chinese takeaway in the next village. Afterwards they'd watched *Mamma Mia!*, one of Eden's favourite films. Lily insisted on staying up until the end of the film and Beth read a chapter of Enid Blyton's *Mallory Towers* as she put her to bed, sending the child into peals of laughter as she mimicked the accent of the French teachers while Eden looked on from the doorway.

Beth turned over the engine and watched her sister tug her cardigan around her shoulders. She seemed brighter; still, the earlier episode unnerved Beth. Eden had tucked the letter away in her pocket and refused to talk about it again, but the mere presence of it was permanently etched on her face. Why would she assume Chris wanted to fight for custody of Lily? After the separation, he'd created distance between Eden and him, corresponding via text, staying in the car when he arrived to pick up Lily, but they'd both tried to protect their daughter, who appeared oblivious to any animosity. It didn't make sense.

The drive to the other side of the village took less than a minute. Mawsley was a modern village, built in the heart of the Northamptonshire countryside almost twenty years earlier, but designed sympathetically with curved lanes and red-brick houses, interspersed with cottages in the traditional Northamptonshire sandstone. Beth steered onto her empty driveway. Darkness seeped out of the windows of her cottage. The thought of sitting in there tonight, all alone, didn't appeal. She retrieved her phone and pulled up the messages to reveal another text from Nick.

Ring me when you get this.

She stared at it a moment, her fingers poised to call back, and then reversed the car, revved the engine and drove off down the road.

23

Beth parked up beside Nick's Spider and crossed the office car park under the obliging light of a crescent moon.

The incident room was crowded, far busier than she'd expected for this late hour. She nodded at some of her colleagues as she wandered through. Nick, who was leaning over an officer's shoulder in the far corner, pointing out something on their computer screen, looked up as she approached.

'What are you doing here?' he asked.

'I got your messages.'

'You didn't need to drive all the way here.' He excused himself and guided her to his desk at the side of the room, away from the others. 'How was Eden?'

Freeman's recent words pressed heavily on her. If she wanted to keep her place on the team, she couldn't afford to let anyone know about possible ongoing problems between Eden and Chris. Not even Nick. 'Okay. It was nothing important.' She wrinkled her nose, but the lie stuck in her throat as it escaped.

'If you need some time off—'

'There's no need.'

'Well, keep me posted. If you do need some family time, I'll square it with Freeman.'

'Thanks. How are things going here?' Beth said. Several detectives were bent over computers, tapping keys, the outline of their frames mirrored in the dark windows encasing the office. 'I wasn't expecting to see so many in at this late hour.'

'Ah.' Nick's face stretched into a smile. 'We've finally broken into the memory stick found in the victim's car. It contains a spreadsheet detailing incomings and outgoings for a boxing promotions company registered to a Mr Alan Jones.'

'How does that link to our victim?'

'Cameron worked in finance, was a professional enabler for investments. We think Jones might be one of his clients.'

'Can we trace him?'

'That's what we're working on at the moment. The business address is a letter-box address. People rent letter-boxes all the time for small companies when they don't have premises.' He nudged up a single shoulder. 'Something to put on their business correspondence, somewhere to have their mail sent to. But we've got the bank details, so we've been in touch with them to track down his home address.'

'How close are you to getting into the phone?'

'We're near. We've cracked the first code. Now we're trying to work out his password. I'm told it's a matter of trying lots of different combinations. Freeman wants a briefing tomorrow morning to see how it all fits in with the wider investigation.'

'That's good news.'

'I do have something else for you though.' Nick turned to the nests of paperwork littering his desk. 'We've been contacted by a member of the response team at Birmingham Central. He'd seen our murder on the news, heard we were appealing for information and remembered being called to the victim's address when he lived on the wharf in May, a prospective criminal damage.'

Beth frowned. 'When Cameron and Monika were still living there? I thought we'd made all the checks?'

'We did. There's nothing on file. He was called by Cameron's next-door neighbour after they heard the sound of breaking glass. They thought it might be a break-in at the time.'

'Why didn't we know about this?'

'It wasn't booked in as a crime. The officer called at the house, but Cameron played it down, said it was an accident. He made a note of it in his pocketbook. The officer remembered him being quite rude. He almost brought him in for Section 5, disorderly behaviour.'

'Can I speak with the response officer?'

Nick checked his watch. 'If you're quick. He's on the late shift, he'll be finishing shortly.' He passed over the handwritten mobile number and rested his hand on her shoulder. 'Then go home and get some sleep. That's an order.'

Sleep eluded Beth that night as thoughts of the case raced around in her head. She shuffled onto her back and stared out into the half-light. The streetlamp out front illuminated the room through the folds of curtain material with a dull hue, creating eerie shadows across the walls and furniture.

The response officer in Birmingham had been surprisingly helpful. He'd made detailed notes of the incident in May and confirmed the date and the fact that the police were called by a neighbour. The obnoxious resident (who she assumed from the description was Cameron) had sent him packing, saying it was an accident. The officer had insisted on seeing his partner before he left, in case it was a domestic dispute and she was injured, but noted she appeared to be okay. On the way out, he'd peered through a broken window at the back of the flat and seen a house brick on the floor in the back room, nestled among fragments of glass. The glass was on the inside, indicating the brick was possibly thrown from outside the property. The circumstances had made him uneasy, and he'd considered booking it on at the time. But it would likely become another undetected crime – a statistic his bosses wouldn't welcome. After she'd ended the call, Beth had checked the date: the incident happened two weeks before Cameron and Monika moved to Northampton.

She cast her mind back, picking through the numerous incidents of criminal damage she'd attended over the years, both on response and during her time in CID before joining the homicide squad. Many of them could be explained by neighbour disputes and family arguments, or they were drug-related. It was incredibly rare for a crime like this to be completely unprovoked and when it was, the victims were usually shaken, visibly scarred by the event. Some even needed counselling afterwards. It appeared significant, yet

Monika hadn't mentioned it when she'd been asked about anything untoward. Why?

Frustration itched at her. She was keen to confront Monika, but with the stark possibility of the incident being unrelated, a late-night call would alarm her and possibly upset the foundations of the relationship she'd been trying to build. No, it wouldn't be prudent to disturb the family. She'd felt a pull to stay at the station and help out with the general enquiries stacking up, but wary of Nick's earlier words, decided to call it a night.

Myrtle padded into the room and jumped on the bed. Beth turned onto her side and folded herself around the cat as it started to purr. It would be interesting to see what Monika had to say in the morning.

24

Monika was in the kitchen feeding the baby when the door knocker sounded the following morning. The clock on the wall read 7.30 a.m. Uncertainty gripped her. She made her way to the front door and pulled it open to a chain's width. The press presence over the past few days had instilled a twitchy sense of caution and, even with the patrol car parked outside, she'd started using the door chain in the evenings when the detectives had gone home. Her shoulders relaxed when she recognised Beth on the doorstep, wisps of wet hair stuck to her forehead from the rain that had arrived first thing.

'Sorry I'm early,' Beth said, as Monika unlatched the chain and let her in. 'I've a meeting at the office at 10 a.m. and wanted to check in with you first.'

Monika didn't answer. Yesterday the detective hadn't arrived. 'On other enquiries,' Warren had said. He didn't expand. Today she turned up with a breezy smile as if nothing was awry. The truth was, the criss-cross visits were making Monika giddy. She'd had enough of the lot of them. She cast a furtive glance down the close, before locking the door and fastening the chain.

The detective opened her mouth to say something, but

her words were drowned out by a crash and the sound of plastic bouncing on tiles. Monika darted back to the kitchen and cursed as she walked through a patch of Weetabix splattered across the white tiles. Jakub was leaning over the side of the highchair, watching the milk seep from the edges of the blobs of cereal littering the floor, clearly pleased with himself. He shoved a Weetabix-covered hand in his hair. So much devastation in the course of so few seconds. Why had she left the bowl within reach? She cursed the door knocker again. When were they to be left alone?

'Oh dear,' Beth said. 'Can I help?'

Monika ignored her. 'Is there some news?' she snapped.

'There is something I need to talk to you about but let me help you clear up first.'

'No, thank you,' Monika huffed but the detective was undeterred. By the time she'd cleaned the cereal out of Jakub's hair, Beth had wiped the cereal from the floor and highchair. When they finally sat down, angry tears filled her eyes. She held them back defiantly and watched the detective retrieve her pad and pen. It was kind of her to help. Perhaps she should offer her a coffee to say thank you. But hadn't she said something about an early meeting? Hopefully if she didn't offer refreshments, she'd be out of there soon and they'd have some peace awhile.

'No Warren today?' she said sarcastically.

'He'll be along later,' Beth said, turning the page in her notebook. 'Monika, we received a call last night from a police officer in Birmingham who claims he was despatched to your flat in Birmingham on the 23rd of May. Apparently, there was some kind of disturbance.' She angled her head, the annoying way she always did when she was expecting a response.

Monika pressed her eyelids together. She knew exactly what the detective was alluding to but couldn't see how it could possibly be relevant now. Jakub wriggled on her lap. She grabbed a padded baby book from the table and placed him on the floor with it.

'This could be important,' Beth continued. 'Can you remember what happened?'

Monika snorted. Surely, she'd already received all the details from the police in Birmingham. She'd put money on it, they'd probably even spoken to their old neighbours; nosey devils, they were. She scratched the back of her neck, vexed at the turn the investigation was taking. It was Wednesday – three days after Cameron's death, yet they clearly had no idea who was responsible, and this smacked of them clutching at straws. 'Shouldn't you be out there searching for the killer instead of dredging up old news?' she said.

'We need to follow up all lines of enquiry. Now, if you could tell me about the evening of the 23rd of May, in as much detail as possible, it would help.'

The detective stayed quiet, her face impassive. Were they trained in this? Trained to stretch out the long silences so that people felt obliged to fill them. Finally, Monika drew a long breath, mustering every last ounce of energy before she squawked out the words, 'Before we moved in May we had a brick thrown through the window of our flat in Birmingham. The police were called, but we didn't pursue it at the time. It was a one-off incident. Kids messing around.'

The detective clicked the end of her pen. 'What exactly happened?'

Monika ran a wary eye over the notebook. 'It was a normal day. Oskar walked himself home from school. Cameron got back around six-ish. Jakub and I were home all day.'

'What time did the incident occur?'

'Around half past ten in the evening, I think. Oskar and Jakub were asleep. Shortly after ten, Cameron and I went to bed. We were talking. The lamp in the bedroom was still on. Suddenly there was an almighty crash. I thought it was outside at first. We both rushed to the window.'

'What happened then?'

'The noise woke Jakub. I went to calm him down. Oskar slept through it.' She shook her head in disbelief. 'Our flat in Birmingham was on two floors. The bedrooms on the first floor overlooked the canal and it was quiet, peaceful out there. Our sitting room, kitchen and dining area was open-plan and ran the length of the ground floor. Cameron found the back window broken and a brick on the floor in the dining area. It looked like it had been thrown from the direction of the car park at the back.'

'Why didn't you tell us about this earlier, Monika?'

'It didn't seem relevant. I wanted to call the police at the time, but Cameron wouldn't let me. He said it was probably kids outside messing around and we should keep a low profile, mend the window ourselves. We were about to exchange contracts and he was concerned it might put off our buyer. I didn't want to lose our new home either. It was our neighbours that phoned the police, but I guess you already know that.'

If Beth detected the sourness in her words, she ignored it. 'Cameron told the police it was an accident. Are you saying it wasn't?'

'I'm saying he thought it was kids.' She notched her voice up a decibel. 'There had been a few incidents nearby around that time: car aerials broken, wing mirrors vandalised. We were moving in two weeks. He didn't want to make a fuss.'

'Did you see anything that evening, after you heard the noise?'

Monika shook her head.

'Did anyone call earlier that day?'

'I don't think so.'

'What about afterwards, and in the days following? Did you see anyone hanging around near the flats?'

'No. It was a one-off. Cameron was convinced we were unlucky because our sitting room was on the ground floor. He stayed home every night afterwards until we moved.'

The detective took an audible breath and eased back into her chair.

'Look, I didn't tell you about this before because I didn't think it was relevant. It was an isolated incident. We left it behind us when we moved from Birmingham.' The legs of her chair squeaked against the tiles. She crossed to the sink, poured herself a glass of water and took a large mouthful. The glass left a watermark on the wood as she placed it on the table and she wiped it away with her cuff while the detective scribbled down the last of her notes.

'Is there anything else?' Beth asked.

'I don't know what you mean. You surely don't think it's connected with what happened to Cameron? It was over three months ago.'

'I don't know. We'll have to look into it. Are you sure there isn't anything else you haven't told us? Because now is the time.' She matched a nod with each syllable rather like a schoolteacher.

'There isn't anything else, not to do with Cameron.' She buried her eyes in the table, expecting the pen to be clicked, the notebook closed.

'What about you?'

'Pardon?' Monika was taken aback. Jakub reached up his arms, but she ignored him.

The detective tapped the pen against the pad a couple of times. 'You do realise, we are looking into your life in Birmingham. It's a necessary part of the enquiry. Only I noticed you looked uncomfortable when we touched on it yesterday morning.'

Monika's stomach clenched. She desperately hoped the look on her face didn't betray her inner self. There was something else, something deep inside and she certainly didn't want to discuss it here. She folded her arms across her chest. 'No.'

The detective's eyes narrowed to tiny holes. 'What about your work in Birmingham? The hospital told us you resigned before Jakub was born. Did you not want to stay on, at least to receive your maternity pay?'

'I couldn't.'

'Why?'

'I wasn't well.'

'You could have submitted a doctor's note.'

Monika swallowed hard. Patches of heat rose up her neck.

'Monika, this is a murder investigation. If something else happened, it could be relevant to our enquiries. You need to tell me about it. Now.'

25

Beth watched Monika rub her hands up and down her face. It was a moment before she spoke. 'I resigned because of a problem with a colleague, but I don't think…'

Beth turned the page of her notebook. 'Go on.'

'I was working in Accident and Emergency. I was a couple of months pregnant, although I hadn't told them at that stage. There was an incident. Look, I really don't think it's worth raking all of this up. It was over a year ago.'

'Tell me, in as much detail as you can, what happened.'

Monika gave a resigned sigh. 'It was Saturday, the 30th of April 2016. The waiting room area was packed. There were people standing in the corridors. We were struggling to cope. I had a string of patients to assess and observe. One of them was a young woman in her early twenties, who'd taken an overdose. We'd already flushed her. She was lucid, calm. My job was to do the observations, blood pressure check, temperature, etc., until a bed was available on a ward. I was worried for her safety. I flagged up my concern with Ian Vaughan, my line manager. I knew I couldn't be in the room with her all the time as I had my other patients to look after. He was rushed off his feet, we all were. He told me to get on with it and do the best I could.' Monika was quiet a moment.

'The woman was found by another nurse in the toilets. She'd managed to cut one of the helpline cords, wrap it around her neck and was trying to hang herself from the lock in the cubicle. We caught her in time, rushed her through to a room, and made sure she was safe. But I was five minutes late for one of my observations on her and Ian accused me of missing the clinical signs of risk. I said I'd flagged it with him and he denied it. It was my word against his.' She took a gulp of water. 'The patient didn't make a complaint. The team wanted to keep it quiet. I was torn. Worried for other patients. I took a few days off. But I couldn't get the incident out of my mind. The mental health teams were in short supply on weekends. The thought it could happen again, to someone else on my watch... As soon as I went back to work, I went to Ian's boss and gave an account of what had happened.' She chewed the edge of her thumbnail.

'Go on,' Beth urged.

'He said he would look into it. I tried to push it all aside and carry on. Several weeks passed. But it was difficult. Members of my shift, the team I'd worked with for the past year or so, people I considered friends, froze me out when they heard I'd taken it further. And it didn't help that I was starting to feel nauseous and tired. I was coming home in tears. Eventually, Cameron stepped up. He told me if I didn't resign, he would go down there and speak to Ian Vaughan. I didn't want to get anybody into trouble. I'd planned to take my maternity leave and resign after Jakub was born, but we were already talking about moving. I felt so ill and work was almost unbearable. So, I resigned on the 2nd of June 2016. I went sick for my notice period and didn't go back. A friend cleared out my locker for me.'

'Wasn't there an enquiry about the patient?' Beth asked.

'Not that I heard. I don't think anyone wanted the paperwork, or the fuss. My record is clear.' Her face turned wistful. 'I love nursing. I want to go back one day. But I'll never go back there, and I'll never work in a casualty department again.'

'Is it possible any of the team you worked with might hold a grudge against you? It must have been a difficult time for all of them.'

'That's the worst thing. I was angry with Ian because he denied I'd spoken with him. But it was a staffing issue, something for management to deal with. I never wanted to make anyone a scapegoat.'

'Have you heard from any of your colleagues since you left?'

'No. I kept in contact with a staff nurse I'd worked with on geriatrics for a while. She told me Ian Vaughan resigned earlier this year.'

'Earlier. When exactly?'

'I'm not sure. Before we moved to Northampton.'

'Could it have been around May time?'

'You're not suggesting he caused the damage at the flat? What would he have against Cameron?'

'I'm not suggesting anything,' Beth said calmly. 'But we will have to look into everything.'

Monika's faced folded. She covered it with her hands. Her shoulders trembled into a shower of sobs. It was pitiful to watch, especially after what she'd been through this past few days. Beth moved to her side and placed a soothing arm around her shoulder. She had to be careful not to get too personal; this wasn't a friendship. Sooner or later, as the investigation wound down, she would have to retreat from the family and she couldn't allow Monika to get too close or rely on her. She made a mental note to email Victim Support and prime them to get in touch.

26

By the time Beth pulled into the office car park, the rain had abated, clearing the sky for pockets of dazzling sunshine. She pulled down her visor, parked up, and stepped over a huge puddle as she climbed out of her car, one of a collection that littered a tarmac full of potholes which desperately needed filling.

She was retrieving her briefcase from the boot when she heard laughter behind her. Chris. Beth cringed, pondering whether she would be able to close the boot and scoot across the car park before being spotted when he called out a greeting. She blinked, pulled the boot door down slowly, psyching herself up for conversation when she realised he wasn't speaking to her at all. He was greeting another colleague who was climbing out of a red Volvo nearby. The woman turned as he approached and smiled. It was Andrea Leary. Beth squinted at them. Nobody had mentioned the senior family liaison officer was returning that morning.

She knew they were acquainted; they'd worked together on several cases, long before her time in homicide. As he reached her she must have pitched some anecdote because they both chuckled. She clapped the side of his arm, nodded in agreement. Beth fastened her boot and made for the door. But she was too late.

'Beth, have you got a minute?' Chris didn't wait for a response. He bade farewell to Andrea and jogged across the asphalt to join her.

She braced herself. Eden had specifically asked her not to mention the mediation letter to him. The last thing she wanted was to fall into conversation, fearful she might say something out of turn.

'Hi. How are you doing?'

'I'm okay, thanks.' She gave a thin smile. 'Is Andrea back now?'

'I don't know.' He whisked his head around to where Andrea's grey-flecked jacket was weaving through the parked cars towards the entrance, then turned back to Beth. 'Sorry, I didn't ask.' They fell in step together. 'I saw Nick Geary's Spider parked outside your house when I drove past the other day. Didn't know you guys were close.'

Beth's shoulders stiffened. She tried to keep her voice light. 'We're just friends.'

'Ah.' He nudged her with his elbow. 'You ought to be careful, you know. That's how rumours start.'

She gave a brief laugh, but although she was pretty convinced he was making small talk, his naïve attempt at humour caught her. It had been a deliberate decision to keep her relationship with Nick private; she certainly didn't want colleagues to think she was currying favour. 'What did you want to talk to me about?' she asked, changing the subject.

His face turned sombre. 'How's Eden?'

'She's been okay,' Beth said warily.

'I'm glad to hear that.'

The late-night phone call she received from Eden on the night Chris left, pulling her from her slumber, tripped into her mind. The long days following when her sister had to be coaxed out of bed and persuaded to get dressed, for Lily's sake. Days that morphed into weeks with little contact from Chris apart from the odd text to make arrangements to see his daughter. The memory irked her. 'Are you?'

Chris was quiet a moment. 'I'm doing my best here, Beth. It's not an easy situation.'

She ignored his comment. They were almost at the door now. A glut of journalists huddled around the entrance, buoyed up by the recent news coverage. They shuffled through, ignoring the questions tossed at them, the microphones shoved in their faces.

It wasn't until they were safely inside and away from the door that Chris spoke again. 'Do you know the reason why Eden and I separated?'

'It's none of my business.' Beth continued along the corridor.

'Beth.' He tugged at her arm and they both halted beside the stairs.

'You decided to go off and shag someone else,' Beth said.

'Eden told you that, did she?'

She looked into his sad eyes. 'Eden didn't tell me about Shelley Walker. I heard it through the rumour mill here at work.' Beth sniffed. Looked away. 'This isn't my business.'

He released his grip, dragged his hand down the front of his face, scratching at the stubble forming around his chin. 'Shelley was only a one-night stand. It was over before it started.'

Beth shrugged a shoulder and turned to go.

'I never cheated on your sister when we were together, Beth.' When she shook her head, placed her foot on the first step, he gave a breathless laugh. 'You have no idea, do you?'

Beth halted. 'I think you need to talk to Eden.'

He ignored her remark. 'We didn't separate because of Shelley. We separated because of Eden. *She* slept with someone else.' His words stopped her in her tracks. While she'd avoided the details of their separation and concentrated on helping with Lily and supporting her sister, Eden always intimated Chris was the one at fault. The words were never spoken but implied in every conversation they shared about the break-up; played out in the rumours about Shelley Walker and the distance he seemed set in putting between all of them.

'She's still seeing him.' Beth reached for the banister rail. Even if he was telling the truth and Eden was seeing someone else, it didn't concern her. 'She's seeing Kyle Thompson, has been for months.'

Disquiet crept its spidery legs over Beth. Kyle Thompson was a local criminal. Older colleagues in the station knew him as a nuisance kid, someone they were constantly picking up for stealing cars and shoplifting from the local One Stop shop when he was young. He'd spent his first spell in prison in his late teens for handling stolen goods. Last she heard, he was working behind the bar at Starling's on Bridge Street after serving a sentence for aggravated burglary.

'How do you know?'

His face contorted, as if he wasn't sure how much to say. 'I know.'

'I don't believe you.'

'Believe what you want, Beth, but it's true. That's why

I'm going to fight for full custody of Lily. I don't want my daughter mixed up with people like him. I thought you ought to know the truth.'

Beth's feet glued themselves to the floor. Chris moved past her, up the stairs towards the incident room, hefty feet tapping the metal lip with each step. After the separation, Beth had encouraged her sister to look up old friends and offered to babysit Lily, so she could enjoy nights out, away from the worry of home. Over the last month or so, she'd seemed to be settling, piecing her life back together. Eden hadn't told her she was seeing someone, but this wasn't surprising since her younger sister rarely shared the finer details of her personal life. Was she using her newfound freedom to build a relationship with Kyle Thompson? Surely she knew about his reputation? She'd certainly know about his prison stretch. Perhaps she thought he was a reformed character. Eden wasn't party to the station intelligence that littered their screens daily, updating officers on the interests of local known criminals. The truth of it was, Kyle Thompson hadn't left his criminal associations at the prison door and was swamped with speculation about drugs trafficking and handling stolen goods. If the intelligence was right, it would only be a matter of time before he was back serving time at Her Majesty's Pleasure, and if Chris was right, Eden was opening herself up to a very dark world.

Pete tapped her arm as he passed on the stairs, bringing her back to the present. 'Are you coming up for the briefing, Beth?'

'Sure.' She smiled. 'I'll be there in a minute.' She listened to Pete's shoes pound the stairs and fade into the distance.

But this was speculation. Chris had made a random allegation and refused to elaborate. A part of Beth couldn't believe Eden would go out with someone like Kyle. Perhaps he'd seen them talking, put two and two together. Although... she crushed the niggling doubts welling up inside. Eden had been quick to jump on the custody issue, even though the letter talked about many issues relating to their separation. If it was true, she would need to speak with her sister, for Lily's sake. But she needed to be sure of their association first. She pushed the thoughts aside and trudged up the stairs.

27

The incident room was rammed when she arrived. Officers occupied practically every seat, others perched on the edge of desks, some even gathered in groups beside the filing cabinets. Practically everybody attached to the investigation had turned out for the 10 a.m. briefing. She moved to her desk at the far side of the room, slipped off her jacket, and greeted a few of her colleagues.

Beth switched on her computer and motioned to Nick who was unplugging his mobile phone charger from a socket in the corner. 'Morning,' he said. 'How did you get on with Monika earlier?' He crossed to her desk, sunk his hands in his pockets and listened to her account of their conversation.

'Interesting,' he said as she finished. 'It looks pretty doubtful there's a link with the murder, all things considered, but we will need to follow up with her former work colleagues. Let's concentrate on Ian Vaughan first.' He scratched the side of his head and called across the room to an attractive woman with a dark bob. 'Right,' he continued when she arrived beside them, 'I can spare you Karen. She'll look into Monika's work background while you're at the briefing this morning.'

Beth smiled at Karen Taylor. She couldn't argue with his choice; Karen was a diligent support officer with a wealth of experience of digging into the background of cases. But it was difficult to hide her frustration. 'Are you sure?'

'Absolutely. Freeman wants you in on this, to see the direction the investigation's taking. I think we're at a turning point. He'll be in the conference room shortly, so you've a few minutes to update Karen before you join us.'

It was a fair point. Beth didn't want to miss out on the briefing, but at the same time she was itching to look into Monika's background. She gave a reluctant nod.

'Okay, I'll leave you two to catch up.' He tilted his head towards the corridor. 'See you in there.'

It only took a few short minutes to fill Karen in and when Beth was confident she understood the task in hand, she sent Warren a quick update message about her earlier meeting with Monika and attached the statement they'd drawn up together. Then she retrieved her notebook, stopped off to fill a cup from the water cooler, and followed the throng of detectives and support staff making their way down to the briefing.

A babble of conversation filled the conference room. Several rows of chairs were arranged to face the oversized noticeboard at the front that was now littered with photos overlapping each other and pinned notes, all underneath the banner 'Operation Hawthorn'. Beth sighed inwardly at the hopelessly impersonal names given to investigations, grabbed an aisle seat close to the back and sipped her water, enjoying the feel of the icy cold liquid slipping down her insides. A few last-minute stragglers filled the empty seats. An enlarged map of the Collingtree Park estate had been placed on the far wall, highlighted with the killer's entry and exit routes.

Voices hushed as Freeman strode in, closely following by Superintendent Rose Hinchin, and tailed by Chris and a tall spindly man who looked vaguely familiar, but Beth couldn't place at first glance.

Freeman held out his hands for the room to hush. 'Okay, people. We've called you here this morning because we've managed to access the information on the phone and memory stick found hidden in the victim's car. Most of you know DC Chris Kirton's been helping us with our digital media on this enquiry. I'll pass you over to him to give us an update.'

Chris finished rolling up his shirt sleeves, nodded his thanks at Freeman and pressed a button on the laptop on the table beside him. A spreadsheet filled the screen at the front of the room.

'The memory stick contained details of incomings and outgoings for a company called Elite Boxing Promotions,' Chris said. 'They correspond with copies of bank statements also found on the stick. The company was owned by a Mr Alan Jones.'

Freeman, still hovering nearby, sunk his hands into his pockets. 'What do we know about Alan Jones?'

'Not much at all. His business appears to be registered to a letter-box address which he also uses as his home address. There's no mention of him on Cameron's company records at Barclay Swift, so it looks as though they were working together privately. We've done all the usual checks, and, for all intents and purposes, it appears that our Mr Jones doesn't exist at all.'

Freeman frowned. 'Are you saying Alan Jones is Cameron Swift?'

'No.' Chris flicked a brief gaze at the spreadsheet before he continued, 'Looking at the poor state of Swift's own bank accounts and finances, I'd say it's more likely Cameron was acting for someone else, a private client, and they've used a false name.' He pressed another button. 'The mobile phone didn't contain any call records, just some texts which appear to be coded.' A sheet of text messages filled the screen, annotated with sender details and dates:

1.7.17 Sender: The mail doesn't look good.

2.7.17 Cameron: It's all in hand.

16.7.17 Sender: Need the post. Now.

17.7.17 Cameron: Don't worry, I'm sorting it.

28.7.17 Sender: Post is well overdue, this is your last warning.

1.8.17 Cameron: Just need a bit longer.

7.8.17 Sender: This needs sorting now, otherwise there will be consequences.

The fact that the last message was sent less than two weeks before Cameron's death wasn't lost on Beth. She scribbled it down on her pad.

'What does all this mean exactly?' Freeman said impatiently.

Chris stood aside and gestured to the spindly man on his right. 'When I saw the list of figures, I got suspicious. I took the liberty of calling in DC Will Drummond. For those of you who don't know him, Will's a financial investigator with the organised crime unit.'

This was the first time Drummond faced the audience front on and Beth recognised him now. Their paths had crossed a couple of times in her early years in the force. Unlike many of the larger than life characters the action and unpredictability of the job attracted, Drummond was a cerebral, quiet man – a thinker. She recalled being crewed up on a night shift with him when they both worked response. She'd exhausted any ounce of interesting conversation within the first hour and it had been the longest shift she'd ever served in the police, even though it was only the regulatory ten hours. He served his time on response and quickly retreated away from the front line, preferring to pick through the finer details of fraud cases and prolonged financial investigations.

'We've done some digging and it looks like the boxing promotions company doesn't actually exist,' Drummond said. His voice was low, nasally. 'It's registered with Companies House, but we've contacted a couple of the venues and there is no evidence of any of the events mentioned in the spreadsheet actually taking place.'

'What about submitting accounts?' Freeman asked.

Drummond held his head high. 'Companies don't have to submit accounts until they have been trading for twenty-one months. Realistically they have around two years before the Inland Revenue chase them. We've found false companies in the past similar to these. They are set up, run like a business and closed down before the two years is up. Especially cash businesses like this one.'

'Are you saying it's a front?'

'The income appears legitimate to the bank – cash deposits for ticket sales for boxing events. Money is transferred to other accounts for expenses to pay for staff, venues, etc., hence the spreadsheet.'

'Okay, okay, detective.' Freeman was struggling to keep his patience intact. 'I get the gist. Is it, or isn't it, a front?'

'I'd suggest it's potentially a mask for a money laundering operation, possibly drugs cash.'

Geary shifted position at the side of the room. He flicked through several papers, stapled together at the corner. 'There are large deposits to Alan Jones' bank account,' he said. 'Some are in excess of eight grand for a single event. Surely the banks would have flagged them up?'

'Banks have their own systems in place to identify suspicious activity. Legally they're required to routinely complete a suspect report for deposits over a certain amount, it's currently around £7000, which are submitted to the police for investigation,' Drummond said. 'There'll be reports, plenty of them I would think, but there are thousands of reports sent through annually. They'll be sitting in a queue or littering a desk somewhere. Unless they're flagged by another suspicious circumstance or a crime, by the time they are looked at the company has usually closed. It's down to lack of resources really.

'I'd suggest Alan Jones is a fictitious name, and the identification used to set up the account is probably fake too.' Drummond's monotone voice continued to fill the room. 'Somebody who's gone to this much trouble is likely to have the right connections to obtain phoney ID details: passport, driving licence, etc. It's quite normal for people who do this to set up a false identity, remove themselves. I'd also suggest that, once we look into it further, we'll find the transactions at the bank, payments for venues, etc. are going to fake businesses too. A vehicle set up to clean the cash.' He let the silence hang in the conference room as the wheels of the detective brains in his audience mulled this over. He was clearly enjoying this far more than they were.

Freeman scratched the back of his neck. 'Okay, so what can we do with this now?'

'We need to follow the money. Search back through each of the accounts where transactions have been made. Sooner or later we'll find a hiccup, trace the source.'

'That sounds time consuming.'

Drummond nodded.

'Well, this is a murder investigation, detective. We have families searching for answers and the press scratching at our door. If our victim was involved in a money laundering scam that wasn't delivering, for whatever reason, it could give whoever he was acting for a motive for murder. It makes sense to a degree. Cameron Swift's own finances certainly don't match his expenditure. We need to track down this Alan Jones, whoever he is. Couldn't be a more regular name,' he added with a sigh.

'That's probably why they used it.'

Drummond opened his mouth to continue, but before he had a chance, Freeman spoke, 'The phone is pay as you go and unregistered, so we can't trace the user through the phone company, but the coded text messages on the phone refer to "mail". It's possible they are referring to mail about payments, clean money that is not coming back as expected. The texts get more threatening towards the end. Let's check the letterbox address and see if there is any CCTV nearby that might show who has accessed it recently. We'll contact the phone company too. Get them to use their mast analysis to site the cell phone where the messages were sent from. That would give us an indication of where in the vicinity our Mr Jones is located.'

'The spreadsheets will need some work, though,' Drummond interjected. 'Again, it's some sort of code.'

'Okay, you can work on that area,' Freeman said. He was pacing the floor now. 'Right, let's get started on this. We need to track down this Alan Jones and find out who he is. Clearly he has had a major disagreement with our victim.' He halted at the side of the room and turned to Nick. 'Get our source handlers back out to check the field for intelligence. If this is a front, and somebody has trusted our victim with cleaning a substantial amount of money and hasn't received the return they were expecting, then they are down a lot of cash.'

Chairs squeaked across the wooden flooring as officers started to move back to the main incident room. Beth shut her notebook and was almost at the door when Freeman called out. 'Beth, check with the families to see if Cameron ever mentioned this boxing promotions company or whether they have received any correspondence or communication from a Mr Jones at home. It's a long shot, I know, but worth a try.'

28

Beth couldn't resist a smile as they piled out of the conference room. The prospect of a possible breakthrough, with the encryption broken, injected a frisson of excitement into the air and colleagues, noticeably weary from the gruelling schedule of the past few days, now moved with renewed vigour. Their enthusiasm was infectious.

She checked her phone, surprised to find two missed calls from Warren, and shuffled to the side, allowing her colleagues to pass while she dialled back.

'Everything okay?' she asked as soon as he answered.

'Where is everyone?' Warren's voice was tight. 'I haven't been able to reach Freeman for the past hour.'

'We were all instructed to put our phones on silent for the meeting. Is something wrong?' He sounded harried, but surely if there was an emergency, he would have sent a message through the incident room or via control.

'Nothing urgent. I need some advice. How was the briefing?'

She passed on the details about the phones and memory sticks. The corridor thinned. 'How are things there?' she asked. 'How is Monika?' The possibility that Monika, Sara, or even both of them together might be connected to the money laundering in some way ate away at her.

'She's okay,' Warren said. His voice lowered slightly. 'Actually, something's happened. Monika took a call from Sara Swift about an hour ago.'

'What?'

'She called on the landline, shortly after 10 a.m.'

'How did she get the number?'

'It wouldn't be too difficult, everything's on the Internet these days.' He sounded exasperated. 'The address was plastered over the papers too. And if the phone was in Cameron's name...' His voice trailed off.

Uneasiness wriggled beneath Beth's skin. Monika was distraught that morning. By the time Beth left, she'd calmed down, but she still looked shell-shocked. It was one of those occasions when Beth was grateful for Warren's presence; she didn't want to leave the woman on her own. She couldn't imagine what taking a call from Cameron's other partner would do to her in that fragile state. Unless, of course, she was expecting it. 'What was Monika doing answering the phone?' Beth asked cautiously.

'I was in the toilet. She said she didn't think, grabbed it automatically.'

'What did Sara want?'

'They had a conversation about Cameron and the children. She's arranged to come and visit Monika this afternoon.'

'What? Where?'

'Here, at Monika's home. According to Monika, Sara thinks they can support each other.'

Beth stretched her neck back. 'And Monika agreed?'

'Apparently so.'

'What time?'

'She's due to arrive at around 2 p.m. I've told Monika I'll need to be present. But I need a briefing from Freeman, to know what role he wants me to take. I've left him several messages.'

Beth did a quick calculation. It had taken her almost three hours to travel from Northampton to Cheshire. She checked her watch. Almost a quarter to eleven. Which meant Sara Swift would have been planning to leave soon, if she hadn't left already. 'Of course, I'll speak with him and get him to call you.'

'Thanks.'

'You're welcome. Don't forget to ask them about the boxing promotions company.'

As Beth ended the call, another thought struck her. The search teams would be going into Sara's house this morning. It seemed odd she'd take the trouble to travel down to Northampton while officers were picking through her home. Either she didn't have anything to hide, or she was confident she'd covered her tracks and they wouldn't find anything.

Freeman's office felt more cramped than usual, with Beth and Nick sat in front of the desk. After a brief respite, the early morning rain had returned, pounding the windows, masking the view of the sports field beyond. Beth had to raise her voice to relay her earlier exchange with Monika about the incident at City Western Hospital, Birmingham.

'How could we have not known this?' Freeman said when she'd finished. He held his head back and stared at the hairline cracks in the ceiling plaster.

'We carried out the usual checks,' Nick said. 'There's nothing on record.'

'The incident at the flat wasn't booked on as a crime,' Beth said. 'Monika resigned from her position at work for personal reasons.'

Freeman closed his eyes, pinched the bridge of his nose.

'If she wasn't officially disciplined, then there probably wouldn't be anything on file. And there's nothing to suggest Cameron was involved, so I can't see how it's relevant,' Nick added.

'Neither can I,' Freeman said. 'But we'll have to look into it.' He rolled his eyes. 'Talk about everything coming at once.'

'There's something else,' Beth said. She shared her phone conversation with Warren. 'Sara Swift is travelling down to Northamptonshire as we speak.'

Freeman looked startled. 'And Monika agreed to the visit?'

Beth nodded.

'I'm not sure about a meet at Monika's house,' Nick said. 'What if it kicks off? Two aggrieved women. Wouldn't it be better for them to meet here at the station?'

Freeman was quiet a moment. 'I think we'll run with it as it is,' he said eventually. 'Bringing them here could make it too formal, put them on guard. Let's use this opportunity to watch their body language, their reactions to each other, check if there are any signs of a previous acquaintance.

I'll make sure there's a patrol car nearby, in case backup's needed.'

'I'll get straight over there,' Beth said. 'See what unfolds.'

'No.' Freeman dragged out the word, still following his train of thought. 'I'll speak to Warren, have him manage this one. I don't know what Sara Swift's motivation for meeting Monika is, but we all know how difficult she can be. The chief constable's furious about the live complaint. Warren is a new face to her, someone neutral. She can't accuse him of taking sides.'

'But, sir—'

'I want you to look into Monika's background. Use Karen to help you. I can't spare another detective at the moment. Let's make sure there's nothing untoward there.'

Beth did her best to contain her disappointment. 'What about Sara Swift?'

Freeman massaged his temple. 'Dig deeper into her background too. Let's make sure she doesn't have any skeletons in the closet either. Okay, people, that's it.'

'There was one other thing,' Beth asked casually. Freeman looked up, his eyes hooded. 'I saw Andrea Leary in the car park earlier. Is she back with us now?'

'Joining us next Tuesday, thank goodness. That's if we haven't caught the bastard by then.'

29

Back in the corridor, Beth nodded at a couple of passing colleagues heading out on enquiries related to the discovery on the victim's phone. Their excited chatter induced a faint sense of longing. Freeman's directive to investigate Monika and Sara kept her in the office for now and it felt as though she was missing out on the action. She'd almost reached the entrance when she heard her name called and turned to find Andrea Leary scurrying towards her.

Beth sighed inwardly. She'd watched Andrea flit around the incident room like a butterfly earlier. Moving from one desk to another, chatting to detectives and support staff. Andrea had worked on the homicide team for a couple of years before her secondment to region, and there was clearly lots of office gossip to catch up on. But Beth was under no illusions. She was also taking her time, learning about the case, sussing exactly where they were so she could plunge right in when she returned.

Andrea halted beside her. 'We need to arrange some time for a handover on Tuesday,' she said. No pleasantries. No small talk. She grabbed her phone, a manicured nail tapping at the screen. 'Shall we say ten o'clock?' Beth nodded. 'Make sure you have all your notes with you. We don't want anything missed on this one, do we?' The question was rhetorical. She lowered the phone, spotted Freeman emerge from his office and moved off towards him, the sharp edge of her suit jacket flapping behind her.

Beth watched her place her hand on her waist as she reached Freeman, tilting her head, swinging her hip out to the side as they fell into conversation. Beth had joined the team shortly before Andrea was promoted to sergeant. They'd barely worked together a couple of months before Andrea left and hadn't had sufficient time to get to know each other. But the string of relieved faces and whispered anecdotes at her leaving party spoke volumes. If the rumours were to be believed, Andrea was fiercely ambitious and liable to trample over anyone who crossed her path. Her return on Tuesday was certainly going to add a whole new dimension to the team.

The hollow sound of laughter pulled her from her thoughts. She followed it, further down the corridor where a door sat ajar and pushed it open. The room was dimly lit, almost like a cinema, and smelt of old food. She recognised the profiles of Pete and Keith, both in shirt sleeves, slouched in front of a computer screen and recalled their absence at the briefing. Empty crisp packets littered the floor. On the table, a used pizza box sat open.

Pete held a remote in his hand. He turned as she entered.

'What are you guys up to?' Beth said, stepping over a discarded crisp packet.

At the sound of her voice the other detective turned briefly, before looking back at the screen.

'Freeman's got us watching CCTV from outside The

Crown, the pub around the corner from where the victim worked. We're logging when he was there, printing out stills of who he was with. Kind of surveillance after the event.'

Ears of popped corn crunched beneath her feet. 'So I see,' she said, a smile playing on her lips. 'How far are you going back?'

'Three weeks initially, then we'll see.'

Suddenly the pizza box and discarded crisp packets made sense. Reviewing CCTV was one of the most laborious jobs in policing. It was so difficult to stay awake and concentrate for prolonged periods that colleagues resorted to caffeine and junk food to alleviate the boredom and keep alert. 'How long have you been at it?' she asked.

Pete checked his watch and stretched his long arms above his head. 'Since this time yesterday.'

'At least you have a fast-forward button.'

'We have to view the inside cameras afterwards to narrow down the dates and times to coincide with any meetings. There are more holes in the victim's work diary than a cracked sieve. His colleagues didn't seem to have much clue of his whereabouts either. They said he called in every day, but rarely visited the office. The company premises aren't huge, they take their clients out to entertain. The Crown was one of our victim's preferred haunts when he was in Birmingham. Freeman wants every person he met logged, in case they correspond to the private details he kept on the memory stick.'

'How much have you done?' Beth asked. She could see the front of the pub and the entrance door clearly on the screen. Rows of colourful hanging baskets hung from its exterior. The other detective fast-forwarded until a figure showed up, then paused and enlarged the image. Pete shook his head and they moved on.

'We've done two weeks so far. We're now starting the week before the murder.'

'Are there many sightings of our guy?'

'A few.' His eyes were on the screen now as they discarded another figure and clicked on. The screen ran to twice the speed. He pointed at a pile of stills on a table nearby.

Beth sifted through them. There were twenty-one pictures altogether, and each had the time and date marked on the bottom right-hand corner. The first showed Cameron shake a man's hand outside the pub entrance, a client she assumed. There were three more of them, taken at different angles, as they chatted briefly and turned to go into the pub. The next showed them leaving together. Two days later, Cameron greeted another man, this time with two women. She flicked to the next photo, peered in closer. One of the women looked familiar. On the next photo, the same woman exited the pub with Cameron, hand in hand. This was a woman of medium height, smartly dressed with coiffured grey hair – not Sara or Monika then. She flicked on, but the stills had caught her off centre and it was impossible to see her face clearly.

She worked her way through the pile again. Something about the grey-haired woman looked familiar. But the stills were hazy, she couldn't be sure. 'Have you seen this woman anywhere else in your footage?' Beth said, passing the photos across to Pete.

'Don't think so. Who is she?'

'I'm not sure. She looks familiar.'

'Do you want us to look out for her?'

'Please, if you could. Let me know if you get a clearer image of her, either on her own, or with Cameron.' She thanked them and left the room, her mind whirling. She couldn't be absolutely sure, but the woman in the photo resembled Sara's friend, Yvonne Newman. The checks on Yvonne had come back clear, she wasn't known to the police, but Beth distinctly remembered her implying she wasn't well acquainted with Cameron. If it was her in the photos, she was lying.

Karen rushed over to Beth as soon as she stepped back into the main incident room. 'Finally,' she breathed, 'I've traced the whereabouts of Monika's old line manager in Birmingham, Ian Vaughan. He left the hospital on the fifteenth of May this year and now lives on the outskirts of the city. Works at a warehouse on the nearby Lowerton Industrial Estate.'

'Have you spoken with him?'

'Yes. He claims he was at work last Sunday morning. We'll need to verify that with his company of course.' Beth was quiet a moment. Karen bit her lip, checked her watch. 'You can speak to him yourself if you want,' she said gingerly. 'He said he'd be home until 3 p.m. He's on the late shift.'

Beth tracked back the dates in her mind. May was also when the brick was thrown through Monika's window. Was it possible his leaving the hospital was connected, that he harboured a grudge against Monika? A grudge deep enough to kill her fiancé? 'Have you got an address?' Beth asked.

'Sure.' She brandished a scrap of paper.

'Great. I think I'll head over there.'

Karen pinched the skin at her throat and looked around the office. 'I haven't run this past the DS yet.'

'Oh.' Beth turned her head towards the door. 'I think he's still with the DCI. They're tied up with this spreadsheet puzzle.'

'Don't you think we should check with him first?'

'I'll call him on the go,' Beth said reassuringly.

'I'll come with you.'

'No, you stay.' Beth swept her arm around the office. Apart from a few officers tapping keys, empty chairs stared back at them. With the break of the encryption code earlier, almost everyone was out on enquiries. 'You're needed here. Plus, somebody needs to monitor the checks on Sara Swift's background.' Karen still looked unsure as Beth crossed to her desk and collected her briefcase. 'I'll let Birmingham Central know I'm on their patch in case I need anything and—' she held up her phone '—my phone will be on.' She reached around and tapped Karen on the shoulder. 'Well done. This is good work.'

30

Edgbaston Villas was one of four tower blocks located within a leafy residential area to the south of the city centre. While the M6 motorway had been surprisingly clear, the roads of Birmingham were clogged nose to tail and Beth crawled to the city outskirts.

She parked up, retrieved her briefcase and checked the clock on the dash. It was almost 1 p.m. The tower block was a seventies construction, with balconies and a pebbledash grey exterior. Some residents had decorated their balconies with colourful pot plants and she imagined them sitting out in the evening, the vista of Birmingham city laid out before them.

A woman carrying a box was struggling to hold the door open and exit the building as Beth approached. Beth rushed over, held open the door for her to pass through, and scooted inside, curling her nose at the smell that oozed in from the trash bins beside the entrance. She stared in dismay at the yellow and black tape stretched across the first set of lift doors, one of only two lifts for the building, and pressed the button for the other. As she shifted from foot to foot, willing it to work, she cast a cursory glance at the staircase. Beth hated lifts, avoided them whenever possible, but Ian Vaughan lived on the ninth floor and she didn't relish the idea of climbing all those steps.

The lift light blinked from the eighteenth floor and cranked into action. The seconds it took to descend felt like minutes. The foyer was a ghost town; the majority of the residents out at work on a Wednesday lunchtime. She couldn't imagine what it would be like on a weekend or in the evenings, when the residents of the twenty-two floors were all jostling to use this one lift with their shopping bags and young children.

The judder the door gave as it opened didn't instil confidence. Beth climbed in tentatively, beads of sweat gathering under her collar as the sheets of metal closed in front of her. A squeak sounded in the distance, making her jump, nudging an old memory to the forefront of her mind. When she was seven, the shopping centre car park lift had broken down between the third and fourth floors and she'd been stuck with her mother and Eden and a man they didn't know. When her mother tried to report the breakdown on the emergency phone, she found it was faulty. The man used his mobile to phone the police to alert security, but the twenty minutes they'd waited felt like hours in the enclosed area and, while Beth had been reasonably calm at the time, the memory of it combined with the clanks and jangles in the background was making her head light. She was relieved when the door finally opened. She'd definitely take the stairs back down.

Number 912 was only three doors up from the lift. The once white wooden door looked in dire need of a paint job. Beth pressed the doorbell and waited. All was quiet. She frowned, checked her watch again. She hadn't phoned ahead and arranged her visit as Vaughan had told Karen he would be at home until 3 p.m. She fisted her hand, rapped the wood, and was just beginning to wish she'd tried the intercom before rising to the ninth floor when she heard a throaty cough. Seconds later the door pulled open.

Ian Vaughan was a tall man, well over six feet, with a mop of wet blond hair that clung to his forehead. He looked like he'd stepped out of the shower in a hurry. A sweat top and joggers hung off his lean frame.

Beth introduced herself and held up her card.

He rolled his eyes, moving aside for her to enter.

She followed him down a gloomy hallway, past several closed doors and into a lounge that was surprisingly bright and spacious. White voile covered the large doors that led out to the balcony, and she could see the outline of a bicycle parked out there. A couple of chairs were neatly stacked beside it.

'Is it always this quiet here in the daytime?' Beth asked, glancing out of the window.

'During the week it is. That's why I like shifts. I do mostly late and night shifts which means I'm out when everyone else is at home.'

'Where do you work?'

'At Benton's. The warehouse around the corner. It's handy.'

She noticed a woman's cardigan draped over the back of a chair. 'And your partner?'

'She's works at Whistles, a boutique in the city.' He placed his hands on his hips. 'Look, I know why you're here. But I can't tell you any more than I told the officer on the phone this morning. I was at work when the shooting took place.'

'When did you hear about it?'

'It's been all over the news. Cameron Swift isn't a common name. I guessed it was Monika's partner.'

'You used to work with Monika, I understand?'

He gave a long sigh. 'Yes, when I was a ward sister at City Western. Monika was one of my team. How is she doing?'

'She's okay, all things considered. How long did you work together for?'

He turned down the corners of his mouth. 'About eighteen months. I'm sure you also know what happened.' He crossed to a sideboard, retrieved a packet of Dunhills and pulled out a cigarette.

'I'd like to hear your account,' Beth said.

He paused and for a moment his eyes bore into her. This was clearly territory he didn't wish to venture into. Beth let the silence linger. Eventually he grabbed a lighter and held it up. 'You don't mind, do you?'

Beth shook her head. The sight of smokers these days was becoming rarer, but ironically it was still a popular habit within the medical profession. She'd seen them on the numerous times she'd visited A&E through work, standing outside the entrance puffing. It was as if their awareness of everything that could go wrong with the human body, and how quickly a disease could befall a victim, encouraged them to indulge all the vices. He pulled open the door to the balcony, stood close by, and lit up.

It took him a while to launch into his story of the night of the incident and when he did the details were scant, summarised, almost as though he'd gone over them a million times in his head this past year or so and was weary of them. He left out the detail about Monika raising the alarm at a patient being at risk and when Beth probed him about it, he gave a hard stare. 'Monika was a good nurse, but she was stressed that night. We all were. It was a one-off incident she couldn't accept. There was no complaint made, no need to take it any further. It's a shame she decided to report it.'

'What happened?'

'If it was pursued, as an enquiry, I would have possibly been facing a disciplinary. If I lost my job, I would have lost my pension and my career. We'd recently been allocated a new matron, tasked with improving our target achievement. He didn't want the adverse publicity, so he buried it for a while. When our targets were announced, several months later, we were so far below expectations he wanted to show he was making a difference and shake things up a bit. I was known for being outspoken, publicly criticising management decisions I thought were unfair or didn't agree with. I didn't fit into his new vision, so I was offered a deal – if I resigned, left quietly and kept the incident out of the newspapers, I could keep my pension. The patient hadn't made a fuss; there was no complaint on record. But he'd kept the details of the incident, in case he needed them.'

'So, you left of your own accord?'

'I resigned, yes. The stress of that year was enough in itself. The weekends were a warzone in A&E. And not knowing whether the complaint was going to lead to a disciplinary...' He inhaled a long drag, then dropped his cigarette and crushed it under his foot on the balcony. 'All the years I'd given to the NHS, all the crap I'd taken for them and there was no support. I decided I'd had enough. I now work in a warehouse and load distribution lorries. I have set hours, a good laugh with my colleagues, and I'm appreciated by my boss. I don't regret the decision, detective, I just wish I hadn't left in those circumstances.'

The door scraped on its runners as he pulled it closed. 'My marriage broke up around the same time. Another decision long overdue. I got the job at Benton's and moved here. Ellie, my partner, has been living with me for about a month.'

'How did you get along with Monika at work?'

'The same as any other member of staff. Like I said, it was a very busy unit.'

'What about after she left? Did you contact Monika, arrange to see her?'

'Monika cut contact with everyone on the team when she left. I didn't have any reason to call her.'

'Did you ever meet Cameron?'

'Not meet, as such. I saw him a few times. He met her from work occasionally, before she was pregnant. Seemed a nice guy. A bit flash.'

'A brick was thrown through their flat window on the 23rd of May this year, before they moved to Northampton. Do you know anything about that?'

'No.'

'Are you sure? It was only a week or so after you resigned.'

'What are you insinuating?'

'My job isn't to insinuate, Mr Vaughan. It's to ask questions. Did you hold a grudge against Monika? Blame her for losing your career?'

His cheeks billowed as he pushed out a long sigh. 'The hospital management were responsible for me losing my career, not Monika. They talk a good fight, make the pretence of offering all the right training, but when you need the resources, they aren't there to do the job. I was very vocal about their shortcomings; hence the new matron and I hadn't got along from day one. Monika's feedback was the catalyst that set it into motion, but if it hadn't been that incident, he'd have found another way to get rid of me.' He closed his eyes, shook his head. 'You can look into me all you like, but you won't find anything. I haven't set eyes on Monika for over a year.'

Beth gathered her things and was approaching the door when he spoke again. 'I wonder what they've done to upset someone.'

'Pardon?' Beth whisked around to face him.

'Well, they must have done something pretty bad to have brought this on themselves.'

31

The exchange with Vaughan played on Beth's mind as she joined the M6 on her way back to Northampton. She called it in to Karen, but something about him troubled her. He claimed he had no argument with Monika: she'd merely highlighted an issue, a problem well overdue. But she couldn't ignore the fact that he'd lost his job and his marriage, and his final words sat uncomfortably. What did he mean by 'they' must have done something bad? It suggested Monika and Cameron had possibly colluded together.

Cameron had built up his own business from scratch. Both Monika and Sara intimated he was charming and charismatic. He was clearly driven and focused too, but also incredibly private, guarding secrets that formed a roadmap through both his personal and professional life.

Her mobile rang out, snapping her back to the present. The line crackled as she answered.

Karen's voice sounded distant. 'I've received the trace back from DWP. Sara Swift was born Sara Kaur in Bradford in June 1984. She moved to London, got married and became Sara Sidhu in July 2006. She's still listed as married.'

Beth baulked. 'Are you sure?'

'Absolutely.'

'How could this not have come to light earlier? I thought the families were looked into.'

'They were, but only their recent background. You have to dig a lot deeper to pick this stuff up. Her last address in London was a flat on the Holloway Road. I phoned there but it's been sold on a couple of times since; the current residents have never heard of her, or him. I've gone back to the DWP for a trace on her husband, to check his current address. Their systems are down for maintenance. I'm waiting to hear when they'll be back up. But I did get the details of her last workplace, a primary school called Easham's in Highgate. The schools are still on holiday and a lot of her old colleagues have moved on, but I managed to reach the headmaster who remembers her.'

'And?'

'It's an odd one. He knew her as Sara Sidhu. She worked there for a few years, looked after a year three class, and then left suddenly. According to him, she just didn't turn up for work one day. No explanation at the time. A letter arrived through the post a few days later, tending her immediate resignation, "for personal reasons," he said.'

'She didn't go back and work out her notice?'

'No. He wasn't impressed. Her husband had no idea where she'd gone either and went to the school looking for her. She'd done a midnight flit, disappeared. She cut off everyone, even her work colleagues at the time who'd considered themselves friends.'

'Interesting. Was she reported missing?'

'I've tracked back. It doesn't look like it. When she was working at Steeples Primary in Manchester, she reverted to her maiden name of Kaur. There's nothing to suggest she got divorced though. Then, seven years ago, she changed her name to Swift.'

'It sounds like she was trying to avoid something. Or somebody.'

'That's what I thought.' She lowered her voice until it was barely a whisper. 'Oh, and the DS is looking for you. Asked me to let him know the minute you called in.'

Beth thanked her and rang off. Her mind raced. Monika and Cameron weren't the only ones squirreling away secrets in their backgrounds. What had happened to make Sara feel the need to leave London so quickly, and keep changing her name? She'd talked openly about marriage plans with Cameron, yet she failed to mention she was already married. Did she take Cameron's name so she couldn't be traced? She drew an excited breath and moved to call Nick when her phone rang out again. To her surprise it was Freeman.

'Beth, where are you?' He sounded stressed.

'On my way back from Birmingham, sir. I should be back at the office soon.'

'What do you think you are doing, taking off without checking in first?'

She ignored the anger that chipped his tone. 'Everyone was out on enquiries. I was following up on Monika's background, as you asked.'

'With a potential suspect, and on your own.'

'It was a statement taking exercise.'

'You couldn't be sure of that. Don't go out again without checking in with me first, you hear me?' He rang off before she had a chance to say that she'd taken precautions and called it in with Birmingham Central in case she needed backup. She clenched her teeth, dialled Nick. He answered on the second ring, as if he was waiting for her call.

'Where are you, Beth?'

'Don't you start. Freeman's just given me a ticking off.'

'I should think so too.'

She opened her mouth to argue when the group of press outside the back of the station, earlier that day, flashed into her mind. They were several days into an investigation that was draining budgets and showed no immediate promise of an arrest. The pressure would be coming from all sides. There was no point in exacerbating the situation. Instead, she swallowed her anger and concentrated on giving Nick an overview of her meeting with Vaughan. 'He might have been responsible for the brick thrown through their window in Birmingham,' she finished up. 'The response officer checked and there were no cameras nearby, so we'll probably never really know. But it doesn't seem enough to give him a motive for murder. His argument was with Monika and not Cameron. He appeared quite sanguine at how things turned out.'

The line stayed quiet.

The information on the memory stick nudged her. 'Is there any news on tracing the owner of the boxing business?' Beth asked.

'We're working on it. We've retrieved cameras from two companies close to the letter-box address. There's loads of footage to run through.'

'Ah.' His heavy tone resonated. A lot of police work was like wading through glue, until a gem of information showed itself and set them on a new path. 'How did the meeting go this afternoon, with Monika and Sara?'

'Still ongoing. I'm waiting to hear from Warren. What time are you back?'

'In about twenty minutes. Have you heard about Sara Swift's background?'

'I have.' He paused a moment. 'It's an interesting story.'

'Isn't it? Shall I call by Monika's on my way back, see if Sara's still there? It'd be good to hear her side of the story.' A beat passed. 'We could do with clearing up the family stuff, especially with everything else going on.'

Nick didn't respond immediately. She could almost hear the cogs in his brain turning as he thought it through. Finally, he breathed a sigh. 'The DCI made it quite clear you weren't to be involved in the meeting with Monika.'

'I know that, but maybe if I meet Sara afterwards, take her for a coffee on the pretence of updating her on current developments—'

'No. Invite her back here. I'll arrange for you to have one of the softer rooms we reserve for interviewing vulnerable witnesses. Give her an update on the case: you can tell her we have some new leads, are moving towards an arrest, but nothing specific. See what you can get out of her then. And, Beth?'

'Yes?'

'Take it carefully. We don't want another complaint saying we're harassing a grieving widow.'

32

As soon as Sara Swift pulled into Meadowbrook Close that afternoon, she realised she'd made a mistake. Gleaming cars lined the driveways of detached houses with immaculate lawns and tamed borders. She wouldn't expect anything less of Cameron. But what really struck her, and what wasn't visible from the media photos and all those views she'd attempted on Google Earth, was the dearth of trees and established hedgerows away from the main road. This part of the estate was modern, only a few years old. Cameron's parents had died a little over eight years ago, within six months of each other. She hadn't gone to either of their funerals, it was before Cameron and she met, but she remembered his raw emotion in the early days of their relationship. He was still grieving for his parents and talked fondly of their family home in Northamptonshire where he was raised. It made sense that he might hold onto their property, rent it out, use it as an investment. Or even stay there occasionally when it was empty, and he was in the area. A small part of her harboured the vague hope that the police had got his late parents' address wrong, and that the incident had actually happened outside their former home after all. But these houses were far too modern to have been his childhood home.

She parked up at the kerb outside number sixteen and cut the engine, appraising the gravelled driveway, the hanging basket bursting with bright coloured petunias. Apart from the red-painted front door it looked similar in style to her home in Cheshire.

It had taken a little over two and a half hours to navigate this route. How many times had Cameron made that journey? Thoughts of him pulling into the driveway, parking up, and wandering to the front door, key in hand, that familiar smile adorning his lips, balled in her stomach. She tore her gaze away, her eyes inadvertently drawn to the tarmac outside where the newspapers reported he'd met his end.

Tears burned her eyes. The last time she'd seen Cameron was at their home in Cheshire, the day before their holiday, a little over three weeks earlier. After he'd cancelled his flight, he'd promised to drive them to the airport to see them off, but the arrangements were foiled by an urgent business engagement, forcing her to take a taxi. She recalled their last exchange: harsh words spoken in low voices, just out of earshot of the children. Over the years, she'd grown accustomed to the schedule changes, ignored the golfing weekends, the business trips, the last-minute meetings. But her girls had been excited about this family holiday and their bitter disappointment had coursed through her. They wouldn't see their father for three weeks. He wasn't even coming on the holiday, the very least he could do was to give them a good send off and show them he cared. But, as with most decisions in his life, Cameron was resolute.

He'd phoned most days throughout their holiday and spoken to the girls, but Sara had been cool with him as she always was when he let her down. She imagined he'd apologise, take them out to dinner and treat them when they arrived home, as he usually did when he knew he'd taken liberties. But now it was too late and her last memory of him was of an argument.

Another gaze at the house. She'd half expected Monika to put the phone down when she'd introduced herself that morning and was astonished when she agreed to the visit. Maybe Monika was as curious as she was. Or perhaps she needed to actually see Sara to believe she existed.

A lump formed in her throat. Did he argue with this woman before he met his end too? Or was their relationship smoother, easier? The notion that they might have shared something together, something more stable, hardened the lump and wedged it deeper into her chest. A twitch of the ground floor curtain drew her forwards. She checked her face in the rear-view mirror, tidied a smudge of mascara beneath her left eye, fluffed up her hair and unfolded herself from the car.

The door was opened by a tall man in shirt sleeves with cropped hair and a sporty stance. 'You must be Sara Swift,' he said, a West Country accent coating his words. Sara looked at his extended hand, unmoving. This certainly wasn't the greeting she'd expected. 'Detective Constable Warren Hill,' the man said, withdrawing his unshaken hand. 'I'll take you through to meet Monika.'

The introduction of police disorientated her, inserting an immediate shift in the arrangements. She'd laboured under the misapprehension this was going to be a meeting of two women, not a vehicle for the police investigation. Yet again she was made to feel like an outsider. The change put her on edge, a feeling exacerbated when she noticed Cameron's grey cashmere cardigan on a peg in the hallway – the one she'd bought him for his birthday last year. A rush of blood to the head. A month ago, that same cardigan hung among her girls' summer jackets in their hallway, back in Cheshire.

Sara gulped a deep breath. The detective ushered her into the front room where an attractive woman with dark features sat on a large sofa. Her face was lightly made-up. The woman stood, freshly washed hair swishing on her shoulders as she did so. 'I'm Monika,' she said. Her voice was low, soft, as if someone turned down the volume. 'Please sit down.' She waited for Sara to settle herself into the sofa opposite, and the detective to sit in the armchair besides, before she continued. 'I hope your journey wasn't too arduous.'

The tension in the room was palpable. Sara wanted to scream, to shout, to unravel the questions she'd lined up in her head on the journey down. But the sight of the cashmere cardigan in the hallway warped her thoughts, folding them around each other and right now she couldn't think clearly. 'Not really,' was all she could manage.

'Can I get you a tea or a coffee?'

The idea of drinking tea out of a mug in this woman's home turned her heart to stone, but Sara needed time. She checked herself, nodded feebly. 'Tea, please. Milk, one sugar.'

Monika nodded and moved out to the kitchen. Sara ignored the detective in the armchair beside her, and scanned the room, her eyes resting on a bookshelf in the corner. Baby books were interspersed with a stream of John le Carré and Ian Fleming novels. The sight of them pinched at her as she recalled a weekend spent at home with Cameron in the early days, watching James Bond movies back to back. He loved his spy thrillers. She worked through the photos: Monika and Cameron standing on what looked like the top of a mountain. They were both wearing shorts and grinning for the camera. Several other pictures showed a boy at various stages of growth; another of a chubby baby, sitting on a beach towel and holding up a spade, deep dimples carved into his cheeks. Tears swelled Sara's eyes as they landed on a family portrait on the wall above the fireplace of Cameron, Monika, and the two boys.

She'd come here, harbouring the notion this was a short-lived fling. Perhaps a woman that Cameron had taken pity on. Maybe she was down on her luck and he'd put her up in this house while she sorted herself out. Even the news they'd shared a baby together hadn't crushed her resolve. They were his real family, her and the girls. This was a passing phase. She'd been convinced of it.

But this was a family home, cemented by photographs of shared experiences, and one where the presence of his cardigan in the hallway showed Cameron frequented often. Maybe even as often as hers. Her eyes flicked around, searching the room, the desperate need to find a flaw overwhelming, when suddenly something about it felt wrong. There was something missing, but she couldn't quite put her finger on it.

The door bumped open, breaking her train of thought. Monika reappeared with a tray of drinks which she handed out. She pulled out a coffee table from the corner and centred it between them, carefully placing down coasters. Sara watched her petite body move around the room. It had taken her over a year to lose her baby fat, yet this woman looked like she'd never been pregnant.

'How long have you known Cameron?' Sara asked as they sat and sipped their tea.

'Two years.' The European edge to her voice gave it an endearing lyrical twang.

'How did you meet?' Monika looked away and squirmed uncomfortably. The air in the room thickened. 'Please,' Sara said, swallowing back the threatening tears. 'I need to know.'

Monika cleared her throat and explained how Cameron had arrived in A&E and how he'd later persuaded her to give up work after she became pregnant with Jakub. She looked down at her hand and twiddled her engagement ring uncomfortably when she explained him proposing to her in the delivery room on the night their baby was born.

Sara pressed her eyelids together at that final remark. Cameron had talked about marriage with her several times in the early years of their relationship. It was something they were always going to do, when the moment was right, but he'd never gone as far as to buy her an engagement ring, let alone a wedding band. And, over recent years, the idea was mentioned less and less. The pain was almost too much to bear. 'You have another son?' she said, desperately trying to hold back the tears.

'Yes, Oskar, from a previous relationship. He's twelve now.'

Silence hovered restlessly. 'What about you?' Monika asked eventually. The words were filled with kind curiosity, but her face looked like she wanted to cry.

Sara drew a sharp intake of breath and spoke through her exhalation. 'We met eight years ago. I was a primary school teacher, loved my job, but struggled to make ends meet. Cameron was exciting, charming. He came from nowhere, right out of the blue, yet…' She shook her head. 'He made it all seem so ordinary.' The knowing look in Monika's eyes stung. 'We have two girls. Zoe is six and Amy is four. I gave up work shortly before Zoe was born. We bought the house in Alderley Edge in Cheshire and I've been a full-time mum ever since.'

'How often would Cameron see you, at home I mean?' Monika asked quietly.

Sara licked her lips and pressed them together before she spoke. 'Two or three days a week. Sometimes he was home on a weekend, sometimes he would be away with work or—'

'Playing golf.'

'Yes.' The joint thought sickened her.

'I don't know how he managed to keep up the pretence for so long.'

Sara ignored the last statement. She realised what was wrong about the room. From the moment she'd arrived home, messages and cards of condolence had dropped through her letter box in Cheshire and now covered every side, every spare surface in her front room. Yet there were none here. Cameron and Monika may have been *together* for two years, but their relationship wasn't established enough to develop a friendship network, people around them that cared. Her shoulders slackened slightly.

'Did you go on holiday last year?' she asked Monika.

'Yes. We flew to the Dordogne, the first week of the school holidays.' Her face turned grim. 'I remember being angry with Cameron. He'd messed up his diary and had to come back a day earlier than us because of an urgent meeting with a client.'

Sara checked the dates in her head and cringed inwardly. It would have been the twenty-fourth of July. Zoe's birthday. He'd arrived in the afternoon, just in time for her party. 'What about last Christmas?' Sara asked, the desperate need to find holes in their relationship compelling.

Monika's eyes switched to the right. 'He was here in the morning. Watched the boys open their presents, had an early dinner and was gone by two o'clock. He said he had to be in Scotland for a golfing day with an important client on Boxing Day.'

Sara swallowed. 'He spent the rest of the day with us. The girls had to wait until evening to open their main presents. We went to the seaside on Boxing Day.'

The next half an hour passed with more dates, more comparisons. Monika paled as she filled almost every gap in Cameron's diary that Sara couldn't account for. Eventually, they sat in silence, weary at the true realisation of their joint situation.

A mumbling sounded, followed by the high pitch of a baby chattering to himself. Monika grabbed the monitor. 'I'm sorry. I need to see to him.'

'Of course you do.' Sara stood and grabbed her bag. The

thought of meeting Cameron's baby son today filled her with dread. She was teetering on an emotional cliff edge. She needed to get out of there. 'Thanks for—' She stood awkwardly, her lip quivering. The baby squawked in the background, ending her sentence.

They'd reached the hallway when she saw them – a pretty array of pastel envelopes, stacked neatly into three piles on the side table: the condolence cards missing from the front room. She'd been wrong. This woman was the same as her, after all.

Sara's departure was as surreal as her arrival. There was no anger, no emotion. The reality of the situation numbed both of their senses. Sara's head spun as she took a slow walk back to her car. Cameron had two families. Two women he claimed to care about. Two sets of kids he called his own. And he never intended for each to know about the other. What kind of twisted mentality would do something like that? But even before she asked herself the question, she already knew the answer. Cameron was exactly the type. Even in death he was able to torment her.

She was almost at her car when she noticed a familiar figure climb out of a black Mini parked behind. Sara turned, shook her head and turned her eyes to the sky. 'I was wondering when you'd show up,' she said.

Monika stood at her bedroom window and watched the woman walk to the end of the driveway. From the minute she'd taken the phone call that morning, the conversation had rolled around her mind, like a song on replay. There was something about the husk in the voice, the calculated pauses and stutters of someone biting back tears that told her it was Sara Swift, even before the woman had introduced herself.

Her first thoughts were to slam the phone down. But a tiny voice inside her compelled her to listen to what Cameron's *other woman* had to say. Her heart pounded when Sara suggested they meet. 'Perhaps we could support each other,' she'd said. 'The children are family, after all.' Inwardly, Monika's head had yelled at her, screaming a resounding 'No!'. But simultaneously that same inner voice quenched it from within. Whether it was curiosity, a niggling drive to get to the truth about their relationship, or a jealous need to expose the cracks in her veneer and cast doubt on her story, she wasn't sure. All Monika knew was, she wouldn't be sure of anything until she'd actually seen this woman with her own eyes.

Misery now tore at her as she watched the slender frame reach the end of the driveway. Jakub whinged from his cot next door, but she ignored him, a torrent of sadness and bitter disappointment wrapping around her, squeezing the air from her lungs. Her life with Cameron had been a façade. How many other women had he done this to? Anger rose within her, anger that swirled into a bitter rage. Tears burned her eyes. How many more secrets were to be uncovered before this was over? She cursed Cameron, then cursed herself for being so stupid as to enter into a relationship with a man she barely knew. She'd always considered herself a strong independent woman. Life was difficult after her last relationship broke down; Oskar was young, she had to work long hours to pay the bills and childcare. Cameron appeared almost from nowhere, all smiles and charm, offering a better future for both of them, a life she could never have imagined living. She'd questioned it a number of times at the beginning. But when she fell pregnant with Jakub she'd accepted that perhaps, finally, this was a true chance of happiness for her family. How could she turn that down? She clenched her teeth. Only now she realised what a fool she'd been.

33

'Would you like a tea or coffee?' Beth asked. She indicated for Sara to sit.

'No, thank you.'

It was a subdued Sara that Beth had met in Meadowbrook Close earlier. It seemed facing her fears in Monika had kicked the former belligerence out of her, and Beth had been surprised at how easily she'd agreed to accompany her back to force headquarters.

Sara raised a single brow at the layout of the room – the sofas and soft furnishings, the Monet print on the wall – but said nothing. This clearly wasn't what she was expecting when Beth talked about finding an interview room for them to talk in.

Beth settled herself into a chair beside her. 'How are you?'

'You said you have some news.'

'Yes, of course. We've been looking into Cameron's business accounts.' Beth talked generally about going through his computer and company records, and the team interviewing recent clients and work colleagues, keeping the specifics to herself. The discovery of the mobile phone and memory stick in the hidden compartment in his car hadn't been revealed to the press, and she didn't want to give too much away at this stage. 'We've discovered he was doing some private investment work. Do you know anything about that?'

Sara shook her head.

'Has Cameron ever spoken about a boxing promotions company called Elite Boxing Promotions?'

'No.' She wriggled in her seat. 'Is that it?'

'Yes, for the moment. I wanted to let you know it's a line of enquiry we're pursuing.'

'Thank you.'

'How did it go with Monika this afternoon?' Beth ventured.

Sara shot her an edgy look, revealing a grain of her usual abrasiveness. 'Why don't you ask your colleague? He was there the whole time.' She looked away. 'To be honest, I wasn't expecting that.'

The sound of the light bulb buzzing filled the room.

'Warren is Monika's liaison officer,' Beth said softly. 'He's supporting her, keeping her updated on any developments. He wasn't there to catch you out.'

If Sara heard her explanation, there was no acknowledgement in her face. She appeared to be distracted, working back something in her mind. Eventually she huffed. 'I couldn't believe it when you told me about Monika and the children.' Her eyes were averted, staring into nothingness. 'Oh, I knew about the affairs. Cameron hadn't been able to keep it in his pants for years. I learned to turn a blind eye. But a family…' Her face was incredulous, as if she was still struggling to deal with the reality. 'That was a whole different ball game. Part of me wanted to hate her, for being the other woman and taking something away from me. But in the end, all I felt was pity.' She met Beth's gaze, her dark eyes vacant. 'She was just like me. She had no idea.'

'I'm sorry,' Beth said. 'Do you know any details about the other women he had affairs with?'

'No. I made a point of not knowing.'

The drone of an engine filled the room as a lorry passed outside. 'How are the children doing?' Beth asked.

'They were up most of the night.'

'We can arrange for counselling, if you think that would help?'

Sara tossed her head. 'I'll deal with it.'

'Where are they today?'

'Yvonne's taken them to an aquarium in Manchester. I didn't want them in the house while your people were searching.'

Beth nodded. Although she'd refused the presence of a detective in her home, the idea of officers rifling through their belongings didn't seem to overly bother Sara. Either she didn't have anything to hide, or she was confident she'd covered her tracks and they wouldn't find anything. 'Have you told them about Monika?' she said.

'Not yet.' Her eyes dulled, the light dimming behind them. 'Can I go now, or do you have more questions?'

Beth was mindful of Nick's caution. She couldn't afford for Sara to clam up. She needed to keep the conversation moderate, avoid confrontation. No mean feat with such sensitive issues to discuss. 'I have got some more questions for you,' she said softly, 'if you don't mind.'

'Well, you might as well make the most of me while I'm here.' Sara pulled the cuffs of her jumper over her hands and sat back in her chair.

'Thank you. Can you tell me about your life before you met Cameron?'

'Why? You think I killed him?'

'I didn't say that.'

'Then why is it relevant?'

'As I said yesterday, we are trying to build up a picture of Cameron's life. You were his partner, the mother of his children.'

'So was Monika.'

'We're asking Monika the same questions.'

'I've already told you everything I know. I lived in Manchester and was working at Steeples Primary when I met Cameron.'

'But you didn't grow up there?'

A shadow flickered over Sara's face. 'No, I grew up in Bradford.'

'Where did you go to university?'

Sara eyed Beth carefully. 'I got an offer from King's College and moved down to London after my A levels.'

'Go on.'

'I stayed on in London after I graduated and worked at a school in Highgate for a while. Then I came back up to Manchester. I wanted to be closer to home. The pressures of teaching were too much, but I still loved the kids and the environment. So, I worked as a teaching assistant. That's when I met Cameron.'

'Where did you live in London?'

'North London. Holloway Road.'

'What was the address?'

She shuffled in her seat. 'I can't remember. It was a long time ago.'

'Why didn't you tell us you were married, Sara?'

A muscle twitched beneath her right eye. 'I didn't think it was relevant. I haven't done anything wrong. Cameron and I weren't married.'

'Tell me about your marriage.'

'What do you want to know?'

'When did you meet your husband?'

She shook her head in disbelief, said nothing.

'What was your husband's name?'

'Look, I don't think this is relevant. It was nine years ago.'

'This is normal practice in an investigation like this,' Beth assured her. 'Was it a happy marriage?'

'For a while. We were young. It didn't work out, so we parted. There were no children, so I can't, for the life of me, see why it needs to come up now.'

'Was it an amicable split?'

'Sort of.' Sara sighed. 'It was a long time ago.'

'And when was this?'

'I was married in 2006. We separated in 2008. That's when I went up to Manchester.'

'Was it an arranged marriage?'

Sara squinted. 'No. My family were happy for me to choose.'

'How did your family feel about your husband?'

'I was raised a Sikh. They were pleased I'd married a Sikh, I guess. They wanted me to be happy.'

'How did both your families feel about your parting?'

'They were disappointed, naturally. My family went back to India before we separated. Anyway, it doesn't matter now. I filed for divorce last year.'

'Why only last year? Why not earlier?'

Sara's face fell. She bent back her wedding finger. 'It seemed like the right time.'

Beth angled her head. 'Do you have a current address for your husband?'

'No. The divorce papers were sent to his family's solicitor. Why?'

'What about names of mutual friends, details of where he worked?'

'No, I left all that behind me in London. It was nine years ago.'

'When did you last see him?'

Sara shifted in her seat. 'You surely don't think he's involved in Cameron's death?'

'I don't know. We do need to eliminate him from our enquiries though.'

She closed her eyes. 'No, no way. He wouldn't.'

'Why do you say that?'

'He just wouldn't. Look, I don't want to talk about this. It was a long time ago.'

Beth dropped her voice an octave. 'Sara, I need to make you aware that we've spoken to the headmaster of Easham's Primary in Highgate. He told us you left suddenly and didn't work your notice. He also told us your husband came to look for you and didn't know where you'd gone. When you moved to Manchester you reverted to your maiden name of Kaur. What happened?'

Sara's face folded. She dropped her head into her hands. 'I think I'll have that drink now.'

34

Sara cradled the Styrofoam cup with both hands. 'His name is Rajinder Sidhu. I met him at university, we shared some classes together.' She paused, lost in her memories. 'I didn't even like him at first, thought he was full of himself. But he grew on me. He was charming, funny.' She grunted. 'Not unlike Cameron, actually. We were in the same circle of friends, and the others were all in couples. It was a natural progression.

'I decided to stay on and work in London after I graduated. Not long afterwards, my grandmother in India fell ill. My brother and my aunt were already living there, looking out for her, but he was doing some high-flying job in finance and she was struggling to cope. They needed help. My grandmother couldn't travel to the UK because she had a bad heart, so my parents decided to go back to India and help to care for her there. They didn't say anything, didn't want to interfere, but I knew they'd be happier if I was married and settled before they left.

'I had doubts, right up to the wedding, but everyone was so happy I didn't want to disappoint them. My family have always been liberal, allowed me a lot of freedom, more than usual for Sikh culture. Rajinder maintained he was liberal too and respected my independence. In the Sikh community it's normal for a new wife to live with her husband's parents after the wedding, but I wanted my own home and he respected my wishes. We rented a flat on the Holloway Road.'

She sniffed, placed the cup on the table in front of her and pulled the cuffs of her jumper further over her hands until they were covering her fingers. 'About a month after the wedding I realised my mistake. It started with silly comments. He didn't like the clothes I'd chosen or wanted me to wear my hair differently. At home he became a stickler for tidiness: the curtains had to be tied back first thing in the morning, the sofa cushions plumped, the bed made as soon as we climbed out of it. I'd never lived with anyone before, apart from house-shares. I thought he was particular, wanted everything to be nice. I went along with it at first. I was having a rough time at work, a combination of budget cuts and changes meant I was working long hours. I thought it was me.

'Time passed. A new headmaster started at the school and I was much happier. But things at home didn't improve. Even though we both worked full-time, Rajinder expected me to be home first and for a meal to be prepared for him. He didn't like me to go out without him, not even with my work colleagues, and insisted on coming along. It was embarrassing. I suspected the pressure was coming from his family. We were summoned every Sunday and expected to attend every festival in the calendar with them. Between travelling to Bradford to see my family, and spending time with his, and work, there was no time left.

'It came to a head when I went for a couple of drinks

with my colleagues after a parents' evening. I wasn't home late, about nine-ish I suppose, but I walked into the house to find him sitting on the stairs in the dark, waiting for me. He didn't shout or holler, just shook his head in disapproval and marched up to bed. He didn't talk to me for days afterwards. When we visited his parents that weekend, they looked at me like I was muck on their shoe. I thought it would blow over, but weeks passed, and I still got the silent treatment. It was suffocating. I tried to tell my parents, but they didn't listen. They didn't want to. Their passage was booked. They'd finally sold their house and were close to leaving the UK. I couldn't bear to upset their plans, so I carried on.'

'Did he ever hit you, or verbally abuse you?'

'No. Never. Rajinder isn't a violent man. He didn't need violence. The continuous sniffs of disapproval were enough. He cut off every lifeline, every ounce of fresh air. Then he started gambling.' Her eyes clouded. 'Card tables, roulette.'

'Did you tell anyone?'

She gave a sarcastic laugh. 'People don't want to know. Rajinder's family were well connected in the Sikh community in north London. Wealthy. I was married, with a beautiful home and an attentive husband – the envy of many of my friends. But they didn't see what went on behind closed doors, the sacrifices I made. Gambling is frowned upon in Sikh culture. He started running up debts, pressuring me to keep silent. He promised me he knew what he was doing. Nobody noticed anything was wrong. Even when I stopped going out, they teased me for being a newlywed, a homemaker.

'It became more unbearable as my parents' leaving date grew closer. The thought of not having my family nearby, being swamped by his…' She closed her eyes, reliving those final moments. 'And the money worries. It was too much.

'I had to do something, I was going insane. So, I planned to leave him the day after my parents' flight to India. I knew he'd never accept it, and it would cause a massive furore in the community, so I kept the decision to myself and tried to play the dutiful wife. We drove my parents to the airport and waved them off together. For weeks I'd been packing a small holdall, tucked away at the back of the pantry. He was quiet when we got back, tired. I waited for him to go to bed and called a cab to the station.

'A friend from university moved up to Manchester after she graduated. I stayed with her for a while. She recommended me for a job at a school – it was only a teaching assistant position, but it was work. Eventually I got my own flat.'

The ensuing silence stretched for almost a minute.

'How did your families react afterwards?' Beth eventually asked.

'My family had already heard about my actions, even before I contacted them. They wouldn't speak to me. Refused my phone calls, ignored my emails. I was estranged from my father until he died in 2010. Only after both my children were born, did my mother acquiesce to a visit. She doesn't approve of my life here. Our relationship is strained. It always will be. I disgraced them. They went along with me when I said I didn't want an arranged marriage. Were happy for me to choose. But separation, divorce.' A tear glittered her lashes as she shook her head. 'They aren't words in their vocabulary.'

'What about Rajinder's family?'

'I should think they were relieved, after the initial shock of it all. They never thought I was good enough for him.'

'When did you last see your husband?'

Sara looked down at her hands. 'I haven't seen him for years.'

'He didn't come to look for you?'

'I don't know. Maybe he was keen to see the back of me too. I changed my name, my address, was careful not to leave any traces.' She gave a deep sigh and looked Beth in the eye. 'I know my relationship with Cameron might sound strange to you. Him being away a lot. The other women. But I lost everything when I left London: my friends, my family, the support of my community. It's difficult to pick yourself up after something like that.' She blinked, wiping a tear from beneath her eye. 'Cameron looked after us. He gave me the chance of a new life, to put the past behind me.'

Beth's feet dragged as she traipsed back up to the incident room. Sara's reluctance for police intrusion, the meagre information, and lack of personal photographs on her Facebook page fitted. Sara was a woman on the run. She'd left her identity behind when she left London, established herself anew in Manchester. It was conceivable, in those circumstances, to understand how she might have been taken in by Cameron's charm, and welcomed his generosity in their early years. Perhaps it also went some way to explain how she'd put up with the secrets and lies that trailed him like a shadow.

Nick was at her desk when she re-entered the incident room. 'What are you up to?' she asked as he clicked away at the keys of her keyboard.

He swivelled in his chair, gave her a quizzical look. 'Is Sara Swift still here?'

Something about the question tugged on her. 'No.' She checked her watch. 'She left a while ago. She'll probably be on the motorway by now. Why?'

He gave a long sigh. 'The traces are back on her late husband.'

'Are you saying he's dead?'

'Yes. He committed suicide. Threw himself off a bridge in February of this year. I've requested the coroner's report. It should be here by the morning.'

35

Dusk was falling, curling its cool fingers around the tombstones of All Saints' churchyard, creating a Gothic eeriness. Beth weaved in and out of the graves, passing slabs of soft marble, old pitted stones, some of which were lopsided and covered in lichen, the words they bore barely readable. A line of mausoleums sat proud at the far side. The sweet smell of freshly cut grass met her as she rounded a gnarled yew tree and reached a stretch behind the church where the most recent burials were stowed. The earth rose into peaks in places there, pulling down protectively on their new wares below.

The frustrations of the day's enquiries gnawed at Beth, wearing her down. She craved peace and calm, and right now this was the only place she could be sure of some tranquillity.

At the end of the second line, Beth halted, unwrapped her flowers and knelt down, pulling out the dead yellow roses from the vase beside the headstone and replacing them with a fresh batch. Yellow roses had been her mother's favourite and a bunch of them had graced their front room dresser on her birthday every year. Beth wiped a fleck of dust from the marble and drank in the gold words.

Jean Elizabeth Chamberlain, 14.10.63 – 17.9.15
Beloved mother to Beth and Eden, and
grandmother to Lily.
Forever in our hearts.

Next month it would be two years since the cruel brain tumour had taken her yet reading that epitaph still embedded a stone in Beth's chest.

The evening dew bled into the knees of her trousers leaving wet circles as she sat back on her heels. Opaque memories of an angry man in shirt sleeves flitted into her mind, the only memories she had of her father. Her mother raised them single-handedly, with the help of their grandparents. It wasn't until after her mother died that Beth appreciated how difficult it must have been for her: to hold down a job, run the home, and raise her girls alone, and what personal sacrifices she must have made.

Absentmindedly, she traced the name on the headstone with her finger. Her mother had known about the tumour, gone through all the tests and been diagnosed terminal, before she'd even shared news of it with her girls. Saving them from some of the prolonged agony of losing her. She even took the trouble to plan her own funeral, in one last act of complete selflessness.

Beth closed her eyes as she recalled her mother's dying request. 'Look after Eden.'

Two years younger than her, Beth watched her sister stretch the boundaries of discipline, time and time again, as they grew up. Eden was the child suspended for smoking cannabis behind the school gymnasium; the fourteen-year-old who kept her sixth-form boyfriend a secret until she was spotted out with him in town. Even as a young child, Eden kept things to herself; never one of those children who talked about their friends or shared even the broader details of their day. When she joined secondary school she became deeper, guarding her personal life like a Rottweiler. Their mother grew accustomed to prising details from her youngest daughter in her teens, of whom she was with and where she was going. 'That child's trouble,' their grandmother used to say to their mother. 'She's going to give you a head of grey hairs before you are forty. Either that or a teenage pregnancy.'

A year after their grandmother passed away, her prophecy came true. Just a couple of months off her twentieth birthday, Eden's bump could no longer be hidden. She'd been seeing Chris for the best part of six months by then and, while he was almost five years older than her, he had a steady job in the police and seemed to be a stable influence. They were married a year after Lily was born and the relief on their mother's face that her youngest daughter's wildness had been tempered, albeit mildly, was palpable.

A combination of motherhood and marriage appeared to mellow Eden. But her grandmother's passing words clung to Beth now, reminding her of the unpredictability that hovered beneath her sister's façade. As a child, Eden was a sucker for anything with an inherent risk. Was that what now drew her to Kyle Thompson? She'd pushed the notion aside, concentrated her mind on the case, but as much as she didn't want to admit it, Chris's comments about Eden niggled away at her. It would go some way to explain why he had gone to such lengths to distance himself from them all. Associations with criminals put officers at risk of all sorts of unsavoury allegations.

Beth looked at the gravestone and implored her mother's spirit to subliminally send her an ounce of the grounded reasoning she'd bestowed upon her so many times when she was living. Kyle Thompson was trouble. He had a string of children littered around the county to different mothers, and a list of criminal convictions longer than her arm, even though he was still only in his twenties. She didn't blame Chris for expressing concern for Lily. Sooner or later, Beth was going to have to talk to Eden. But she needed proof of the association first.

36

Beth's phone rang before the alarm sounded the following morning. She clamped her gritty eyes together a moment and reached out for her phone, her hand tapping across the bedside table until she found it. It was 6.50 a.m.

'Beth?' Nick's voice sounded urgent.

'You're in early.'

'More like didn't leave.'

She suppressed a yawn. 'Have you had a breakthrough?'

'Not exactly. We've been working through the bank statements and spreadsheets most of the night. No, I'm ringing about your lady, Sara Swift.' Beth sat up and was blinded by a glint of sunshine squeezing through the gap in the top of the curtain. She shaded her eyes. 'The coroner's file is here for her ex-husband. One of their cops lives locally and dropped it off last night.'

'Thanks. I'll be there as soon as I can.' She rung off. Her head was thick, woolly. Yesterday's enquiries had tossed themselves around her skull like clothes in a tumble dryer for most of the night. Both Monika and Sara harboured secrets they hadn't shared with the investigation. Continuing enquiries at the hospital with Monika's old work colleagues hadn't uncovered anything new. Sara's ex-husband, a man scorned, a man who could possibly have a motive to hunt her new family down, was dead.

Warren had included notes of the two women's meeting in the report he'd emailed her last night. He'd watched their body language throughout the time they spent together and saw no indication of any previous association, no evidence of guilt or malice. They both claimed to have no knowledge of the boxing promotions company or Alan Jones, although, if past experience was anything to go by, she couldn't rely on either of them to be completely truthful.

Less than an hour later, Beth was back in the conference room at the office, leafing through the coroner's file for the late Rajinder Sidhu. The clouds outside had conjoined, blocking out the early sun and making for an overcast day. She hadn't bothered to put on the light and a gloomy greyness hung in the room, mirroring her mood. She pulled out photographs of the scene and stared at Archway Bridge, a known suicide spot in north London. Some years ago, the local council had erected railings along the top to stop people jumping, but they didn't stop the most determined. She laid it beside a photograph of the victim, supplied by his family.

The statements were harrowing. His doctor confirmed he'd been taking citalopram, an antidepressant, for some years. Financial checks showed he was in debt up to his eyeballs when he died. A statement from a friend said he was struggling with debts he couldn't sustain due to a gambling habit. His family were aware he was on antidepressants but seemed to know nothing of his financial situation. He appeared to have maintained the front of a loyal hardworking man who visited his family at weekends. There was no note, no explanation. Beth's stomach twisted. She'd attended enough suicides in her career to know it was a common misconception that depressed people reached out, or always left a note. Often people worked hard to maintain a front so as not to upset their loved ones and even believed their death would be saving their families further heartache. The sadness and utter desperation wrenched at her.

During their discussion yesterday, Sara Swift hadn't given any indication she'd known about Rajinder's death. Beth worked it back, re-listened to Sara's account in her head. Offenders and witnesses often slipped up in interview and inadvertently talked about the person in the past tense, but Sara never did that. Not once. Was that because she didn't know he was dead, or because she was carefully hiding the fact? There was certainly nothing in the file to suggest Sara had ever been contacted. The only family member to mention her was Rajinder's mother who said they'd been separated for around nine years and had no contact.

Rajinder was pronounced dead at 11.30 p.m. on the 20th of February 2017. One witness, a pedestrian, saw him jump. Beth recalled Sara mentioning she'd filed for divorce a year earlier. Rajinder committed suicide six months later. Not a knee jerk reaction to her call for a divorce then. In fact, the more she looked, the more there didn't appear to be any correlation between the two.

The flap of the door turned her head. Nick's face appeared. He flicked the switches beside the door. The bulbs

THE OTHER WOMAN

flashed a few times before they flooded the room with light. Beth blinked as her eyes adjusted. 'I don't know how you can work in this half-light,' Nick said as he strode down the room. He paused beside her and peered at the papers scattered across the desk. 'How are you getting on?'

Beth relayed a summary of her findings. 'Not much there to help us, I'm afraid.'

'Okay.' He waved a sheet of paper in front of her. 'What is interesting though is that we've found a payment from Cameron's bank account to a Rajinder Sidhu for £10,000. It was made on the 19th of December 2016.'

'Really? That was two months before he died.' She cast her mind back. 'Sara said she hadn't seen Rajinder in years.'

'Maybe she hadn't. But Cameron had been in contact. What we need to know is, why?'

'I can feel another trip to Cheshire coming on,' Beth said.

'I've got something else,' Nick said. 'What do you know about Yvonne Newman?'

'She's Sara's friend, lives around the corner from the family in Alderley Edge.' The still photos Pete had found of a woman that resembled Yvonne on the CCTV footage from Birmingham jabbed at her. If it was the same woman, she was more familiar with Cameron than she'd admitted. She passed on the details. 'Why, do you have something on her? I've already checked, and she's not known to us.'

Nick scratched the stubble on his chin. 'I'm not sure. The spreadsheets from the boxing promotions company show a payment of £200 in June to a YN for bookkeeping services. When we traced the payment to the receiving bank account, we discovered it was made to a Yvonne Newman.'

Beth recalled Yvonne's protective attitude towards Sara when she first visited. 'That's interesting. When I asked her, she claimed she barely knew Cameron.'

The door opened, and Freeman's face appeared. He nodded at Beth and called to Nick. 'You got a minute?'

'Sure.'

He marched down the room to join them. This was the first time she'd encountered Freeman since his irate phone call yesterday and she was relieved to see his attention diverted; he appeared to have put the conversation behind them.

'Another source in the field has just advised their handler that Nigel Sherwood has met with Cameron Swift on several occasions over the past year or so,' he said. 'Also, we've cell-sited the phone that sent the text messages. They were sent all within two hundred yards of either Nigel Sherwood's home or the casino he owns.'

'That links in with the anonymous call we had pointing us in Sherwood's direction.'

'It does. We've a lot more work to do, but if they've been working together and our victim upset him, it gives Sherwood a reason to want him out of the way.' He paused a moment, looked down at the line highlighted on the spreadsheet. 'What have we got here?'

Beth chipped in, recounting their discussion.

'So, all we have on Yvonne is some possible photographs indicating a liaison with the victim and this payment into Yvonne Newman's bank account?' he clarified.

'That's right,' Nick said. 'But it does show a closer connection than she was letting on.'

'Okay. Yvonne Newman is a married woman and a family friend. There are lots of reasons why she might not have been totally truthful. It doesn't necessarily give her a motive for murder. At this stage, I'm more interested in what she can tell us about the boxing promotions company. The indicators point to a contract killing. Our current priority is to find out why. So, let's take this gently.'

'Why don't I go and see her at home?' Beth said. 'Interview her as a witness, take a statement. If we bring her in, she might clam up or go no comment, depending on whether or not she was involved, and we won't find out anything.'

'I agree,' Freeman said. 'Interview her informally. See if you can ascertain her relationship with the victim and what you can find out about the boxing promotions company or the victim's connection with Nigel Sherwood. I can't see her role being huge, the payment is relatively small, but anything she can tell us about it right now could inform the wider investigation. Make sure she's aware she's being interviewed as a witness. Take a statement. If at any time you detect anything suspicious, we'll bring her in.'

37

Yvonne's house was grander than Sara's, with a mock-Tudor frontage, latticed windows, and a long, block paved driveway; stone jardinières containing colourful pot plants sat either side of the entrance. The front door was set in the middle of the property beneath a wide porch. As Beth rang the doorbell, she couldn't help but wonder at Yvonne rattling around in all this space, with her children left home and her husband away for most of the working week.

She stood for a while. Rain had started to fall, soft droplets splattering her jacket. She rang the bell again. Its chimes echoed around the inside walls. But there was still no answer. Beth heaved a sigh, turned on her heel and surveyed the empty driveway. She'd made a point of phoning ahead. Yvonne was expecting her. Why the hell wasn't she home?

After a third try at the doorbell, she returned to her car and slung her briefcase in the back. There was only one other place she could imagine Yvonne might be this afternoon.

She drove around the corner, surprised to find the gates of number twelve Knighton Lane wide open, and rolled her eyes when she saw Yvonne's white Audi A4 on the driveway. She was crunching across the gravel to the front door, when it opened to a thin gap. Yvonne's pinched face peered out.

'Ah,' she said. 'I'm sorry, I'm going to have to cancel our appointment today.'

Beth continued towards the door, ignoring her statement. 'There's still time,' she said, placing her briefcase down. The fine rain was gathering momentum, dampening everything in sight, and she was grateful for the wide porch canopy.

Yvonne didn't flinch. 'I'm afraid we'll have to rearrange. Sara's had some bad news.'

A face appeared out of the shadows pulling the door open wider. Sara looked like she'd been crying. 'This isn't a good time,' she said.

'Why, what's happened?' Neither answered. 'I'm sorry, but I have more questions,' Beth said, undeterred. 'For both of you.'

Sara and Yvonne exchanged a glance, but neither of them made any attempt to move. Beth pushed on the door, a gentle nudge but enough to show she wasn't awaiting an invitation. She hadn't driven all this way for nothing, and she certainly wasn't going to return to Northampton empty handed.

Sara turned her eyes skyward. 'You'd better come in then,' she said, her voice laced with sarcasm. 'But make it quick. I don't want my girls upset any more than they need to be.'

The house was eerily quiet. Beth's footsteps clicked against the black and white hall tiles as she followed Sara into a front room that looked remarkably different from her last visit: bereavement cards covered the mantel, the window ledge, the hearth. It looked like half of the estate had expressed their sympathy.

Sara caught her eye. 'They think we were separated.' She

extended a hand at the cards. 'Every one of them. They push their cards through the letter box in the gate, and rush away. No one knows what to say. They've all seen the news and know about his other family. I've even had a couple of calls from reporters, asking if I've anything to add, as Cameron's ex-partner.' She placed an emphasis on the 'ex'. 'It's surreal.'

Was that why she was upset, because she was being hounded by the media? 'Have you spoken to any of the reporters?' Beth asked.

Another headshake. 'I don't have the energy right now.'

'Good. We'd be grateful if you could leave that to us for the moment. How are the girls doing?'

'All right, all things considered. They're upstairs playing with Lego.'

Nobody offered Beth refreshments, and although she'd have loved a coffee after her long car journey, she didn't want to delay her questioning by requesting one. Instead she moved to the sofa beside the window and sat, indicating for Sara and Yvonne to sit on the sofa opposite. Sara sat, but Yvonne stood by the door, her face wary, as if she wasn't sure what to do.

'I can talk to you separately, if you would like?' Beth said eyeing her.

Yvonne straightened and sat beside her friend. 'That's not necessary,' she said.

Beth paused a moment. She'd intended on speaking with Yvonne first, discussing the payments found on the bank statements, but now she was here, in Sara's home, it felt more appropriate to update Sara. Plus, something about the young woman's manner didn't feel right. 'Sara, I'm sorry to have to tell you that your husband, Rajinder Sidhu, is dead.'

Sara blanched. 'Oh, my goodness! When? How?'

'He jumped from a bridge on the 20th of February this year. A coroner's enquiry recorded a verdict of suicide. I'm so very sorry.'

'I had no idea.'

Quiet fell upon them. Beth had delivered numerous death messages over the years, enough to know there wasn't a standard response: a woman, whose teenage son had wrapped his car around a tree, fainted on the spot when she was told he died at the scene; a daughter, whose mother had died of a stroke in a supermarket, looked at her in disbelief, saying, 'I only spoke with her this morning,' as if they must be mistaken. But watching Sara right now, there was no response at all. Just a pale numbness.

Yvonne leaned over, pulled a tissue out of a box on the side table, placed her arm protectively around her friend's shoulder, and held it out with her free hand. Sara took the tissue and surveyed Beth. 'What happened?' she asked.

Beth explained the events from the coroner's file in as much detail as she was able.

Sara shuddered as she finished up. 'Poor Rajinder.'

'I'm so sorry,' Beth said again. 'Can I get you a drink?'

Sara shook her head and looked towards the window. The rain had gathered in droplets across the glass, masking the view of the garden out front. Seconds passed. Beth allowed them to. Even though they were separated, and clearly had their differences, this was a man Sara had been close to for several years and the shock tunnelled deep.

Eventually, she looked up. 'I do have some more questions, I'm afraid.'

Sara gave her a glassy stare.

'We found a payment of £10,000, paid into Rajinder's account, at the end of last year. The payee was traced back to Cameron.' A hint of apprehension travelled across Sara's face. 'Do you know anything about the money?'

Sara gave a quick head shake.

'Had Cameron ever met Rajinder?'

Sara closed her eyes a moment. When she opened them, her pupils were dilated. 'I don't think Cameron ever met him. He gave him the £10,000 because of me.'

'Why?'

It was a moment before she answered. 'Rajinder turned up on our doorstep about…' She paused a moment, working through the dates in her mind. '…December last year. A week before Christmas. I didn't recognise him at first. He looked so skinny. I thought maybe he'd received the court papers and wanted to talk it through. I know solicitors take ages. But I was wrong. He'd ignored the court papers. He was recently separated from another woman and gambling hard. He'd got himself into more debt, and now he knew where I was, he wanted money. He said if I wanted a divorce, I had to pay him off.'

'Why didn't you call the police?'

'I don't know. I threw him out, told him to leave us alone, and he said he'd come back, he'd keep coming back unless I paid him. He also said he'd let everyone in our community in London know where I was and who I was with. I didn't know what to do. I wasn't frightened of him, not at all. I wasn't really bothered about the old community either, not after all this time, that's why I didn't ask the solicitors to keep my address confidential. I was sick of hiding away. But then he mentioned my mother.' She hung her head. 'My mother moved house a couple of years ago. I didn't realise anyone knew where she was living in India now. I didn't think for one minute she'd have told Rajinder's relatives in London her new address, especially after what happened. I've worked hard to rekindle some kind of relationship with my mother for the sake of my children. The shame of him contacting her, exposing my life here to people in her community back in India.' She flinched. 'They would find out Cameron and I weren't married and see my children as illegitimate. It would inflict more pain, ruin what we'd built.'

'Are you saying your ex-husband tried to extort money from you?'

'I don't know. I just knew that if we didn't pay him, he wouldn't go away and leave us alone. I can't believe I was such a fool, to allow my address to be known. When Cameron phoned that evening, I was hysterical. He made me pass on the details, said he'd deal with it. I never heard from Rajinder again.'

'What details?'

'A mobile phone number. That's all I had.'

'Do you still have it?'

Sara shook her head. 'I gave everything to Cameron. I couldn't bear to even think about it afterwards.'

Beth's phone rang. She excused herself and moved out into the hallway, surprised to see a number she didn't recognise flash up on screen.

'DC Beth Chamberlain,' she answered.

'Beth, it's Pete from the office. You wanted me to contact you if we found any more footage of that woman.'

'Ah, yes.' Beth stepped further down the hallway. 'What have you got?'

'Several stills from two different dates. About six of them are reasonably clear – it's definitely the same woman. The victim and her were very familiar,' he said.

Beth held her breath. 'What do you mean?'

'Well, I'd put money on it they were not having a business meeting. Not to talk about investments anyway.' He chuckled at his own joke. 'I'll email them to your phone.'

He rang off and Beth tapped her foot, waiting for the email to come through. She opened it up, waited for the images to download, and scrolled through. There was no doubt the woman was Yvonne. The first photo showed a kiss on the cheek, probably a greeting. There were two, later on the same day, one where they'd emerged from the pub, another showing an embrace outside. She moved down to the next images, recorded the following week, in the days running up to Cameron's death. The first was an embrace, taken at an angle showing his eyes closed; an affectionate gesture, betraying a close friendship. The next, taken seconds later, showed them from the rear, entering the pub, his hand in the small of her back. But the third was where Pete's familiarity comment derived from. It was over an hour later and they were outside the pub, her head twisted slightly, lips pressed on his in what looked like a prolonged kiss.

Beth's thoughts raced as she shut down her phone. The stills were recorded during the two weeks before Cameron died. While Sara was on holiday in Goa.

Back in the lounge, the air was still and quiet. Yvonne looked up as Beth eased herself back into the chair. 'You had some questions, for me, I believe.' The harsh edge that made Beth want to slap her face had returned to her tone. She folded her hands in her lap, looked up expectantly.

It felt unfair to question them, in the same room together, especially after the news she'd delivered to Sara. But Yvonne's tone caught her. Perhaps she could test the water ...

'Yes, could you tell me about your relationship with Cameron?' Beth said.

Yvonne looked at Sara and then back at Beth. 'I'm sorry. I don't know what you mean.'

'How well did you know him?'

'I've already told you, I'm a family friend. I met him here, several times, at gatherings. I didn't know him as well as I know Sara, obviously.'

Beth gave a single nod. 'When did you last see him?'

'I can't remember exactly. What's all this about?'

'Last time we spoke, you said you hadn't seen Cameron for several weeks. Is that right?'

Yvonne looked rattled. 'I don't know what—'

Beth retrieved her phone and pulled up the photo of Yvonne and Cameron outside the pub. The edge of a window box filled with orange begonias sat in the background. She was careful to select the right photo, keeping the more intimate ones out of view, before she held it out at arm's length.

Yvonne's eyes widened. 'Where did you get this?'

Beth ignored the question. 'You can clearly see the date and time at the bottom. It was taken last week.'

'What?' Sara's face crumpled.

'This was taken outside The Crown public house on Clarkson Street in Birmingham,' Beth said. 'Would you like to tell me what you were doing there?'

'Yes, what were you doing in Birmingham?' Sara said. She edged away, creating a small gap between her and her friend.

'Oh, that.' Relief laced her voice. 'Cameron was giving me some advice on my investments.' She waved her hand in the air and addressed Sara direct. 'I'm sure I told you, lovely.'

'You didn't.' Sara's face tightened.

'I'm sure I did. It's the money from my mum's estate, you know.'

'Your mum died last year. What were you doing meeting Cameron while we were on holiday?'

She looked at Sara. 'It's nothing really, darling. It's taken a while to sort everything out. He's been doing me a portfolio.'

'You never mentioned it.'

'Didn't I?'

'Not once.' A muscle flexed in Sara's jaw.

Yvonne turned back to face Beth. 'Is that it?'

'How many times did you meet Cameron in Birmingham?' Beth asked.

'Oh!' She shook her head as if it was a mere formality. 'Just a few.'

'A few!' Sara looked astounded.

'Well, there were things to sort out.'

'I bet there were,' Sara said, arching her forehead.

'No, you misunderstand.'

Sara looked at her incredulously. 'What? What do I misunderstand? That you met my partner in Birmingham a *few* times and never thought to mention it. What was going on, Yvonne?'

Yvonne looked taken aback. 'Nothing, I promise.'

Sara's jaw dropped. 'You, of all people. You were my friend. You knew what Cameron was like.'

'You're getting the wrong idea.'

'And what idea is that exactly?'

Beth didn't like the direction the interview was taking. She snapped her phone closed, slipped it into her pocket. She desperately wanted to confront Yvonne about her other visits to Birmingham and her connection to the boxing promotions company, but now wasn't the time or the place. Before she could intervene, Yvonne spoke to Sara again.

'You're upset over Anthony.'

Who was Anthony? Beth didn't recall his name being mentioned in their earlier discussions. But before she could ask, Sara stood and rounded on Yvonne. 'Get out!'

'Oh, don't be like that,' Yvonne said. 'I can explain.'

'Get out of my house now!'

A thud sounded from above. Sara ignored it.

Yvonne swallowed, smoothed down her skirt and stood. 'If that's what you want. But it's not what you think.'

Sara turned away, her back tense with anger, as Beth followed Yvonne out of the room.

In the hallway, Beth addressed Yvonne directly. 'I need to ask you to stay at home this afternoon. I'll be visiting later to talk to you further about your visits to Birmingham.'

Yvonne's face was flushed. She gave a sharp nod and walked out of the front door. Seconds later, the sound of an engine revved and the Audi sped out of the driveway.

38

Sara was standing beside the window when Beth walked back into the front room. Her eyes were wide and heavy, as if somebody had punched her in the stomach and she was still reeling from the pain.

'Can I get you anything?' Beth asked. 'A glass of water maybe?'

'No, thank you.' She moved over to the sofa and sat, staring into space.

It was a moment before either of them spoke. 'Was she shagging him?' Sara asked eventually, levelling her eyes on Beth. 'I'm sure you know more than you're letting on.'

'I don't know,' Beth said quietly. 'They may be business meetings, but I do need to interview her, to verify her connection with Cameron and the dates of her visits to Birmingham.'

'She must have been shagging him. Why would she keep it a secret otherwise?' The words hissed out of her mouth.

Beth didn't answer. She was mentally working through the list of Cameron's associates Sara had provided at their first meeting. She couldn't recall the mention of an Anthony.

Something wasn't right: Sara's tear-stained face on her arrival, the thick atmosphere in the room, even before she'd delivered her news. Something had happened. 'Sara,' Beth asked slowly. 'Who is Anthony?'

'What?' Sara was barely listening, her eyes unfocused.

'Yvonne mentioned him just now. It sounds like you two are close.'

'Oh.' She blinked. 'No, not really.'

'But you do know him?'

She took a deep breath, exhaled with her response. 'Briefly. I met him at a school event, the opening of the library, about five months ago.'

'Anthony what?'

'Mullins.'

Beth scribbled down the name. 'What was the nature of your relationship?'

'We were… friends. Our kids were friends. He dropped his off a few times for play dates, we got talking.'

'How many times have you met him?'

'I don't know. Ten or twelve.' She shook her head. 'Maybe more. I didn't keep count.'

'Always with the children present?'

'Is that relevant?'

'I'm afraid so.'

Sara covered her eyes, didn't answer.

'Why were you upset over him?' Beth continued.

'I don't want to talk about it.'

'I'm afraid we have to. Even if he's only an acquaintance, we need to interview him, to eliminate him from our enquiries.'

'You can't interview him.'

Beth tilted her head. 'Why?'

When she dropped her hand, her eyes glistened with fresh tears. 'Because he's dead. He was found hanging in his bathroom this morning.'

'Tell me about Anthony,' Beth said as she passed over a tissue.

Sara wiped her eyes. 'Our children went to the same school, they became friendly. He called around with the kids occasionally and we talked while they played. Sometimes he came around without them. He was good company, made me laugh.'

'Did Cameron ever meet him?'

'No. Never. I didn't mention him to Cameron.'

'Did you have an affair with him?'

Sara pressed her lips together. 'I'm not sure if you could call it an affair. We slept together sometimes, when the kids were out, at parties and such like.' Her gaze softened. 'He was kind and gentle. It was nice to have someone appreciate me for a while.'

Beth baulked inwardly. Both Monika and Sara's phones and bank accounts would have been routinely checked to ensure there was no suspicious behaviour, nothing that would give them a potential motive for murder. How did they miss an affair? 'Did you talk about Cameron together?'

'No. He knew my situation. We mostly talked about films and books. He read loads, was always recommending books to me.' A sadness filled her eyes. 'I couldn't keep up.'

'Sara, do you know where he was on the morning of Sunday, the 20th of August?'

'I know what you're thinking, but you're wrong. He couldn't have killed Cameron. He was in Portugal, a holiday with his girls and his parents. They'd been there for two weeks. They only arrived back the day before yesterday.' Beth jotted down the details and made a mental note to contact Cheshire police and get his alibi checked out.

'When did you last see him?'

'The weekend before I went away. He talked about the future, us doing something together, maybe going away for a weekend when he came back. I confided in Yvonne. She'd said she would babysit the kids.' She closed her eyes.

'How did you hear about his death?'

'One of our neighbours told Yvonne he'd committed suicide. His wife found him in his bathroom.'

'Was he depressed?'

'He was going through a messy divorce. But he seemed good, given the circumstances. He was doing well.'

'Did he contact you while you were away in Goa?'

'No.'

'What about since you've been back?'

'He called around yesterday morning.'

'He came here?'

She nodded. 'We've only ever communicated in person, never by text or phone. I didn't give him my number in case Cameron looked at my phone and saw the messages. Anyway, he'd heard about Cameron and wanted to check if I was all right. Amy answered the door. I told her to send him away, said it wasn't a good time. When Yvonne heard the news from our neighbour today, she came straight around. She'd only told me about twenty minutes before you arrived.' She placed her head in her hands. 'I can't understand it. He was talking about the future, making plans for when his divorce was through. What happened to make him do something like that?'

39

After she'd taken a statement and left Sara to rest, Beth pulled out of the driveway, rounded the corner and parked up kerb side. It was nearly 3 p.m. Her phone vibrated with a text from Eden.

Don't forget Lily's swim comp tonight. 7.30 p.m. at Corby pool.

Beth's heart sank. She was almost two and a half hours north of Corby, traffic permitting. She'd need to set off within the next hour and a half if she had any hope of catching the competition.

She rested her hands on the steering wheel and stared out into the afternoon, gathering her thoughts. What was it about Sara Swift? The lies and deceit surrounding her were becoming more and more tangled. Just when she'd thought she'd got through to her yesterday, she realised she'd still only scraped the surface. The gates were open when she'd arrived, although she clearly remembered advising Sara to keep them closed. Was she telling the truth this time, or weaving another tale? And what else hadn't she told them? Three deaths in six months, two of them in the last five days, and every one of them connected to her. Sara was out of the country for Cameron's attack, claimed she hadn't seen Anthony since before her holiday, and didn't appear to know about Rajinder's death. But the fact of the matter was, she was intimately connected with all of them.

She reached for her phone and dialled Freeman. This was more than she could deal with alone.

Freeman answered on the second ring, his voice sharp. She could hear the sound of phones ringing off the hook in the background and guessed he was in the incident room.

'Sir. Have you got a moment to talk?'

'Hold on, Beth.' The phone line crackled. She heard him bark a command and the background noise dulled. 'Okay, go ahead.'

Beth poured out the results of her conversation with Sara and Yvonne.

Freeman held his tongue until she'd finished. 'Good work, Beth. Where are you now?' he asked eventually.

'I'm still in Alderley Edge, about to question Yvonne Newman again. I need someone to check the details with Cheshire police on the Anthony Mullins case.'

'Leave that with us,' Freeman said. 'I'll get someone on it.'

A raised voice in the background caught her attention. 'What's going on there?'

'It looks like we might have found a match for our Mr Alan Jones from the boxing promotions company.' There was a hint of excitement in his voice. 'You interview Yvonne, see what you can find out there, then head back and get some sleep. We need you in early. We'll be doing a raid at 7 a.m.'

Beth ended the call with a grateful sigh. Perhaps she'd make the swim gala after all.

Yvonne was sombre when she answered the door. Mascara smudges decorated the wells beneath her eyes. She led Beth through an opulent hallway, with open beams and an apex roof, and into a sitting room that could have been an advertisement for Laura Ashley. Beth sat on an oversized armchair and retrieved her notebook and pen. Yvonne didn't offer refreshments. She obviously didn't want to prolong the meeting for any longer than was necessary.

'You know why I'm here,' Beth said as she settled herself. 'I need to ask you some questions about your contact with Cameron Swift.'

Yvonne gave a short sharp nod.

'How many times have you met Cameron without Sara present?' Beth asked.

Yvonne slid a piece of A4 paper off the mahogany occasional table beside her and handed it over. 'I've put together a list of the dates and places Cameron and I met,' she said. 'I've consulted my diary and put the times beside.'

Beth eyed her warily, took the paper and cast her eyes down the list. There were numerous occasions, at different locations, all in Birmingham, dating back into the previous year. 'Did you meet alone?'

'What do you mean?'

'You said you were discussing an investment. Was your husband or anyone else present at any of the meetings?'

'No. We met alone. My husband doesn't know about it. He's away on business a lot himself. I didn't like to bother him.'

'What did you talk about?'

'I told you, money. That was his job, you know.'

'What was the nature of your relationship?'

'I don't think I'd call it a relationship.' An ounce of petulance crept into her voice. 'It was more a series of business meetings.'

Beth looked down at the sheet in front of her. 'There are a lot of dates here. Did you ever meet any of Cameron's colleagues, or clients?'

'I may have done, in passing perhaps. I don't remember.' Yvonne took a deep breath, sat tall.

Beth retrieved her phone and brought up the images Pete had sent through earlier. She passed them over and watched Yvonne's expression fall as she slowly scrolled down. When she reached one of the more intimate photos her face twisted uncomfortably. She passed the phone back.

'I'll ask you again,' Beth said. 'What was the nature of your relationship with Cameron?'

Yvonne stole a deep breath before she responded. 'We saw each other, from time to time. Look, I'm not the sort of woman to have an affair. I love my husband. But his work takes him all over the world and we barely see each other. When he is home, he doesn't notice me. I'm convenient, the woman who keeps his house, organises coffee mornings for charity, the mother to his children. Cameron was...' Her face softened. '...Sweet. He could be very charming.'

'He was also your best friend's partner.'

A muscle twitched in her cheek. 'I'm not proud of myself.'

'Why did you meet in Birmingham?'

'It's where he works. I met him there initially on business, I really did have my late mother's legacy to invest. And it's not too far to travel to from here.'

'How did the affair begin?'

'The first time I met him was at The Crown. We'd never been alone before. He was more relaxed than at home, friendlier. I travelled down again about three weeks later. I had rather a lot to drink that night and stayed over in a hotel. He stayed with me. I thought it was a one-off and didn't expect to hear from him again, but he sent me a text the very next day.' She shook her head. 'I don't know. There was something different about him when he was alone. He oozed charm, had the ability to make you feel special. Afterwards, I travelled down a couple of times a month. Occasionally there were things to sign, to do with the investment portfolio. Otherwise we went out for dinner and talked. I never thought of it as an affair. Not really.'

'When was the last time you met him?'

'Last Thursday. I couldn't believe it when I saw his death announced on the news on Sunday.' Tears leaked out of her eyes, dribbling down her face. 'I couldn't get hold of Sara for ages. Those poor children.'

Beth had dealt with numerous character types during the course of her police career, from sociopaths to cold-blooded killers, yet Yvonne's ability to mentally switch from the man she was having an affair with to a maternal concern for his partner and their children shocked her. It was almost as though she was talking about a different person. Was that how she'd reconciled the situation to herself? She brought up the photos on her phone, scrolled through. The latest still was recorded last Tuesday. The sheet of dates finished on Tuesday too.

'Thursday. Are you sure?' Beth said.

'Yes, you won't have a photo.' Her face turned sheepish. 'We didn't go to The Crown that day.'

'Where did you go?'

'Do we have to do this?' Her voice was quiet, brittle.

'May I remind you that you have already hampered the investigation by denying your relationship with the victim? Perverting the course of justice is a serious offence.'

'But I didn't mean…' Her voice cracked. 'That is to say, I didn't do anything illegal.'

'Where did you meet last Thursday?' Beth repeated.

'The Marriott. Cameron booked a room.' She hung her head, closed her eyes. When she opened them, fresh tears streaked her cheeks. 'Oh, God. What have I done?' She reached across to grab a tissue revealing arced nail indentations in the pads of her hands as she did so.

'We'll need to check out all the dates and match them with Cameron's diary.'

Yvonne gave a weak cough. When she looked up her eyes were desperate. 'Is there any way we can keep this to ourselves?' she pleaded. 'My husband—'

'This is a murder investigation. I can't guarantee anything,' Beth said. 'Is there any possibility your husband knew of your liaisons with Cameron?'

'No, not at all. It was always when he was away.'

'Where were you both last Sunday?'

She cast her eyes to the floor. 'At my daughter's in Manchester.'

'Did you ever do any work for Cameron?'

Yvonne frowned. 'I don't know what you mean.'

'We've uncovered some accounts in Cameron's records that show a payment to you for bookkeeping services.'

'Oh, that.' She sniffed. 'At one of our meetings, Cameron was complaining about paperwork. He said he hated accounts and bookwork. I used to do my husband's books, years ago, before the company expanded. I said if he ever wanted any help, then I'd be happy to assist. It was a flippant offer; I didn't expect anything to come of it. The next time we met he gave me a carrier bag of receipts. All he wanted me to do was to catalogue them and enter them into a spreadsheet.' She shrugged. 'It was easy really, only took me a couple of hours. I didn't want paying, I told him so, but he insisted. Cameron could be very persuasive when he wanted to be.'

Beth narrowed her eyes. 'What sort of receipts?'

'Fuel, restaurant bills, stationery.' She turned down the corners of her mouth, 'The usual business expenses.'

'What business were they for?'

'I don't know. I presumed they were for some freelancing work he'd done, and he wanted to keep his accountant's bills down. I didn't ask questions. I worked through them as I was asked and passed them back.'

'Have you ever heard of a company called Elite Boxing Promotions?'

'No.'

'The payment on your bank statement came from that company.'

'Ah. Yes, I remember now. I asked Cameron and he said it was a business interest of his. I didn't pay a lot of attention. He seemed to have fingers in lots of pies.'

Beth sat back and stared at her a moment. 'Has Cameron ever mentioned the name Nigel Sherwood to you?'

'No.'

'What about Alan Jones?'

'No, why?'

'Did you ever meet any of his colleagues from this boxing promotion company?'

'No.'

'Do you still have a copy of the spreadsheets?'

'I might have on the computer.'

'I'll need to see them.'

40

Beth took advantage of a break in the races to squeeze through the tiny gap between the seats filled with parents and relatives, lining the viewing area at Corby Swimming Pool. By the time she'd taken a statement from Yvonne Newman and emailed all the information back to the station it was late, and she hit the rush hour traffic leaving Cheshire, plus there were added tailbacks all the way down the M6. It was well after seven by the time she arrived back in Northamptonshire and the gala was already in full swing. She'd spotted Eden in the tiered viewing area, in the middle of a row, with an empty seat beside her, but had to wait in the wings for a suitable time to move through.

'You took your time,' Eden said, folding down the empty seat for her sister.

Beth settled herself. 'Sorry, I got held up on the motorway.' The scoreboard flickered on the wall opposite. 'What have I missed?'

'Six races. We're about two thirds through. Lily's front crawl is up after the next race.' Her voice tailed off as the umpire announced the start of another race.

Beth reached down, shoved her bag underneath her seat and shuffled to get comfortable on the hard plastic. It was warm in the pool area and the chlorine tickled her senses, bringing back memories of her own mother driving her around the county to attend races when she was young. A part of her missed the exhilaration of the race; the camaraderie with her teammates afterwards and she felt an all-encompassing longing to be in the pool again. It was ages since she'd taken time out to swim and she missed the gentle release of endorphins clearing her head as she moved through the water.

The earlier meeting with Yvonne weighed heavily on her mind. She'd lied about her relationship with Cameron when they'd first met, and maintained she had no knowledge of the boxing promotions company. Both her and her husband's accounts and phone records would now be scrutinised to see how far her involvement in the money laundering operation went and whether she should be arrested, and their movements routinely checked in connection with Cameron's death.

'Here she is!' Eden said, grabbing Beth's forearm, pulling her from her thoughts. Lily was small for her age, a fact accentuated by her fellow competitors, although the regular swimming routine had built up the muscles around her shoulders giving her slender body a sporty shape even at her tender age. She dived in and her body became musical, in tune with the water as she glided along. Pride spread through Beth's veins; she was clearly a natural swimmer. They were on the edge of their seats, eyes glued on Lily as she tumble-turned. It was neck and neck on the way back. Four pairs of hands touched the end bar almost at the same time. Beth and Eden were on their feet. Eden's eyes were on the scoreboard. Beth watched Lily who looked up, unsure. Finally, the leader board flashed showing her in first place. Lily jumped up and down and waved at her mother and auntie who were on their feet, clapping and yelling.

Beth was itching to go down and congratulate her, poolside, but the coach wouldn't let relatives through until all the races were complete, so she sat back in her seat. Eden wriggled next to her.

Beth glanced askance at her sister. She hadn't seen or spoken to her since the evening before last when she'd produced the custody letter. 'How are things?' she asked.

Eden returned her gaze. 'All right, thanks. You?'

'Good. They're good.' Chris's comments about a potential relationship needled her. 'How was your night out last Saturday? I haven't had a chance to ask you, with everything's that's happened.'

'Same as usual. We all had too much to drink and ended up scraping our heels on the dance floor in Ruben's Bar.'

'Meet anyone interesting?'

Eden gave her a strange stare. 'No, not particularly.' Beth was about to fish further, when Eden added, 'Oh, look. There's Olivia, Lily's mentor.'

Another race started, and Eden stood to cheer on Olivia. As soon as the race was over, Eden reached down to collect her bag.

Beth grabbed her arm. 'I need to talk to you about something.'

'Oh, me too,' Eden said, pulling her arm back and tugging at her collar. 'Let's get out of here, shall we? This heat is oppressive.'

The corridor was heaving outside. All the swimmers' families sharing the same idea. 'What was it you wanted to talk about?' Beth said over the throng.

Eden waited for the crowds to thin. 'I wondered if you could have Lily tonight for a sleepover. I've got loads to do in the morning, would appreciate the time.'

'Not tonight. I'm sorry. I've got to be up at the crack of dawn. We've got some early morning knocks to do.'

'Never mind.' They halted at the changing rooms. 'I'd better get an early night then. We'll have a quick drink and shoot off.'

Beth crossed to the far side of the door, out of earshot of the other parents, and was about to mention Chris's concerns about Kyle Thompson when Eden said, 'Oh, look there's Olivia's mum.' She waved. The woman came over and they chatted about the swimming club and upcoming galas. Frustration was starting to grate at Beth. Every opportunity was thwarted by someone taking her sister's attention.

Olivia emerged from the changing room, said hello to Eden, told her Lily was on her way, and moved off with her mother. Finally, they were alone.

Beth opened her mouth to quiz her sister when the door pulled open and Lily appeared, beaming. This wasn't a conversation to have in front of the child. Beth heaved a heavy sigh. Another moment lost.

After fuelling up, the route to Beth's home took her through the far entrance of Mawsley Village. Lily had twittered like a bird all the way through the drinks after the gala; there'd been no opportunity to bring up Kyle Thompson.

Beth was weary, the long hours over the past few days starting to take their toll. She looked into Chancery Court as she passed, half expecting Eden's home to be encased in darkness after her talk of an early night and was surprised to see lights burning in all the front rooms. And even more surprised to see a dark BMW M5 parked on the driveway, beside Eden's car. She slowed to a stop. The wheels screeched across the asphalt as she reversed. The windows of the car were blackened out; the registration included the number 42. It looked very similar to the BMW she'd almost collided with the other day.

She punched the registration plate into her phone. Was it Kyle? Was that why Eden wanted Lily to come to her for a sleepover? She changed gear and was about to turn the corner when her mobile rang.

'Hey, I'm at your house,' Nick said. 'Where are you?'

'Around the corner, but there's something—'

'Good because dinner's ready.' Beth sighed as he rang off. She longed to knock on Eden's door, warn whoever it was about their erratic driving the other day, if nothing else to find out if it was Kyle Thompson inside. But the phone call grounded her thoughts. Eden wouldn't welcome the intrusion into her evening, especially if it disturbed Lily. Plus, if it was Kyle, she would dig her heels in, get defensive. There would be no reasoning with her and they'd end up rowing. No, the erratic driving gave Beth a legitimate reason to check the number plate back at the station tomorrow. If it was him, the association, however mild, would be proved and she could ask uniform to pay him a visit, give him a cautionary warning, and then pick her moment to speak with her sister.

Nick was in the kitchen when she arrived back at the cottage. Bent over the hob, gyrating his hips to a Queen song blaring in the background, he didn't notice the door open and close, or hear Beth drop her briefcase, kick off her shoes in the hall. In fact, she had to make her way to the kitchen and tap him on the shoulder before he was aware of her presence.

'Hey,' he crooned, swirling the wooden spoon in the pasta pan.

Beth turned down the music and chuckled. 'Are you really cooking?'

'I am. Pasta frenzy. It's my speciality.' He bent down, kissed her cheek.

Beth recognised some chopped mushrooms and leaves of spinach among the ribbons of linguine in the pan, alongside other chunks of colour that looked unidentifiable.

'Thought I'd feed you up,' he said. 'We've got an early morning tomorrow.'

The food tasted better than it looked, and Beth shovelled it down. For the last few days she'd grazed, picking up convenience bites on the go and the warm plate of home-cooked food was hearteningly welcome.

Nick looked across and raised a brow. 'My, you were hungry. How did it go with Yvonne Newman today?'

She gave a quick overview of her meetings with both Sara and Yvonne. 'I emailed all the statements back to the office. I'm surprised you haven't seen them.'

'Ah. I've probably got them, just not had a chance to read them yet. We're prioritising.' He scraped the last remnants of food from his plate and pushed it aside. 'We've confirmed the link between Nigel Sherwood and the victim.'

Beth's stomach dipped. That meant the enquiries on Anthony Mullins were likely to be treated as low priority. She thought about the noise in the background when she'd spoken with Freeman on the phone, and pictured Nigel Sherwood's hefty frame in her mind. Sherwood was an established local gang leader, astute at keeping his distance from the organised crime groups he managed. 'What did you find?' she asked.

'The messages on the phone referred to "mail". There's a camera on one of the garages, opposite the letter-box address. We've trawled through the CCTV footage. It showed both Sherwood and our victim accessing it on different occasions over the past few weeks. The dates Sherwood visited correspond with when the text messages were sent.'

Beth recalled the text messages talking about mail on the phone, the final of which mentioned consequences. 'Are you suggesting Alan Jones is the false identity for Nigel Sherwood? That Cameron was investing cash for Sherwood and syphoning it off? If the company has been running for two years, surely it would have come to a head before now?'

'Maybe it was a two-year investment and Cameron was helping himself to the money. We know Cameron's bank records don't support his lifestyle. It's possible he was trying to make back what he'd taken through a high-risk investment and it didn't work. Then he couldn't pay up.'

'So, Nigel Sherwood murdered him?'

'Along those lines. People in the field are starting to talk. Sherwood's down over £500,000. It wouldn't look good; he has a reputation to uphold. I doubt he would have done the shooting himself, he wouldn't want to get his hands dirty, but he's got all the right connections to order a contract killing. And he'd be pretty keen to send out a message too, to warn off others.'

'But Sherwood's pushing sixty.'

'Exactly. The sources reckon he's setting himself up for retirement. If Sherwood was making plans, he would need legitimate investments, a source of clean income for his retirement. It links in with that anonymous call we had connecting the victim with Sherwood. We initially thought it was maybe Cameron gambling, but this makes a lot more sense. Plus, we know the text messages were sent from two locations, both within the vicinity of Sherwood's home address and the casino.'

'Why haven't we picked him up?'

'We've considered it. There's no doubt Sherwood had motive, means, and opportunity, and we can link him to Cameron. But he's a slippery customer, as you know. We need to catch him by surprise and link him to the phone if we can. The casino is at its quietest around 7. a.m., after the night rush. Freeman's organised warrants to hit everything at once. We're to pick him up *and* do a raid on both his home and his businesses at the same time. That will give him less chance of covering his tracks, and us the best opportunity of finding what we're looking for.'

41

Beth adjusted the straps of her stab vest. At 5.30 a.m., she'd normally expect to find the conference room full of bleary-eyed detectives, especially after the hours they'd put in over the last week. But, although some of them held the lingering aroma of sleep, on the whole, a familiar buoyant excitement and anticipation filled the room. Finally, the scent of an arrest was close.

Freeman's paunch pressed onto his own stab vest. Unlike many of his peers, he struggled to restrict his presence to the office. When he was sending his unit out on a raid, he insisted on being there with them, barking communications through his radio. 'Okay, we'll have three teams, one each for the casino, the snooker hall, and Sherwood's home,' he said. He pointed to a new board set up at the front of the room, covered with a map indicating each of the locations. 'We all go in simultaneously at 7 a.m. Each sub team has been allocated an officer in charge who will coordinate events at their location. I'll be with the casino team and available on my radio should anyone need me.

'Let's be clear, we are looking for something to link Sherwood to Cameron Swift. Seize all the computers, mobile phones, CCTV footage, and anything with the remotest possible connection, even if you are not sure. We need to corroborate the evidence we already have, and let me tell you, once Sherwood knows we are onto him, we won't get this chance again. The team going to Sherwood's home are bringing him in for questioning.

'Okay, let's split into our sub teams, study each of the locations, and get started. Good luck, everyone!'

Just over an hour later, the van rattled over a pothole as they pulled off the ring road towards Sherwood's home. While the house raid of a suspected murderer and gang leader carried its own adrenalin rush, it was without doubt that the location of choice and the best chance they had of finding any evidence was likely to be the casino. Beth felt a pang. Once again, she was missing out on the core of the action.

Nick's knee knocked beside her, undeterred by the lesser location, an embodiment of the throb of underlying excitement that filled the van.

Sherwood lived in Flore, seven miles outside Northampton, and as they passed the village sign, the van juddered with officers shifting about, preparing themselves. Beth looked out of the rear window at the vehicle travelling behind. The target was Sherwood's family home and while a risk assessment indicated no pet dogs, often a problem in house raids, and intelligence suggested no threat of firearms, Freeman had allocated them a specially equipped tactical support unit. He wasn't taking any chances.

Sherwood's home was a converted public house that straddled the corner of two streets in the heart of the village.

It was an ancient building, with a whitewashed front and a thatched roof. Cars lined the kerb all around and they cruised to the bottom of the street, past a line of cottages and houses with curtains tightly drawn, before they parked up, streamed out, and doubled back to take their positions. Beth watched two officers dash around the back to cover the rear. Nick checked his watch. At exactly 7 a.m., he nodded at the pair of officers at the front door.

The collection of thuds at the door were enough to wake the entire street and followed up by the call of, 'Police. Open the door or we will force entry!' The officer stood back a moment. Beth held her breath. A curtain twitched in the top window. After a few moments passed, Nick nodded at the other officer who lifted the battering ram. He swung it back, about to force the door, when the sound of a chain rattled.

The door opened to reveal an auburn-haired woman, struggling with the cords of a fluffy, grey bathrobe. She rolled her eyes.

'Hello, Lisa. Is Nigel home?' Nick said.

She shook her head indignantly as he proffered the warrant. 'Nope. He's already left,' she said, spitting out the words as officers streamed past her. Two of them rushed into the rooms downstairs, the others marched up to the landing to check the bedrooms.

Lisa Sherwood padded into the kitchen and flicked the switch on the kettle. Something about her untroubled approach, playing the ill-fated wife, didn't seem right. Beth followed her. Footsteps thudded through the rooms above as officers prepared to check the loft space, a common hiding place for criminals seeking refuge. Having studied detailed plans back at the office, Beth knew the house layout and her eyes quickly found the door to the cellar. Her boots clicked the stone steps as she rushed down, Nick at her heels, her torch illuminating a tunnel in the darkness. The room was long, open-plan, and ran the length of the house, with a low roof. The beer barrels that had once crowded the area had been replaced by rows of different sized boxes stacked high and haphazardly, interspersed with a collection of what looked like discarded family junk. The mountains of boxes cast dingy shadows in the torchlight.

'Mr Sherwood!' Nick called as he pressed the light switch. To no avail. Either the bulb was broken, or the wiring no longer worked down there.

The scraping and scratching of the officers above was the only sound to penetrate the room. Beth moved her beam around the area, checking it in sections. There was so much junk that she had to move systematically to check every nook and cranny.

'It's going to take an age to work through all of these,' she shouted to Nick, pointing at the boxes when her toe caught something. The lip of another box. She tripped, put out her free hand to steady herself. Scraped her arm down the side of a wooden crate as she saved her fall, sending it toppling over onto the floor in front of her. Beth was about to scream an expletive when she heard a shuffle. She gritted her teeth, shook her hand, and turned to Nick, tilting her head at the far corner.

Beth lifted her flashlight. It landed on the external door, once used for beer barrel deliveries when the house had been a pub. The plans indicated the external door had long since been bricked up; the only entrance or exit to the cellar now was the internal door from the kitchen. It looked undisturbed.

Another shuffle. Beth followed it with the strobe of light. And saw a pair of eyes.

'Stop! Police!' Sherwood ignored her, darting up, pushing at what looked like a hatch opening at the top of the wall above him. Beth could hear Nick call through on his radio, alerting the officers outside, as she rushed towards Sherwood. 'Nigel, stop!' She was almost on him when she slipped, her feet rolling on a mound of balls underneath the hatch. Coal. Sherwood had built his own coal hatch. A coal hatch that doubled up as an escape route. That wasn't noted on the plans.

By the time Beth reached the hatch, Sherwood had heaved out his torso. She scrambled towards him, grasped for his boots. But they slipped her grip and disappeared from view. Beth cursed and followed him, hauling herself up and out of the gap. The wooded edging was un-sanded and rough, snagging at her trousers.

Finally, she was out. The hatch led into the street that ran down the side of the house.

Beth checked frantically up and down. Apart from the odd parked car, the pavements were bare. Which way had he gone? A scraping behind her was followed by a thud. Nick was out too. He pointed left. She took right, her feet pounding the pavement as she ran. Her breaths came fast and quick, ripping at her lungs. Flore was an old village and the cottages and houses were interspersed with alleyways and waste ground, all perfect hiding places. She frantically scanned them as she passed and stopped at the top of the road, turning on her heel 360 degrees. Nick had called out to the officers at the front and rear to check those areas. His stealthy stride was now pounding back up the road to assist her. She placed her hands on her hips, bent over to catch her breath. Sherwood was a heavy-set man. How could she have lost him? She was beginning to convince herself he'd gone into one of the other houses, when a thump sounded nearby. It came from behind a Volvo parked opposite. Nick was still twenty yards down the road. Beth moved forwards gingerly and was just rounding the vehicle when a fist flashed up and struck her. She tumbled, grabbing hold of the torso in front of her with all her might. The bony edge of an elbow connected with her cheek. Still she held her grip. Another fist, to her ribs this time. Yells in the distance. Beth mustered every ounce of energy and brought up her knee. It connected below the groin area but was enough to fold him.

He took her down with him. The pavement was cold and hard. Beth scrabbled to focus. She couldn't let him get away, she was so close. She was aware of a babble of grunts and scuffles nearby. Sherwood's body turned limp. Beth turned to find Nick beside her, wrestling with his handcuffs. He clicked them on Sherwood, turned to Beth and smiled breathlessly. 'Do you want to lock him up, or shall I?'

Back at headquarters, Beth winced as she pulled the last of the splinters out of her forearm and held it out. Clear liquid oozed out of the jagged grazed lines. She checked her cheek in the mirror. A swelling the size of an egg was turning the left side of her face indigo. She ran a finger over it, relishing the cool feel against the angry skin. She hadn't felt the pain at the scene, but now the adrenalin rush had passed, her cheek was starting to smart. She dabbed a tissue on her grazes, pulled down her sleeve gently and took another look in the mirror. Shame she couldn't wear a cover over her face too.

A low-bellied roar sounded as she entered the incident room. A couple of her colleagues clapped her on the back. Keith nodded at her face and said, 'I hope you gave worse than you got.' Beth laughed off their jibes and crossed the office to her desk.

Nick was nowhere to be seen, no doubt preparing Sherwood for his interview. The searches were likely to take some time and many of the desks around her were empty. They worked through the first tranche of belongings brought back from the house, cataloguing their findings. Time passed easily. She was on her second coffee when the door flapped open and a team of officers marched through. They looked weary, demoralised. It wasn't until she saw Freeman's face at the door that she realised it was the team from the casino.

She called across to Pete who was making a play of wriggling out of his stab vest. 'Hey. Any news?'

'It was a no go. The place was clean. The cabinets in the office practically empty. Looks like someone tipped them off. We've left a small group there. Freeman's told them to rip it apart, pull up the flooring in the staff area if they need to, but there's nothing so far.' He stretched his arms back. 'Worst of it was, he'd sent his heavies in to mock us.'

'What do you mean?'

'Sherwood's grooming some guys to take over managing the casino.'

'Who?'

'Bloody Kev Richardson.'

Richardson was an unusual combination of muscle and brains. According to their intelligence, when he wasn't in the gym he was heavily involved in drugs supply. He'd been arrested several times, but he always seemed to wriggle out of a charge due to lack of evidence. Beth gave a disappointed smile. So far, the search teams at Sherwood's house in Flore hadn't found anything concrete either. They were holding out for something from the snooker hall, the sooner the better. Sherwood had been booked into custody and the clock was ticking.

She turned back to Pete. 'Who else was there?'

'What?'

'At the casino. You said, "guys".'

'Oh, Richardson's new sidekick. What's his name?' His brow furrowed in thought. 'Kyle Thompson.'

Beth's blood ran cold. She switched back to her screen, her mind racing. What was Kyle Thompson doing at Nigel Sherwood's casino? The car registration number from Eden's drive pressed on her. She dug into her bag for her mobile phone, retrieved the details, and clicked a few buttons on her computer, counting her breaths as she waited for the results. Colleagues wandered around her, carrying more boxes. Her eyes didn't leave the screen. Finally, they came up. And Beth's heart pitted. The car was registered to Kyle.

She clicked another button. After Chris's revelation the other day, she'd been dying to check out Kyle's record. But the police code of practice was strict, controlled by an audit trail and while officers were party to daily intelligence, they had to prove a legitimate reason to look up an individual's record. Only last month, a detective had been dismissed for taking a peek at her brother's new girlfriend's status. The erratic driving now gave Beth a reason.

She logged in, typed his name and selected his profile. Having been out of the office so much, she'd missed the recent intelligence updates, and for Kyle there had been a lot of updates. A shiver ran through her as she read how a line of intelligence had come in yesterday, mentioning Kyle Thompson aligning himself with Kev Richardson. Another source, questioned in connection with the murder investigation, confirmed they were working together and learning the ropes at the casino. Looking to take over from Nigel Sherwood.

42

Beth's stomach clenched as she tapped Freeman's door. Freeman's head shot up abruptly, his attention dragged away from the papers he was sorting through on his desk. He tempered his scowl when he saw Beth. 'I'm sorry, Beth, is it urgent? I'm bogged down with this interview brief right now. After three search warrants and an arrest, so far, we have little to put to Sherwood in interview, apart from an assault on a police officer.'

'I think it might be my fault.' Her words were barely audible.

He noticed her forlorn face, pushed the papers to one side and invited her in. 'What do you mean?'

She ignored his extended hand, indicating for her to sit, preferring to stand, and ran through the details of the car at Eden's yesterday. The same car that had been there the other day. 'I checked the licence plate earlier. It belongs to Kyle Thompson.'

'Did you know they were associated?'

'No, yes...'

He sat back in his chair. 'Which is it?'

'I heard a rumour the day before yesterday. I was going

to confront Eden and check with her, once I was sure, but I didn't get the chance.'

'Where did you hear the rumour?'

Beth pressed her lips together, strained her face. She was stuck with nowhere to go. She'd have to take the punishment, but whatever she thought of Chris she wasn't about to take anyone down with her. 'I'm not sure. It was just on the grapevine.'

Freeman narrowed his eyes. 'Does Chris know?'

She took a deep breath. 'I don't think so.'

He pushed his tongue against the side of his mouth a moment. 'Exactly how would this affect our operation this morning?'

'Eden and I watched Lily at a swimming gala last night. She asked me if I might take Lily home with me afterwards, have her sleep over.'

'Is that unusual?'

'Not in itself. I turned her down, said I had an early start. I saw the car on her drive on the way home and thought it was a friend.' She dropped her eyes to the floor. 'I'm sorry, sir. She knew I was on this enquiry. If she mentioned it to him…' The sound of a car passing down the driveway nearby filled the room. 'I knew Kyle Thompson had a history but had no idea he was punching that far above his weight,' she added.

'None of us did. Apparently, he's paired up with Kev Richardson, one of the guys vying to step into Sherwood's shoes when he retires. Looks like he's stepping up in the world.' Freeman chewed the side of his mouth a moment. 'I appreciate it's only recent, but have you filled in the form, declared your association?'

Beth reeled. 'Not yet. I didn't want to until I was sure.'

Freeman let out a long sigh, sat back in his chair and pressed his hands together with the tips of his fingers touching his nose. Seconds crawled past. 'Okay,' he said eventually. 'You did the right thing coming forward. We'll have to bat on with what we have. But you must know I can't have you attached to this now.'

'So I'm off the team?'

'Not the team. This enquiry. It may or may not be your comment to Eden that gave Sherwood the reason to clean up. There is always the possibility there could be a leak elsewhere. But I have to be seen to treat everyone equally and safeguard the case. And I will have to feed this back. I'm sorry, Beth. If I were you, I'd have a quiet word with Eden. Try to get her to review her friendships. Associating with a known criminal won't do her any good.'

'Who's going to work with Warren?'

'Don't worry, we'll amble along for now. Andrea Leary's back on Tuesday.'

Beth tried not to look crestfallen. Even if he didn't personally consider her a risk, once word seeped out, others might, and he had to remove the appearance of compromise. She knew it was the right thing to do, but it didn't temper the sting that penetrated deep. Especially when he mentioned Andrea taking over.

'I heard it was you that apprehended Sherwood in the end,' Freeman said, nodding at the bruise on her cheek. 'Do you need to get that looked at?'

Her stomach was starting to ache from the hefty punch she'd taken. 'No, it's fine.'

'Well, get the force medical officer to examine and document it, will you? We'll get Sherwood for assault, if nothing else.' Freeman mustered a weak smile. 'Okay. Why don't you take the next few days off? You've put in a lot of extra hours this week. Take some time owed.' It wasn't a recommendation, it was an order.

Beth was awoken later by a tap at her bedroom door. She groaned and pulled the duvet up to her chin.

'Beth. I know you're in there.' Beth sighed and checked the clock. It was a few minutes to eleven. The curtains were undrawn, and the evening darkness crept into the bedroom, painting everything with brushstrokes of murky grey. She turned away from the door and snuggled back under the duvet. As soon as she'd arrived home she'd climbed straight into bed fully clothed and fallen into a heavy slumber. There was no reason to get up now.

Nick's voice bellowed through the door. 'I'm coming in.'

'I'm tired.'

A crack of light from the hallway illuminated the room as he pushed the door open. 'I'm sure, but you need to eat sometime.'

'Who are you, my mother?' Her words were muffled by the bedclothes.

He crouched down beside the bed and stroked the back of her head. 'You haven't answered my messages.'

'I haven't answered any messages. My phone is switched to silent.'

'Don't you want to know what's happening? It's not

like you to keep your nose out,' he added. Beth yawned. She blinked as she sat up. 'Why didn't you tell me about Kyle Thompson and Eden?' Nick said. His voice sounded distant, confused.

'I wasn't sure.'

'Have you spoken with Eden?'

Was he talking to her as her sergeant, or her friend? Right now, she couldn't be sure. And the crossover made her uncomfortable. She dug the heels of her hands into her eyes. 'I don't want to talk about this.' She lowered her hands. 'Go on then. I can see you're dying to spill it out. What happened at the office with Sherwood?'

Nick pushed the duvet back, forcing her to shuffle across so he could sit beside her. 'We've charged him.'

'You've what?'

'We've charged Nigel Sherwood.'

'With what?'

'Conspiracy to commit murder with persons unknown, pending further evidence. Plus, the assault on you.'

Beth's mind raced. When she'd left the office that morning, they had nothing to implicate Sherwood apart from a bunch of circumstantial evidence. 'Did he make admissions?'

'Not exactly. But Freeman was incensed this morning. Told them to pull the casino offices apart, take the carpets up, everything. No expense spared. If there was something there he was determined to find it. And they did – wedged down the back of the drawer of a desk they found the packaging for a SIM card.'

Beth frowned, but said nothing.

'The packaging matches the SIM that sent the messages to Cameron Swift. The threatening messages.'

'How do we know it belonged to Sherwood? Loads of people must have used that office.'

'It also had a fingerprint on it. We fast-tracked it through the system. It belongs to Nigel Sherwood.'

'And that's enough?'

'Not on its own but put together with the information on the memory stick, the phone, the CCTV footage that shows him accessing the letter-box address, and the intelligence that he was down over £500,000 on his investment, it shows an association and gives him a motive. He's made threats. The CPS reckon it's a runner. He appears in court tomorrow morning, but I'm guessing it'll be a formality. Nobody's going to give him bail when we are talking conspiracy to commit murder, certainly not with his attempts to avoid capture today.'

43

An hour later they were sitting around the table in the kitchen, tucking into takeaway pizza. 'Did everyone go to the pub to celebrate?' Beth said, scooping up another slice.

'No. It was late when we got finished, everyone was shattered. There's a big bash planned for tomorrow night though.' He smiled. 'You are going to join us?'

'I'm not sure.'

'Aw, come on, Beth. Even the superintendent's coming along. There will be some sore heads on Sunday morning, mark my words.'

Beth snorted.

'Talking of the super, her bulletin should be on the late news.'

They cleared away the pizza box and moved into the front room. The news headlines were gracing the screen as Nick switched on the television. Beth plumped up a cushion and sat. The screen changed to a petite woman in a trouser suit, reading out a statement.

Nick turned up the volume. 'We're on.'

Beth focused on Superintendent Rose Hinchin as she

announced the charge of conspiracy to murder. She missed off the full charge: conspiracy to murder 'with persons unknown'. Very conveniently, Beth thought. Reminding the public they hadn't apprehended the actual killer wouldn't do their PR any good at all. Hinchin's public voice differed to her office voice, the tone crafted, affected, as if a boiled sweet was lodged in the side of her mouth. 'This was a shocking attack in a quiet residential area,' she said. 'I'd like to thank members of the public for working with the police to bring it to a speedy resolution, and to reassure the people of Northamptonshire that it was an isolated incident, a personal attack.' She went on to thank her team of officers who had worked around the clock this past week to track down the people responsible. When asked about images of the body shared on social media, her face turned grave. 'We condemn the sharing of images of this nature. This has been a complex case and I would ask that members of the press and the public respect the privacy of the families at this difficult time. Thank you.'

Beth reached for the remote and turned down the volume as the superintendent disappeared from view. Elements of the case wriggled themselves up from the depths of her mind. 'What I don't understand is, if Cameron's murder was ordered by Nigel Sherwood, why did the killer share it on social media?'

Nick rested his head back. 'As an example, maybe, to put off others? Intelligence indicates he'd scammed a lot of money off Sherwood. Drummond's still analysing all the financial records, but he reckons Cameron dipped his hand in, probably to help finance his own lifestyle, then moved some into a high-risk investment that didn't yield the return. He panicked. Kept putting Sherwood off. A man like Sherwood has a reputation to uphold. He'd want to warn off others.'

'Maybe, but the message said, "*Who was Cameron Swift?*". Why invite you to look into his life when there was a distinct possibility you might be implicated somewhere down the line?'

'I don't know. Maybe the killer was asked to send out a simple warning message and took it too far. People make mistakes.'

'It doesn't make sense.'

'You think too much.'

'What about the real killer, the guy that pulled the trigger?' Beth pressed.

'We'll keep looking, naturally. But Sherwood would have hired a professional. That's why we struggled to track his route in and out of the estate, why he disappeared off the cameras, and why we can't trace the murder weapon. He'll have planned well. Sherwood's gone no comment in his interview. He isn't the type to talk.'

'Are you saying we might never find them?'

'It wouldn't be the first time.'

'What about the families? Isn't it possible they are at risk? Sherwood might send someone out to search for some of his missing cash. I doubt being in prison will stop him from pulling strings on the outside.'

'If that was going to happen, it's likely they'd have had a visit by now. Their houses were pulled apart during the police search and we found nothing to indicate they were involved or knew anything about his arrangement with Sherwood. Cameron was secretive about his business affairs. That'll be why Sherwood chose him. Freeman's pretty convinced this was an assassination, to send out a message, a single attack. There's nothing to suggest the families are at risk.'

Her mind wandered to Monika and Sara and the revelations about each other the case opened up; the painful secrets in their own backgrounds that the investigation uncovered. Most people were killed by someone they knew, someone close to them. As an investigation progressed, families were scrutinised in more and more detail. She thought of Sara's affair with Anthony Mullins and Ian Vaughan's comments placing a question mark over Monika. Both women had kept secrets. The charge appeared to exonerate them both of involvement, yet their lives had been picked apart this past week. 'I presume someone has been out to the see the families?' she said.

'Warren went to see Monika this evening.'

Beth could almost see the creases of relief in Monika's face. Relief that would be tempered with anxiety when she was informed of the details of the case, and later when she discovered Cameron's financial situation. She'd be concerned for her family's security. She was a named beneficiary in the will, but from the poor state of Cameron's finances, there wasn't going to be much of a pay-out, unless there was a hefty life assurance policy they didn't know about.

'What about Sara Swift?'

'Freeman phoned her himself. I think he's trying to get her to drop the complaint.'

Beth raised a brow. 'How was she?'

'Steely. I think that was the word he used.'

'Someone should still visit her, even if it's only a welfare call.'

'We'll get her home force to keep an eye out.' He reached out an arm, pulled her close. 'Don't worry.'

44

Beth sneaked into the conference room the following morning and sauntered down to the boards at the far end. Photos of the victim, snapshots of Sherwood, the casino, the letter-box address and the map of Collingtree Park all glared back at her. In many respects, the arrest fitted: Cameron was an asset manager, a financial enabler. He'd built up an association with Sherwood and together they'd set up a false business to launder his illicit cash. The phone messages indicated Sherwood wasn't getting his money. It gave him a clear motive. But the Twitter message and use of social media still bothered her. It was a large chunk of the case that made no sense. Was it really as simple as the killer going too far?

She worked from one board to another, desperately trying to piece everything together to make the puzzle complete and was so absorbed that she didn't hear the door softly open. Was oblivious to the footsteps creeping up the room. It wasn't until she felt a presence beside her that she turned and jumped.

'Chris, what are you doing here?'

'I could say the same to you.'

She looked back at the door. 'How did you know I was in here?'

'I saw your car in the car park.'

'I left some stuff in my desk yesterday, the power pack for my phone and things,' she fudged. The last thing she wanted was for rumours to start that she was obsessed with the case, couldn't let it go.

'Of course.'

She watched him glance at the boards, guessing the real reason why she was here, but he gave her the courtesy of not mentioning it. Perhaps he wasn't confident with the arrest either. 'What are you up to?' she asked.

'I'm off the case too, just gathering my stuff.'

'I don't understand. I didn't mention you when I talked about the relationship between Eden and Kyle.'

'I know. Freeman said you were very tight-lipped. Thanks. But you didn't need to say anything, Beth. Freeman thought it prudent to move me anyway.' He shrugged. 'It doesn't matter to me now. My work was pretty much complete. It'll be up to the case builders to put it all together for the trial.'

They stood in silence a moment. 'Why didn't you declare Eden's association with Kyle Thompson when you found out about the affair?' she asked. 'She's your ex-wife. There were bound to be inferences drawn.'

'I'm not sure really. I didn't believe it myself at first. Then I suppose half of me hoped it was a fleeting misjudgement, a fling that would soon pass. When it continued, I made every effort to remove myself.' He dug his hands deep into his pockets. 'I'm sorry, Beth. I should have been more honest, made you believe me earlier. I shouldn't have put you in that position.'

'No, you warned me. I just… I guess I wanted to think better of her.'

'Me too. Do me one favour?' He met her gaze. 'Talk to Eden, make her see sense. I don't want things to get messy, for Lily's sake, but I can't have my kid around people like him.'

'I'll do my best.'

His phone buzzed. He rummaged in his pocket, checked the screen. 'I need to get this.'

'Of course.'

She watched him stride down the room and disappear. Chris was a big personality, prone to irritating bouts of brashness at times, but straight down the line; not a man she'd ever imagined would be drawn to someone like Eden. She'd wondered over the match when they first announced their relationship, but he was a good father to Lily, and had been a steady husband and a calming influence on her sister. And Eden's familiarity with a convicted offender certainly explained the distance he kept with the family after they separated.

Beth sucked her teeth. Damn Eden. It was one thing protecting her from the wrath of their mother by keeping her boyfriend a secret in her teenage years, or covering for her when she was grounded and wanted a night out. But quite another sorting out her life when she was fraternising with a known criminal and fighting a custody battle over her daughter. The promise to her mother was beginning to feel like a hefty load she could no longer carry. It was time to confront Eden. But there was something else niggling her that she needed to address first.

'Hello.' Beth turned to see Nick marching down the room. 'I heard you were here.'

'News travels fast.'

'So it seems. What are you doing, Beth?' He peered at the bruise on her cheek as he drew nearer. 'You should be resting.'

'I'm fine. I came in to collect a few things. It's not like I'm suspended.'

'I didn't mean that. I meant what are you doing in here?'

'I don't know. I was trying to settle it all in my mind.'

'And?'

Beth ran the tips of her fingers around the edge of her bruise. 'I'm worried about Sara Swift.'

Nick's tone hardened. 'We've been through this. Freeman's spoken with her.'

'Somebody needs to check on her.'

'And her local force will. You need to leave it now. You're off the case, remember?'

'All thanks to Eden.'

'Have you spoken with her?'

'Not yet.'

'I'd say that's your priority right now.' Beth looked away. 'Listen, do you fancy a coffee? I can't finish for another couple of hours, I've got to write up these last few reports, but we could grab a coffee before you go?'

'Thanks for the offer but I can't. I've got loads to do. I'll catch you at the pub later.'

'No worries. Should be a good night.'

45

Monika stared at the spaces lingering between the half-used packets of pasta and rice, and array of old tins on the cupboard shelves. She opened another door, picked up a pot of baby milk powder and shook it, listening to the fragments tinkle against the bottom. Warren had remarked yesterday that they were almost out of milk and brought in some 'essentials', as he called them, waving a carrier bag around when he'd arrived that morning. He'd offered to set her up online, arrange for the rest of her shopping to be delivered. Monika declined. In her previous life, food shopping was one of the highlights of her week. She loved planning family meals, visiting the supermarket and selecting fruit and vegetables. Cameron laughed at her, called her old fashioned. But to her a large part of the cooking process was about selecting the right raw produce.

She closed the cupboard doors and leaned her back against the cold marble work surface. After the arrest yesterday, everybody seemed more relaxed. Warren had nipped back to the office to collect some papers; Oskar was asleep in his bedroom. Should she take advantage of the time to walk Jakub to the shop on the estate? It was only a fifteen-minute walk and the air would undoubtedly do him good. She looked down at him, bouncing in his baby chair, poking at the string of mobile toys in front of him. He caught her eye and smiled, pushing his chest out, as if welcoming her thoughts.

Although… her heart pounded. She hadn't been out of the house since Cameron died. It would be hard enough to walk down the driveway, following his last footsteps, around the patch of tarmac where he took his last breath. Thoughts of the flutters of curtains being whisked back filled her mind. The eyes of Meadowbrook Close glued to her, sending a chain of whispers down the road as they consumed her movements, dissected her actions. How did she look? Where was she going? Would they have questions after the news bulletin last night? Amanda's visit to deliver the lasagne skipped into her mind, 'We've all been worried about you,' she had said, the words accompanied by a head tilt and soppy eyes. Genuine enough, sure, but at moments like this, it didn't stop Monika feeling like a tragic painting in a gallery, the new exhibit for people to discuss.

She pictured the piles of cards towering on the hallway table. Some of them bore stamps and postmarks, but many of them were hand-delivered. Cards that she couldn't face opening. She knew people meant well, but why feel the need to record their thoughts in a card and send it to the bereaved family? Did they think it might be a comfort to them, to be told how much Cameron was thought of by a group of people he barely knew? Everyone knew it was a tragedy and Cameron would be missed. She didn't need half the damn estate to tell her that.

She ambled into the lounge and peered around the edge of the curtain. It was a bright day, a few puffy clouds decorating a cornflower blue sky. The patrol car was no longer parked outside. The police seemed to have relaxed after the charge yesterday. The killer was still at large, but they felt sure they had the man responsible for organising the murder and targeting Cameron. Surely if the police weren't overly concerned about their safety, then she shouldn't be. It was just after 12 p.m. The close was usually at its quietest at this time of day.

A thought struck her. Her car was still parked in the garage. She could load Jakub into his car seat and slip out through the connecting door from the house. Warren wasn't due back for at least another half an hour. Oskar was sleeping upstairs. It was possible she could make it to the supermarket and back without either of them knowing. She tiptoed up and checked on her eldest son. He was sprawled across the bed. Resolved, she made her way back down, left him a note on the table and lifted Jakub out of his chair. Oskar was a sensible lad. She'd left him on his own for an hour on odd occasions in the past. She'd lock the doors, he'd be fine.

A few moments later, her chest tightened as the electric door to the garage raised and she cruised towards the end of the driveway. The phone calls from reporters, earlier in the week, picked at her. Later, when the road was reopened, they'd gathered at the end of the driveway until the detectives moved them on and made it clear they weren't to call at the house. She'd been shielded from their lenses and their intrusive questions. Were they still around? Lurking behind cars and vans, waiting to jump out? The murder of a family man outside his home was high-profile, the social media message grabbing widespread attention. A quote from her, or even a quick photo would probably make front page news. She pulled her sunglasses over her eyes and taxied down the road, relieved to find it empty, and turned at the bottom. By the time she'd worked through the estate and reached the dual carriageway, her shoulders relaxed. It was a busy Saturday afternoon and she merged into the blur of traffic.

The supermarket car park was clogged. With no spaces anywhere near the front and none in the parent and child area, she had to drive to the far end to park. Jakub fought against going into the trolley and at one point she thought he might scream and attract attention, but she managed to find a soft book in the back of the car to divert his attention.

As she crossed the threshold, dark glasses still covering her eyes, she blended in, another mother out grocery shopping with her child. Her photo hadn't been in the newspaper, so it would only be local residents of Collingtree Park that would possibly recognise her. And right now, Collingtree Park and Meadowbrook Close felt as though they were on the other side of town, even though they were less than a mile away.

Monika strolled up and down the aisles, collecting items, placing them in the trolley. For the first time she felt an ounce of the tension of the last few days trickle out of her shoulders. She picked up packets and tins, examining the labels, the simplicity of the experience temporarily cleansing her of the sadness that had dogged the last few days. It was a moment out of life, a welcome hiatus.

She pushed into the baby aisle. Smells of cotton wool and talc and scented nappy bags filled the air. Jakub, who'd long since lost interest in his book, pointed at a row of colourful teethers, hanging off the edge of a promotional side rack. Absentmindedly she grabbed one and passed it to him, not flinching as he shoved it straight into his mouth. Something she would never normally do, but today she needed to keep him quiet. The less attention they attracted the better.

By the time she reached the tills, Monika was more relaxed than she'd felt in days. She couldn't erase the past; the gaping hole of Cameron's death still sat there, a constant reminder of the indelible change to her life. But for a short time, she'd managed to push the pain and struggles to the side, and she began to realise just how suffocating it had been.

She busied herself with packing everything away in bags and working through in her mind what she could rustle up with the ingredients she'd bought for dinner. Perhaps she'd make a lasagne. Oskar would enjoy that, it was his favourite.

Monika had inserted her card into the pay machine when she heard a voice behind her. 'Oh, no. The bag's split. Could you get me another?'

She froze, desperately hoping she was mistaken when it sounded again, 'No, that's fine. I'll have the same.'

Monika's heart plunged into the depths of her stomach as her suspicions were confirmed. The strong tone with the hint of an Australian accent – it was Janine, her neighbour from across the close. They'd met at Amanda and Jack's BBQ, where Janine told Monika all about how they'd emigrated to England with her husband's job and moved into the close when the houses were first built, having her pick of the plots which is why she had the best rear-view over the golf course beyond. 'How nice it will be to have another baby nearby,' she had said, fussing over Jakub. Afterwards, every time Monika walked down the close with the pushchair, or ventured out into her front garden, Janine would be there – admiring Jakub's clothes, his dark curly locks, how much weight he'd put on. And once she started chatting it was near on impossible to get away.

Monika took a deep breath and pressed her pin number into the card machine. She could hear the sound of the blood rushing through her ears. The shopping was packed in the trolley. If she was quick she could slip out without being noticed.

'It's declined.' The sales assistant cut through her thoughts. Her tone was harsh and too loud for her petite frame.

Monika looked at her, confusion turning to apology as she battled to put her card in again. 'I'm sorry. I must have used the wrong number.'

'Monika!'

She ignored the call behind her, half hoping Janine's attention would be distracted elsewhere, lifted her sunglasses onto her head to make sure she could see the buttons clearer, and keyed again, quicker this time. The machine flashed up 'approved' as a hand rested on her shoulder.

Monika jumped, and cursed her frayed nerves.

'Monika, it is you! I thought so.' Janine looked back at Jakub and gently cupped his chin. 'I'd recognise those cheeks anywhere.' When she turned back to Monika, her face crumpled, deep creases forming in the folds around her eyes. 'How are you feeling, darling? We've been so worried about you.'

This was the question she'd been dreading. How was she supposed to feel? Grief-stricken, sick? In truth, she felt nothing right now, her insides empty. The days merged together, her mind working automatically, as a separate entity, programmed to channel what little energy she had into sorting out her children. With Cameron gone, she'd forced herself to resist feeling. Because when she started to feel, let things sink beneath the surface, she knew she'd be in grave danger of imploding.

But nobody wanted to hear that. They didn't want to hear her scream and holler about the unfairness of the situation imposed on her, didn't want to hear about the tight jacket she woke up in every morning. So, Monika buried her thoughts and answered the only way she could muster. 'I'm okay, thanks.' She tried to push away, indicating an end to the conversation, but Janine wasn't going to be dismissed easily.

'I'm surprised to see you here after what you've been through,' she continued. The eyes of the shop assistant and those of everyone at the tills nearby were now on her. Prying eyes, pausing to watch and wonder what 'she'd been through'. There wasn't even a queue behind to save her.

'I have to keep going. For the children.'

'Of course, you do. But we can help. You look so pale.'

Monika swallowed and nudged the trolley, an action that would usually cause even the most thick-skinned of people to move. It had the desired effect as Janine reversed. An assistant bustled up to the till beside them. 'Here we are, madam. We've got your rice,' she said to Janine, holding up a bag as if it was a winning lottery ticket.

Taking advantage of the distraction, Monika edged forwards causing Janine to automatically step aside.

'Ah, thank you,' Janine said. She switched back to Monika who was hooking her handbag on the edge of her trolley and grabbed hold of her arm. 'Wait for me by the entrance, will you? I'll help you lift those bags into your car.'

Monika nodded and moved away. Her pace quickened as she reached the exit, so much so that Jakub squealed in delight as she raced out to the car. She wasn't prepared to discuss Cameron's case with a neighbour she hardly knew. She drew a ragged breath. Although right now there was something else bothering her, blotting out the Janines of this world. She'd thought she could slip out in sunglasses, incognito. But if she was that easily recognised, if people started to pick her out in a crowd, it reinstated her vulnerability. It wouldn't be too long before the press found her. When would this be over? She flung the bags into the boot, tucked Jakub into the car, her fingers fumbling with the straps on his car seat and fled the car park.

46

Sometimes the lines between right and wrong blurred. Beth was wary of Nick's caution as she passed the services heading north on the M6 later that day. Sara Swift was a tricky customer. Her past had not only toughened her, but worn her down, leaving an abrasive edge. When Beth persevered and probed beneath that harsh exterior, she found a woman with vulnerabilities whose life had been turned upside down by the events of the past week. A woman who wanted the best for her children. Since her training, she'd attended a couple of the family liaison officer network meetings, where other trained officers got together and talked through the highs and lows of their role. Many of them talked about visiting the families afterwards; it was difficult not to get close and build a bond when you spent so much time with people in their darkest hours. But this wasn't about becoming attached, more an underlying responsibility.

Freeman had met their minimum requirements by phoning and updating her on the charge, contacting Cheshire force and requesting a welfare visit. But with current policing cuts, the family of the victim of a case from another force would be low priority. Even if they did visit,

Sara didn't know them and would probably turn them away at the door. Victim Support would be alerted, but again it was unlikely they'd make it over the threshold. Sara had been through so much in her adult life; she was constantly let down – by her family, by Cameron, by Yvonne – and she didn't accept help easily. Beth's training reiterated the point, time and time again: ensure victims' families are offered the right support. Warren had visited Monika to update her on the case, advise her of the charge. Surely Sara deserved the same treatment, even if it was only a welfare call to persuade her to accept some of the support offered.

For a brief second, she considered calling it into the station, wary of Freeman's harsh words about her visit to Birmingham the other day. But he wouldn't approve of her going behind his back either. No. She glanced at the clock on the dash. It was almost lunchtime. She was less than an hour away. It wouldn't be too difficult to check on Sara, give her all the necessary assurances, and then hotfoot it back for the evening out tonight.

Beth rang the doorbell of 12 Knighton Lane and waited. It was early afternoon and the front of the house was in full sun, the breezeless air heavy and clammy. A rivulet of sweat trickled down her neck. She looked around the driveway and rang again, shifting from foot to foot when she heard something. A faint whisper. She angled her head, concentrated hard. Yes, definitely a whisper. The words played on the periphery of her hearing, barely perceptible. Not enough to make out what was being said, but enough to decipher it was a child's whisper. Sara was a bolshie woman, with a quick temper and a sharp tongue. But, from what Beth had witnessed, she was a good mother. She surely wouldn't leave her girls in the house alone.

Beth rapped the front door with her knuckles. More whispers. Louder this time. Footsteps slapped the tiled flooring.

The chink of metal was followed by the sound of a bolt screeching as it drew back, and the door opened. Beth looked down at Zoe's sleek cheeks. Wisps of dark hair had escaped from the hair tie at the nape of her neck and hung messily around her face. Beth stooped slightly, rested her hands on her knees and smiled. 'Hello,' she said. 'Is Mummy home?'

The child backed away, twisting her body around the edge of the door frame, leaving only half of her face visible.

'Who is it?' Beth recognised Sara's rasp in the voice that called from beyond.

Beth and the child exchanged a look. Neither answered, as if they were playing a game.

'Zoe. Who is it, darling?' The voice grew louder, and Sara Swift appeared on the stairs, barefooted in a flowing vintage dress. 'What happened to you?' she asked Beth as she approached.

Beth remembered the bruise on her cheek. No wonder the child had backed away. 'Oh, it's nothing. Looks worse than it is.'

Sara pulled a disbelieving face. 'Is there some more news?'

'Not exactly. Can I come in?'

Sara's face hardened. She raised her hand, shielding her eyes from the blistering sunlight that streamed into the hallway. 'We were about to go out.'

'It won't take up much of your time.'

Sara inhaled and pulled her daughter back, wrapping her arm around her shoulder protectively. Staunch. For a moment the two women stood there, the child watching them eye each other. Until Sara puffed out her cheeks, exhaled a huge sigh, and stood aside.

It was cooler in the house but just as sticky. Beth followed them into the front room where Amy sat on the floor, surrounded by a collection of tiny dolls in various states of dress. She continued her game, muttering under her breath as she moved the figures around in front of her; the source of the earlier whispers.

'Zoe, take your sister upstairs a moment,' Sara instructed.

'There's no need,' Beth said, but Sara ignored her comments, her face stiffening as she looked at her daughters.

'May I?' Beth motioned to the sofas after the children had left. On Sara's sombre nod, she took a seat. Sara sat across from her and smoothed her dress. Apart from the change in clothes, they were in exactly the same positions they had been the other day, when there were still so many question marks over the investigation. When Beth was on duty, still attached to the case. The irony was not lost on her.

She placed her bag on the floor beside her. 'I understand DCI Freeman phoned you yesterday to advise you we'd made an arrest?'

'He did. I saw it on the news last night too.'

'I wanted to come up here today to make sure you understand the charge and are fully updated with the investigation.' Sara raised a brow but said nothing. Beth took that as a cue to explain the charge in as much detail as she was publicly able.

'What about the gunman?'

'The DCI is hoping Sherwood's associations will lead us to him. But this is a major breakthrough,' Beth said with as much assurance as she could muster. 'Sherwood had a clear motive to order an attack on Cameron.' She leaned forwards. 'How are you doing?'

It was a while before Sara answered. 'What do you think?' She shook her head, looked away again. 'The police came to see me this morning.' Her voice was distant.

'Oh?'

'They wanted to talk about my relationship with Anthony Mullins.' Her eyes filled. 'You told them, didn't you?'

'I was obliged to pass along any possible connections.' A muscle flexed in Sara's cheek. 'What did they want to know?'

'My movements since coming back on Tuesday. When I last saw Anthony. That sort of thing.'

'They're tying it all up. It's routine.'

'I still can't understand it. I mean he had no reason, gave no indication.' She sniffed and wiped her nose with the back of her fingers. 'What is it about me? Rajinder committed suicide. Cameron was killed. Now Anthony takes his own life. Three men I've been close to, all gone.'

Her shoulders hunched, and the tears started to flow. Beth threw caution to the wind, moved in beside her and hugged her tight. However difficult and manipulative Sara Swift was, she'd been through so much in her life, and now she not only had to come to terms with her loss, but also carve out a future for herself and her girls. Even Yvonne, her main source of support, hadn't turned out to be the loyal friend she initially appeared.

Beth wasn't sure how long they sat there. A clock chimed in the dining room next door. Sara raised her head and glanced out of the window, her eyes swollen and red. Slowly she spanned the room, brushing the cards that littered every flat surface. 'You thought I'd organised this,' she said, resting her gaze on Beth. 'I felt it after your first visit. You thought I'd arranged for my own partner, the father of my children, to be killed. If only I'd had the guts.'

'What do you mean?'

'The lies, the infidelity, the cheating. You think I didn't know?'

'You said you didn't know about Monika.'

'Not Monika. That bloody floored me. The thought that he'd made a new home with a new family. That my children had stepbrothers and didn't even know. No, he excelled himself there.'

'Were there many others?'

'Plenty of them. Cameron was all smiles and charm for the first couple of years. He couldn't do enough for me. I thought I'd finally found my glimmer of happiness until my children were born and my life was taken over by babies and routine. He felt left out and pouted, like the neglected only child.'

'When did you first find out he was cheating?'

She pulled her face southwards, injecting a sharp edge to her voice. 'I'm not sure exactly. A year or so after Amy was born, I guess. He'd always travelled with his work, but he was away from home more often. And when he was back he was distracted, less attentive. He declined dinners and social events we were invited to, we went out less. Sometimes he'd arrive home the morning after he was expected and complain a meeting had overrun or he'd been sitting in traffic.' Her nostrils flared. 'He always had an answer for everything. Laughed it off. Said I was being paranoid. But one day I found a false nail while emptying the contents of his trouser pockets for washing.' Her eyes switched to the side. 'Lilac with a row of diamond studs on the tip.'

'What happened?'

'I confronted him. I'll never forget that evening.' A bitter smile played on her lips. 'I put the girls to bed early, much to their dismay, and sat in this very chair.' She turned her head from one side to another. 'I was seething. I watched the front window, waited for him to come home from the golf club. It was after 9 p.m. when he arrived. He marched in, dropped his golf bag in the hallway as he always did, and mocked me for sitting in the dark. He even bent down to kiss my forehead, but I ducked away and stood, facing him, waving the nail in front of his face. Triumphant that I'd finally been proved right. Expecting him to apologise and assure me it wouldn't happen again. Or make up some inane story as to how the nail found its way into his pocket.'

Sara's face darkened. 'But he just stared back at me and said, "If you don't like it, you know where the door is." The following morning, he left early for another business trip. I considered leaving, even packed a bag for the girls and me. But where would I go? I knew Yvonne would take us in, but I couldn't stay there indefinitely. I didn't work and, apart from the allowance Cameron gave me, I had no means to support us in the short term.' She gave a shudder. 'I lived in a dingy flat before I met Cameron, with a broken venetian blind that clattered against the front window because it didn't close properly, and mould crawling up the bedroom wall. I couldn't take my girls somewhere like that. I wouldn't.

'So, I kept my mouth shut, turned a blind eye. Ignored the lipstick marks on his shirt, the perfume on his jacket. I stopped questioning him about where he was staying, what he was working on, and he stopped telling me. When he was away, he was working, or networking if it was a holiday – well, that's what I told the girls. It wasn't easy, but I couldn't see another way out.' Her features softened, a faraway look on her face. 'Then I met Anthony and it didn't bother me so much. He was so gentle and caring, so different to Cameron.'

The patter of feet running across the floor above broke the silence. The girls were getting restless. 'Would you like a glass of water?' Beth asked.

Sara nodded. 'Let my girls down please. I don't want them shut away.'

The girls were sitting on the stairs, peeking through the banisters when Beth opened the door. She smiled at them both, opened the door wider and indicated for them to rejoin their mother.

47

Beth padded into the kitchen. She was relieved she'd made the decision to come; Sara clearly needed someone to talk to. Now all she had to do was to persuade her to speak with Victim Support who could help her in the upcoming days and weeks. The girls' voices twittered from the front room as she found a glass, filled it with water. She was considering texting Nick to tell him where she was when a knock sounded at the front door.

Beth stilled. Sara had said they were getting ready to go out when she arrived. She hadn't mentioned she was expecting visitors.

The sound of quick breaths was followed by shrieks as Zoe and Amy raced to the front door in a scatter of laughter. It rattled as they pulled it open, still chuckling.

'Who is it?' Sara called through from the front room. When no reply came, Sara's voice grew louder. 'Girls, who is it?' Beth could hear her in the hallway now. She approached the kitchen door, was about to swing it open when she heard Sara gasp.

'What are you doing here?' Sara said, a trembling undertone to her voice. Beth pressed her face to the crack in the doorway. A man was on the doorstep. Only the edge of his stature was in her vision, but she could see enough to identify he was Asian and of medium height. Her mind raced. Sara had said her brother and mother were in India. Had someone come over to visit?

Sara made to shut the door in his face, but he was too quick for her. He thrust out an arm, pushing the door back on its hinges. His mouth curled into a bitter smile. 'You thought you'd got away with it, didn't you?'

Sara stepped back. Short, jagged movements. Pushing her girls behind her. He moved into the hallway. That was when Beth spotted the gun.

Beth held her breath and pulled back further behind the door to ensure she wasn't seen. He held the gun high, tilted it towards the front room. Sara obeyed his command, shuffling through, her arms still wrapped around her girls. Beth ducked back and held her breath a second. When she looked again, they were gone. The door to the front room was left open. He must have assumed her Mini, still parked on the drive, belonged to Sara because he clearly didn't realise Beth was there.

She scooted back behind the door. Who was that? The look of sheer horror on Sara's face was mixed with familiarity. She knew him.

'You thought you'd got away with it.' His words sliced into Beth with a grave sense of foreboding. Cameron's killer was still at large. Had Sara been involved in his death all along? She certainly had motive, if her accounts of their life together were to be believed. Perhaps she'd been involved in the money scam too, realised it was going wrong and organised Cameron's death. Or maybe she'd double crossed them, and the killer thought there was money to be recovered there.

Beth moved back to the door. The few beats that passed felt like long minutes. She dug her hand in her pocket for her mobile phone when Sara's voice filtered through from the front room. 'Please! I have children.'

The voice that responded held a gravelly undertone. 'You should have thought of that before.'

A high-pitched scream followed. One of the girls. 'Tell them to shut up,' he said.

Beth searched her pocket. And the other. Where was her phone? Her stomach plummeted. It was still in her bag in the front room.

She cursed. Her training drummed into her. Whenever you are on duty, keep your phone on your person for emergencies. Except she wasn't on duty today. She'd visited in her own time. And she hadn't retrieved her phone from her bag when she arrived.

Beth glanced frantically around the kitchen. Sara's landline was also in her front room. With no phone, she had two choices: either sneak up on the gunman, attempt to disarm him, or break out and get help. She was torn. She didn't want to leave Sara and the girls. But if she failed to disarm him, she would put them all at risk. The best she could hope for right now was to escape. As soon as she'd raised the alarm, she'd come back for them.

She darted to the back door and rested her hand on the handle. It was locked. She cursed again, her eyes scanning the kitchen for the key. She crept around until she noticed a small wooden cabinet beside the cooker and hooked it open. Bingo! A row of keys hung before her. She worked her way through, selected one that looked as if it might fit and rushed back to the door, inserting it into the lock.

She didn't see the black and white cat climb in, wasn't aware of its presence beside her. Until the cat flap snapped back, a noise reverberating through the house. Beth jerked forwards. She couldn't stop. Not now. The key was in the door, she made to turn it, when a gravelly voice rang out behind. 'What do we have here?'

48

It was shortly after 2 p.m. when the call from Cheshire major crime unit came through. Nick was finishing up, planning to hotfoot back to Beth's for a quick nap before the festivities later. He was sitting back in his chair, hands behind his head, stretching his elbows wide while he read through his report, when Pete called across the office, 'Sarge, there's a call for Beth from Cheshire major crime. Is she contactable?'

Nick finished up the last dregs of coffee in his mug before he replied, 'What's it about?'

'Something to do with Sara Swift.'

Nick's stomach twisted. He hoped this wasn't a bad omen. 'I'll take it,' he said.

His stomach dipped further when the caller introduced himself as Detective Chief Inspector Carl Redgrave.

'Hello, Beth's not here right now. You're speaking to Nick Geary, her sergeant. What can we do for you?'

'Your detective chief inspector contacted us about an incident in Alderley Edge, an Anthony Mullins. He wondered if it might be linked to your enquiry. He asked me to contact a DC Beth Chamberlain if I needed any details.'

Nick wracked his brains. He recalled reading Beth's report about her visit to Sara Swift and the death of her boyfriend locally. 'Yes, I remember,' he said. 'The suicide. He was linked to one of the families in our case. I can give you their details, if that would help?'

'Ah. That's just it. I'm afraid it's not suicide. Right now, it's looking more like murder.'

'What? I thought he'd hung himself in his bathroom?'

'That's where his ex-wife found him. But when we had a chance to take a closer look, the chair he would have used to get him into the required position was too far away from the body. It would have been awkward for him to kick it in that direction. Our pathologist confirmed our suspicions when he examined him yesterday afternoon and told us the ligature marks on his neck don't match the rope of the noose he was hanging from. It appears somebody killed our Mr Mullins and strung him up afterwards to make it look like suicide.'

Nick pinched the bridge of his nose. 'Right. I'm not sure how much we can help you there though, other than give you the contact details of Sara Swift. Beth met with her the day she received the news of Anthony Mullins' death. She was quite distressed, and said they'd been having an affair.'

'We've spoken with Sara Swift already. I wanted to check out the details of the case you've been working on.'

'How do you mean?'

'I understand you've made an arrest for conspiracy to murder and the killer is still at large?'

Concern wrapped around Nick as he explained the assassination type killing of Cameron Swift and gave the chief inspector an overview of their case.

The chief inspector took a moment to digest the information before he said, 'Is it possible Mullins could be linked to your enquiry, your victim or the organised crime leader you've arrested?'

Nick clicked a few keys. 'That name hasn't come up in the course of our enquiry. Well, not until Beth visited Sara on Thursday. What are you thinking?'

'Is it possible Sherwood's still giving orders from the inside?'

Nick felt the blood drain from his head as he ended the call and placed the phone on the cradle. He thought about the concerns Beth raised with him last night, the concerns she had reiterated in the conference room that morning. The killer was still at large. Freeman was pretty sure it was a contract killing; the file would be kept open, but it was unlikely they'd ever apprehend the perpetrator. Sherwood had denied all allegations and gone no comment. Could it be possible they were so keen to charge, so keen to reassure the public they'd caught the man responsible, they'd overlooked the possibility that the killer wasn't working with Sherwood? Yes, the finances didn't add up. Yes, Sherwood had a motive and had made threats. But what if they were wrong? Perhaps Sherwood planned to kill Swift, but someone else got there first. Someone close to the family.

Nick grabbed his mobile and called Beth. She'd been unconvinced of Sherwood's guilt, made a good point questioning why he would send the Twitter message. A point he'd pushed aside in the exhilaration of making a charge. He cursed when it went to voicemail and pressed redial. Where was she?

49

'Police,' Beth said, raising her hands above her head. She surveyed the slight build of the man in front of her: the plaid shirt tucked into his jeans, the grubby laces hanging out of his Converse. 'Please put down the weapon.'

The face that returned her stare was taut, unmoved. Until it broke. The ensuing cackle chilled her to the bone. Just as quickly it tightened again. 'This gets more interesting,' he said. He nudged the gun at the door, indicating for her to move into the front room.

'I asked you—'

'Move!'

The sharpness in his tone made her stomach clench but she was careful not to show it. A musty aroma wafted up to meet her as she walked up the kitchen and past him. The nose of the gun dug into her back. He followed her into the hallway.

Sara was beside the window when they entered the front room. Amy was on the ledge. Zoe held the frame as she attempted to haul herself through the gap. Sara darted in front of them, trying to shield their futile attempt at escape.

The man didn't speak, didn't make a single sound. Instead he gave Beth a hard shove and pointed the gun up.

The blast reverberated around the room, rooting everyone to the spot.

Zoe screamed. Sara folded herself around her children, tremors running through her body.

He finally spoke, his voice squeezed through tight teeth. 'Get them down. Now!'

Sara jumped, her breaths coming hard and fast as she lifted each of her children to the floor.

'Right. Everyone on the sofa.'

Sara obeyed his command, grabbing the hands of each child, dragging their ragdoll bodies across to the sofa. They crashed into the cushions.

He pushed Beth again, indicating for her to join them, and waited until they were all in situ.

'Place all phones on the table in front.'

Beth pulled her bag towards her and scrabbled inside. Her fingertips brushed the smooth screen of her phone. She feigned a search of the side pockets with her right hand, while blindly trying to work her security code with her left. If she could at least make contact… She swiped once, twice. One last try when, 'Now!' His eyes bore into her. She was out of time. She pulled the phone out of the bag. It tapped the hard surface as it landed beside Sara's.

She held up a reasoning hand. 'You don't have to do this.' He ignored her. 'Whatever it is, I'm sure we can sort something out,' Beth continued.

'What? Like life imprisonment?'

'Let the family go,' Beth said, leaning forwards,

desperately trying to close the gap between them. The closer she was, the more chance she had to disarm him somehow.

'They're not going anywhere.' He flicked his gun, stopping her in her tracks.

'Look, there are police officers on their way as we speak. Let them go, and you and I can talk, as adults.' He stared at her a moment, surveying her. Beth swallowed. 'You can keep the gun if you like.'

'No.'

'It would be much easier if—'

'I said, no.'

Beth glanced at the window in the vague hope the sound of the gunshot might attract attention. But the predatory look in the eyes of the man in front of them made her heart pound her chest. He wasn't troubled about the sound of the gunshot. He hadn't even bothered to close the window. He'd lost all connection with reality.

The sofa squeaked as Sara pulled her children close. 'What are you doing here, Jagdeep?' The words stuttered out of her mouth.

'I think you know the answer to that question already, don't you, Sara?'

Beth's mind reeled. The look that passed between them chilled her to the bone. She recalled the name from the coroner's file on Rajinder Sidhu. Jagdeep was the name of his brother. How was he involved in Cameron's death? And what was Sara's part in it all?

'What do you want?' Sara whispered.

'What do I want? Hmm. That's an interesting question.'

He drew out the final sentence, enjoying the sound of the words playing in his mouth. 'What did my brother want when he came to visit you last year?'

Sara's face crumpled. 'You're looking for money?'

'Money won't bring my brother back.'

'What then? Please, Jagdeep. I have children.' The desperation in her voice was heart wrenching.

'You don't deserve them.' They all ducked as he swung the gun around the room. 'You don't deserve any of this. Look at you, playing the grieving widow in your swanky house, surrounded by cards of condolence. These people don't care about you. Nobody cares about you.' A line of spittle flew from his mouth. 'You're vermin. You take people in, drain them dry, and when everything's gone you move on.' He cocked his head. 'Not unlike your dead partner actually.'

'I don't know how I can help you.'

He scoffed. 'I'm not looking for your help. I don't want anything from you. You killed my brother.'

Sara shook her head, short jerking movements. 'I-I didn't. Rajinder killed himself.' She looked across at Beth. 'I only found out the day before yesterday.'

'Because of you.' He drew out the words, enunciating every syllable. 'You ruined him. Humiliated him in front of his family, his community.'

'I left London nine years ago.'

'But you've seen him since then, haven't you?'

'He only came here once.'

'Once was enough.' He paced the floor. 'Oh, you hid yourself well. It took him years to track you down. Years of people laughing behind his back, laughing behind all our backs.' She cowered as he closed in on her, a sneer curling his lip, exposing a line of yellowing teeth. 'My father died less than a year after you left. Can you imagine what it was like for my mother, living in a close-knit community where people whispered about her behind the backs of their hands, watching her son's slow demise while grieving for her husband? How could you do that to him? You were his wife!'

Sara flinched as his spit showered her. Zoe hid her head in her mother's shoulder.

He moved back, stood tall. 'Then you come up here, change your name, meet a rich man and make a whole new life for yourself. Did you think he'd never come looking? That we'd never find you?'

'You don't understand.'

'What don't I understand? That you left my brother in cold blood, broke him in front of everybody he holds dear? And when he finally tracked you down, he finds this?' He waved his arms wide. 'You were never good enough for him. We all tried to convince him before the wedding, but he wouldn't listen. And when you left, he vowed to find you. Tried for years. It crushed him. We all tried to help him pick up the pieces and move on. He was starting to recover, pull his life back together, when he received that solicitor's letter. It dredged it all back up. But it also gave him an address.'

'Please, Jagdeep. Don't do this.'

'Don't do it? It's already done. My mother died three months after Rajinder.' His eyes turned to dark pools, unfocused. 'I found her on her kitchen floor, a crumpled mass. A heart attack, the doctor said. But we all knew what she really died of – a broken heart. You didn't only break him, you broke all of us, one by one. I couldn't let you get away with that.'

Sara swallowed. 'Jagdeep, I never meant for any of this. You have to believe me.'

He ploughed on, ignoring her interruption. 'I found his emails after he died. The correspondence he had with your new partner. Learned about the money he was paid to keep his silence. To stop the old community finding you and showering more shame on your family in India. But still my mother wouldn't let me come to you. She said you'd get your comeuppance in the end. God would see to it. But now she's gone. And you're going to watch your family suffer before they die, just like she did.'

Zoe let out a shrill cry. Sara tightened her grip on her children.

He turned on his heel, dismissed the interruption. 'Tracing you wasn't enough. I wanted to learn about you, follow your journey. You did pretty well for a runaway. Created the perfect life. So, I set about taking it apart, bit by bit.'

His face eased. 'It's interesting what you find when you dig deep. Your dear partner and his beloved second family was a revelation. I enjoyed myself watching him travel from one to another, and soon realised that neither of you knew about each other. He was always going to be my first target, but it made the game all the more interesting.' He stared into space a moment, an actor commanding his audience. 'I could peel away the layers, one by one. Expose this perfect life you now lived and watch the events unfold vicariously from afar. And Anthony Mullins...' A cruel smile tickled his lips. 'He put up a good fight. It was an impressive end. Honourable even.'

Warm liquid seeped onto Beth's thigh. Amy's tiny frame quaked beside her.

'It was almost like directing a theatre production, watching it play out.' He drew a deep breath, spoke through his exhalation. 'But everyone knows that all performances have a finale.'

50

Beth's mind was reeling. Cameron didn't die because of his shady dealings, laundering money for local criminals. He was murdered as part of a personal vendetta. Rajinder's brother had set himself on a course to avenge his family's honour. And he was focused on executing his plan, whatever the consequences.

She stole another glance at the window, yearning for colleagues to be gathering outside, preparing to make contact. The child squirmed beside her on the sofa, sending a line of urine down its leg. Urgency and indecision beat Beth with their wicked sticks as she watched the pee pool on the floor. She had to do something.

'Eeny, meeny, miny, mo.'

He moved down the line, pausing to point the gun at each target. Sara elbowed her girls behind her. The look in his eyes chilled the back of Beth's neck. Thoughts whirled around her head. Nick. How she'd ignored him earlier that morning. He thought she was going to see Eden. If only she'd told somebody where she was going.

The chime of a clock nearby indicated two o'clock. The line of urine crept slowly across the floor.

'Eeny, meeny, miny, mo.'

The gun hovered on Zoe. Sara's face contorted. She shot out a hand. The laugh that emitted from his mouth was like being plunged into an ice bucket. Sara gasped, pushing herself in front of her daughter. 'Please, don't hurt her.'

At the last minute he changed his mind. A brief flick of the wrist, switching the gun to Amy. He'd chosen the youngest, barely a month from her fifth birthday. The air in the room tightened. Sara wailed.

Jagdeep gave a menacing smile. He was clearly enjoying himself.

Guilt peeled away the layers of Beth's conscience. This was a scene no child should ever have to endure. She thought of her mother, risking her life, racing through the traffic to save others. The image was replaced with Lily, poised to dive into the pool, her young face taut with concentration. Amy had her whole life in front of her. She couldn't allow this to happen. But she couldn't rush at him either. One bullet and she'd be gone, unable to save the others.

Nobody saw the cat slink in through the gap in the doorway. Until it leapt onto the back of the other sofa. It caught Jagdeep by surprise. He turned. Beth took advantage of that split second to hurl herself at him.

Pain splintered her brain, tiny fragments spreading through her consciousness. For a moment everything was still, like somebody had pressed the pause button. They toppled over onto the sofa. She had hold of the forearm with the gun and, with all her might, was pushing it away. The sofa juddered, tipped back, and crashed to the floor. The cat squealed and scurried away. The room swirled as they scrabbled across the floor. Still Beth couldn't let go of his arm. She wanted to call to Sara for them to make a run for it, but all her energy was consumed in holding back the gun. She drew up a knee, made for his groin, but he was too quick for her. A blow to her stomach hit the old bruise. Beth doubled over. But didn't release her grip.

Beth wasn't sure whether she heard the sound of the gun being fired or the scream first. A wailing grew in the background. The air in the room tensed. She had no idea who was hit, whether they were alive or dead.

Her grip loosened. She'd lost him.

He was back on his feet. A trainer headed for her face. She ducked back. The pain was excruciating as it connected with her shoulder. Another met her chest. She could taste blood.

A cruel smile looked down on her. Yellow teeth. Hot breaths. The gun pointed at her head. Her eyes were blurring. Someone had muted the volume. She clawed the floor for focus.

Her hearing returned to a cacophony of noise. Screams. Screeches. Howls. All merged into a din.

Her sight sharpened. Jagdeep was no longer standing over her. Now it was Sara. In her hand she held the pewter statue of the man with the shotgun, the Labrador at his feet, the one Beth had noticed on the dresser the first day she'd come here. The side of the statue was covered in blood.

She became aware of a crumpled mass beside her. Jagdeep. His eyes were closed. Instinctively, Beth reached out and grabbed his wrist. A faint beat pulsed against her fingers. 'Call an ambulance!'

Sara looked down at her, blood stains soaking the left side of her shirt. But instead of dropping the statue and moving to the phone she heaved it higher. Beth could see the determination in her face. She turned back to Jagdeep. A line of blood trickled from behind his ear. One more blow and he'd be finished. She was tempted to leave Sara to it, let her finish him off. He'd subjected her to a cruel tirade of violence. Pointed a gun at her children. Yet something inside Beth cracked. It was wrong. To die now would be too easy.

Beth hauled herself between the limp body and the poised statue above. 'Call an ambulance. And the police. Now!'

Sara's eyes widened. She wavered, toppled forwards, and folded to the floor.

51

Beth could feel a throbbing nearby, pulling her from the depths. She opened her eyes and was dazzled by a bright light, forcing them closed again. Pain spiked her forehead. The throbbing wasn't nearby. It was inside her head.

She forced herself to open her eyes, blinking several times. The blur in front of her cleared to reveal a hospital room. Flashbacks of the scene in Alderley Edge entered her mind. Pain. Gun shots. Blood. So much blood.

The frightened faces of Sara Swift's children, huddled in the corner.

The police had arrived with the ambulance. Jagdeep's pulse was waning. They took him first. Another arrived for Sara. The stray bullet had caught her arm in the fracas. She'd lost a lot of blood, the shock causing her to faint. The children were uninjured thankfully, but they'd bear the mental scars of that afternoon for years to come. A final injection of adrenalin set Beth into action. She organised for social services to come and take the children into temporary care. She'd considered contacting Yvonne, the only person she could think of who the children knew. But Yvonne's involvement in the money laundering was still under investigation and although she'd never shown any propensity for violence and they could find nothing to link her to Cameron's death, after everything that had happened, she couldn't imagine Sara being comfortable leaving her children in Yvonne's care. By the time the scene was clearing, the pain in her head was starting to sear.

Nick had rushed up to Cheshire last night when the news broke. Indistinct images of him beside her bed moved in and out of her mind. She wasn't sure if she was dreaming at first. He'd told her he'd been alarmed by a phone call from Cheshire police and when he hadn't been able to reach her, he'd guessed she'd travelled to Cheshire to see Sara. In view of the question marks the Cheshire DCI placed over the Anthony Mullins case, he'd requested an urgent despatch to check on them all. If only they'd tried earlier, Beth thought. If only she'd had her mobile in the kitchen. But nobody could have known, nobody could have predicted what she was to face there. She'd read the coroner's file on Rajinder's death herself and there was nothing to indicate the family bore any malice towards Sara, or that they'd even seen her in years.

A shiver spiralled through her shoulders as she recalled Jagdeep Sidhu's menacing gaze. After his mother died, he'd set himself on a course to ruin Sara, but hadn't seen any merit in killing her immediately. Instead he'd taken time to watch, wait, and learn about her new life, then set about unpicking it, stitch by stitch. The Twitter message was intended as the beginning of a public exposé, part of a systematic plan intended to ruin every aspect of Sara's life and pull her family apart as he believed she had done to him. He wanted to draw attention to her through Cameron, torment her from afar as she learned about Cameron's other family, remove the only source of genuine love and friendship in her life by killing Anthony Mullins and making it appear a suicide. All a series of steps to make her suffer, eventually culminating in killing her children before he took his ultimate victim. Would he have killed himself if his plans hadn't been scuppered at the last minute by the coincidental presence of a police officer? They'd never know now.

If she closed her eyes she could still see the blood, puddling around his limp body. Was he still alive? She hoped so. Because he needed to face his punishment. The families deserved justice.

A single knock at the door. The sight of Eden and Lily brought a faint smile to her lips.

'You have to walk a mile to get a coffee in this place,' Eden said.

Beth blinked, desperately trying to clear the fug in her head. They'd hotfooted up to Cheshire to see her that afternoon. Their plastic chairs still sat beside the bed. She cursed herself for the intermittent dozing.

Lily sat herself down and swung her legs back and forth, one at a time, hands tucked into her lap.

'How are you feeling now?' Eden said to Beth, placing her coffee down on the bedside table.

'All right. It looks a lot worse than it is, believe me.'

'Do you want to watch my county final race?' Lily said.

'That's sounds like a great plan.'

The bruises in her stomach pulled as she pushed herself up the bed. Lily skipped around, waiting for her mother to set up the iPad and fast-forward the footage to Lily's freestyle. They gathered around to watch. By the end of the first length, it was tense. Beth's eyes were on her niece on the screen. She watched her arm lift, slice through the water and disappear. She jerked forwards, just in time to see the young girl surface from her tumble turn and race back up the pool. It was neck and neck, Lily and her opponent both pushing for the finishing line. 'Lily!' Beth exclaimed, jerking forwards again, then, 'Ouch!' as the bruise in her stomach tugged.

Lily placed a hand on her aunt's shoulder. 'It's okay, Auntie Beth. We can press replay.'

'I know.' Beth placed her hand over her niece's and screwed up her eyes. 'I wish the screen was bigger.'

'It's even tense when you know the outcome,' Eden said, balling the blanket in her hand as the race ended. Beth passed Eden and Lily a quizzical look.

'Wait a minute,' Eden said.

A blank scoreboard filled the screen. It flickered but stayed empty.

Beth winced. 'Oh, this is too much.'

'You were the one who wanted to watch the race before we gave you the result.'

Beth ignored her sister and hitched herself back up the bed. Coloured digits filled the screen. Her heart sank. Lily was in second place. It couldn't have been closer. 'Oh, honey. I'm sorry.' She turned to her niece and hugged her close. 'I thought you had it.'

'It's okay,' Lily said. 'I beat my personal best.'

'That's brilliant,' Beth said, biting back the tears that swelled her eyes. 'You did amazing. Even to make the county final at your age is a massive achievement.' She kissed Lily's head and waited for the child to sit up. 'I wish I could have been there.' She attempted a smile. She'd been sceptical about her niece seeing her face so battered, but the young girl seemed to accept the explanation that her aunt had been in an accident and made a play of mothering her.

'Me too. You'll come next year, won't you?'

Beth gave her a wink with her good eye. 'You try and keep me away.'

A hand thrust out and moved the iPad off the bed. 'Okay, people,' Eden said, 'that's enough excitement for one day.' She plumped up Beth's pillows. While Beth was grateful they'd made the journey up to the Cheshire hospital to see her, she wasn't enjoying being fussed over. At all. 'Somebody needs to rest.'

'I'm fine.'

Eden examined the gash on her forehead. 'You still need some rest.' Beth rolled her eyes as she tucked in the bedclothes around her. Finally, Eden sat back. 'Are you sure there isn't anything we can get you before we head off?'

'I'm sure.'

Lily excused herself to go to the toilet. A heavy silence hovered in her wake.

'Are you sure you're okay?' Eden said. 'You gave us such a shock.'

'I'm fine. The doctors are only keeping me in for observations because of the bang on the head. I should be out within a couple of days.' Beth squirmed in her bed. She could no longer bear the strain. Every time she'd tried to broach the subject of her sister's relationship, something else got in the way: a phone call, an interruption, Lily's presence. 'How long have you been seeing Kyle Thompson?'

A muscle twitched beneath Eden's right eye. 'I don't know what you mean.'

'Don't play games with me.'

'I'm not playing games. I'm not seeing Kyle. Well, not anymore.' Her eyes dropped to the floor.

'But you were?'

'It's none of your business.'

'On the contrary, it's exactly my business. I was taken off an enquiry because of your relationship with a known criminal and I didn't even know about it.'

'Yes, I heard. I'm sorry.'

'You heard?'

'Chris told me. He arrived at the house yesterday evening to tell us what happened to you.' She huffed. 'First time he's crossed the threshold in months and, after he delivered the news and told me you were safe, he decided to have a moan. He told me about your conversations.' There was pain behind her eyes when she lifted them. 'You had no right to get involved in my relationship.'

'Kyle's bad news,' Beth said gently.

'He's changed. He deserves a second chance.'

Beth recalled the intelligence reports back at the office, the links to Sherwood. 'Believe me, you don't have any idea what you were getting into.'

'Then tell me.' Eden was defiant. But Beth's lips were sealed. She was already paying a price for slipping up, mentioning an early start when they'd carried out their dawn raids. She wasn't about to repeat the error and give away confidential police intelligence. 'No, I thought not,' Eden said when she didn't reply. She folded her arms.

'This is serious, Eden.' Anger flared in Beth's chest. 'You

must have read the news reports when he went to prison last time. He was sent down for aggravated burglary. The woman was eighty-seven!' Eden looked away. 'Did you read what they did to her? It was well reported in the papers.' Beth didn't wait for an answer. 'They hit her over the head and threatened her life. All for a few hundred pounds she kept under the mattress. She had to go into a nursing home afterwards because she couldn't bear to go back home, for fear it might happen again.'

Eden flushed. 'Kyle wasn't in the house.'

'No, he was the lookout. Which makes him just as culpable as the rest of them.'

Eden swallowed. The muscle beneath her right eye twitched again.

'Why Kyle?'

'He's trying to turn things around. He's a good man.'

Beth shook her head. 'I thought you were better than this. What would Mum have said?'

'This has nothing to do with Mum. And it has nothing to do with you.'

'It has everything to do with me.'

'Well, you needn't worry about your reputation at work anymore because it's over. Anyway, you're a fine one to talk.' A sneer lifted the edge of her mouth. 'What about you, with your sergeant?'

Beth's stomach rolled. She hadn't told Eden about Nick because there'd been nothing to tell. It was casual. Nothing more. 'Nick is a friend.'

'Yeah, right. You can try that on Lily, but it won't wash with me. I've seen you guys together.'

'And?'

'Oh, come on, Beth. You're deluding yourself.'

'He's a friend,' Beth said firmly. But the suggestion sat uncomfortably. Especially after Chris's comments, only a few days earlier. She'd dismissed his remarks at the time, thought he was playing with her. But if Eden and Chris had made assumptions, or noticed something, maybe others had too. 'Anyway, this isn't about me. It's about you. About Lily.'

'Leave Lily out of this.'

'Lily can't be left out of this. Because if you don't sort out your life, you'll lose her.'

Eden stiffened. The door opened, and Lily wandered back into the room, her innocent steps oblivious to the harsh exchange.

'Get your things together, darling,' Eden said avoiding Beth's gaze. 'We need to get going.'

52

Later that afternoon, the mist in Beth's head was starting to clear when another knock sounded, and a familiar face appeared around the door frame. 'How are you feeling?' Nick said, returning her smile.

'All right. I'll be better when I get out of here.'

'Do you feel up to visitors?'

'Sure, come in.' She was surprised to see Freeman shuffle in behind him.

'Well, you certainly look better,' Freeman said awkwardly. She doubted that. She'd examined her face in a mirror when the nurse had woken her earlier. The lump on her cheek was like a golf ball, blooming from the fresh punches. Her lip was split, her left eye so swollen it only opened to a tiny crack and a stitched cut on her forehead resembled an upside-down smile. She'd been told some of the bruising on the rest of her body penetrated deep and would take weeks to go down.

'Thanks for coming to see me.' She pulled herself into a seated position while they moved into the chairs beside the bed. 'Any news on Sara Swift?' she asked.

'She's doing okay,' Nick said. 'The bullet clipped the

flesh on her right arm but didn't touch the bone thankfully. They're hoping to discharge her later.'

'That's great news.'

'It is. She's full of praise for you. Wouldn't stop talking about how brave you were.'

Beth shrugged it off. 'She was pretty brave too. How about Monika?'

'Warren went out to see her last night, after the news was confirmed. She's already been in contact with Sara to check on her. The two women are planning to meet up again soon.'

'Wow.' Her face turned grave. 'What about Jagdeep Sidhu?'

'Still in intensive care, but stable. We're hoping he'll pull out of the coma soon, so we can interview him.'

Beth's eyes turned to Freeman. She'd never seen him look so uncomfortable. 'How are things back at the office, sir?'

Freeman cleared his throat. 'Good. Sherwood's charges have been reduced to money laundering and the assault on you, but we've managed to keep him in custody and the CPS are pretty confident he'll get a decent sentence.'

'That is good news.'

He nodded. 'Are you sure you're okay, Beth? Everyone's been asking about you.'

'I'm fine. They're only keeping me in for observations. I'll be out of here in no time.'

His shoulders relaxed, but the stress still showed in his face. 'You've done a sterling job looking after the families on this one. Sergeant Geary told me about the trips you made to Monika's home in Northampton, and to Cheshire. It's a great start in the role, certainly something we can expand on at a later date. We just have to work on your communication skills. Next time you consider leaving the office on police business, I don't care who you're speaking to or who you visit, make sure you call it in, eh?'

The split in her lip stung as she attempted a full smile. 'You'll let me loose again soon then?'

Freeman didn't answer. He couldn't. He'd been forced to pass the details of her undeclared association with Kyle Thompson up the chain where it was referred to the Professional Standards Department. She knew it was routine. They needed to be sure she hadn't been compromised. But he couldn't give her any guarantees until they'd completed their investigation. 'We're all very proud of you, Beth,' he said.

'Thanks.'

The trill of a mobile filled the room. Freeman dug into his pocket, checked his phone and held it out. 'I need to take this.' He rested a hand on Beth's forearm. 'I'll see you later.'

'How is Eden doing?' Nick asked after Freeman had left. 'Chris insisted on being the one to go out and deliver the news to her about your incident last night.'

'She's okay. She was here earlier.' Beth shifted uncomfortably. Eden's remarks about a relationship with Nick bothered her. She thought they'd been careful. But if Eden had noticed something awry, had others too? What about her work colleagues? With Professional Standards already investigating her, she didn't need rumours circulating, putting her honesty and integrity into question.

He leaned over and gently kissed the split on her lip. The gesture was soft, tender. 'Are you sure you're okay, Beth?

You had me going for a while back there.' To her surprise, his eyes filled.

'I'm fine.' She pulled back and picked at the folds in the bedsheet. 'I think we need to cool things for a while.' His face fell. 'I'm sorry, Nick. But I'd rather keep this,' she pointed at him, then herself, and back again, 'whatever it is, between us. I can't afford for it to get out right now.'

He looked across at the door. 'Don't worry. Freeman hasn't got a clue.'

'Even more reason to keep a bit of distance.'

'I don't understand.'

'Look, I've already got Professional Standards on my back. It wouldn't look good if they discovered I was creeping around behind people's backs, sleeping with my sergeant.'

A muscle flexed in his jawline. 'It's not a disciplinary offence to have a relationship with a colleague.'

'It's not a good idea right now.' The hurt in his eyes caught her. She turned away, faced the wall. 'We need to take a break. At least until all of this is over.'

The chair squeaked against the floor as he stood. 'If that's what you want.'

Her face was still fixed on the wall when the door clicked closed behind him. She reached up and swiped a tear from her cheek.

Epilogue

The woman's heels clicked a staccato rhythm against the flagstone tiles. Her dark dress moulded over the curves of her breast and hips, nipping in at the knees, showing off her slender figure.

Sara Swift, oblivious to the crowds gathered in the tiny church, barely reached halfway down the aisle when she paused and looked back over her shoulder, peering from beneath an elegant net-veil that reached down from her box hat. She waited, craned her neck, the expression in her face easing as her two girls emerged in matching blocked cream and black dresses, their skirts swishing around their calves as they quickened to catch her up. The youngest reached for her mother's hand and they proceeded further down the aisle together.

They approached the front row where another woman stood and held out welcoming arms. With her dark hair neatly folded into a French pleat, Monika looked calm and relaxed. She was several inches shorter than Sara but carried the same elegance in her movements.

Beth fidgeted in the pew she'd squeezed herself into at the back, the wooden seat beneath her cold and unforgiving, and watched Monika fold her arms around Sara. The embrace was long and touching. When they drew back, they stared at each other, passing a subliminal message, before shushing and herding the girls into a pew beside Oskar who held baby Jakub in his arms. The children sorted, Monika guided Sara to a seat beside her.

Beth's gaze wandered. St Luke's was a small church, originally built in the 1100s to support the once village community of nearby Duston, before the town's expansion swallowed it up, and not designed for the droves pressing themselves inside on that September morning. The pews filled early, leaving late arrivals to stand at the back and spill into the aisles. Carved statues, punctuated by headstones, lined the walls. A kaleidoscope of colours streamed through the stained-glass windows, highlighting the dust motes that danced above them.

Beth had been surprised by the detailed nature of Cameron's will, his request for a traditional funeral and a Christian service, followed by a burial in the churchyard beside his parents. She'd never considered him a religious or spiritual person; his business associations and lifestyle certainly didn't suggest it. But there would be no pallbearers, no coffin today. Jagdeep Sidhu had admitted murder initially, an admission he rescinded later. With nothing to lose, he'd decided to fight, plead self-defence on the shooting in Cheshire and claim police coercion in the former admission of guilt with Cameron's murder. Now Cameron's body would be retained at the morgue, pending trial. A legal anomaly, in case the defence needed to clarify any of the wounds or request further examination.

Three weeks had passed since the incident in Cheshire, putting an end to their nightmare, and whether it was a desire to give friends and family the opportunity to lay Cameron's memory at peace, or the necessity to put this chapter in their life behind them, Beth wasn't sure, but Sara and Monika had decided to go ahead and arrange a memorial service. They seemed an unlikely alliance. Both women had alluded to Cameron's heroic qualities – he'd lifted them out of the grind of life, given them beautiful homes and families of their own. But he'd also controlled them, pushed them to the edge.

When Beth visited Sara last week, she had spoken about moving to Northamptonshire to be closer to Monika. With her relationship with Yvonne irrevocably broken, Beth suspected there was little to keep her in Cheshire. She surveyed them, huddled together in the pew. Two women putting aside their differences, for the sake of their children, and forging a relationship out of the worst possible circumstances. Hope bloomed at the prospect of some future happiness for them.

The vicar's robes flapped around his ankles as he emerged from the side of the font and approached Sara and Monika, taking time to speak to them and their children individually, before resuming his position at the front.

The service, with its hymns of 'Jerusalem' and 'The Lord's My Shepherd', seemed misplaced somehow. The vicar talked of Cameron being a good father, a shrewd businessman. There was no mention of the Cameron Swift that had emerged from their enquiries: the lying, conniving conman with dirty fingers in so many unpalatable pies.

It never ceased to amaze Beth how funerals eulogised people, pushing aside the faults of even the most unsavoury characters.

Freeman stood solemnly beside her, singing along brazenly to the hymns despite being tone deaf. He'd barely let her out of his sight since she'd returned to work this past week. Never a day passed when he didn't check on her like an overprotective father, the guilt over her injuries etched into the furrows of his brow – unlike Nick, who'd kept his distance in the office and been professional, perfunctory. When their shoulders brushed in the corridor an awkward uneasiness sat between them. Occasionally, she felt his eyes on her and the sadness behind them tugged at her. It was only ever meant to be casual, a fling, a bit of fun; an extension of their friendship. But during their break, she realised just how much she missed their time alone. The smell of his sporty aftershave. The way he tucked her hair behind her ear before he kissed her; the way he laughed at her stupid jokes. His impromptu visits. The erratic and unsociable hours of the job made it difficult to maintain regular friendships outside the force. During the past months, Nick had not only been her lover but also her friend, and she missed the closeness they'd shared.

Eden called or texted most days, but her tone was off, still aggrieved by the connection between her lover and the circumstances surrounding the murder case and wounded at being warned off by her ex-husband. Was she still seeing Kyle? She said not, but Beth couldn't be sure and had taken to driving past Eden's house on her way home of an evening to check to see if Kyle's car was parked on her sister's drive.

She was tied to Eden, for the sake of Lily if nothing else, but their relationship was strained, guarded.

The service ended. Sara and Monika led the procession out of the church, flanked by their children. The air was fresh outside, clean. Beth watched the two women float about expressing their gratitude to their guests, then said goodbye to Freeman and moved off towards her car.

Later that afternoon, Beth closed the door behind her and leaned against the wall, pressing her back against the cool plaster. For the past hour, she'd sat opposite the poker faces of a sergeant and inspector in the Professional Standards Department while they fired a barrage of questions at her: When did you first find out about your sister's association with Kyle Thompson? When did you last see Kyle? What was the level of your contact? All questions they'd asked before. But this time it was a formal interview and her answers were recorded. It was three weeks since she'd spoken of the possible compromise with Freeman, a week since she'd returned to work after the incident at Alderley Edge. Professional Standards had latched onto her association with a convicted criminal, however tenuous, and seemed set on digging deep.

Her heels clattered the stairs as she descended. PSD were tucked away in the far corner of the top floor of Wootton Hall HQ. She imagined the pointy faces of the sergeant and inspector standing at the window, fixing their hawk-like eyes on the officers passing through the courtyard below.

A draft funnelled along the corridor at the bottom, billowing her jacket, inducing a shiver. She was almost at the exit when she spotted a figure in the distance. It was Sergeant Andrea Leary.

Disquiet gripped Beth. Her involvement with the Swift case and the incident at Alderley Edge had been well talked about in the office since her return, and Andrea's discomfort at Beth's success in a role she considered her own was obvious.

Beth considered turning back. But that would take her towards the PSD offices.

Andrea slowed as she approached. 'Hi, Beth.' She lifted her head, gave a backwards nod, but her face was flat, and her disingenuous tone touched a nerve. Andrea glanced towards the staircase behind her. 'How'd it go?'

Beth didn't answer. She wasn't about to chew over the remnants of her interview with PSD with someone who'd gone out of their way to avoid her since she'd returned to the team. She pulled back her sleeve, viewed her watch. 'I have to be somewhere.'

'Of course.' Andrea shuffled aside for her to pass and continued up the stairs.

Beth didn't look back. As soon as she was out of the door, she passed the exit barrier and trudged up the drive, gulping lungfuls of fresh air. When she reached the offices at the top, she turned and surveyed the vista. It was only now she realised how fond she'd grown of the hum of the traffic from the dual carriageway, the view of the headquarters building across the sports fields. All part of the architecture that made up her workplace. Her breaths hitched. She turned on her heel, back towards the car park when she spotted a familiar face waiting for her.

'Hello, stranger.' Nick Geary was leaning against the

driver's door of her Mini, arms crossed against his chest. His face was solemn. 'How did it go?'

'Difficult to say. I answered all their questions. Again.' She sighed. 'They're looking into my old cases. It's almost as if they want to find something.' A siren rose and fell nearby. 'I saw Andrea as I left.'

Nick shrugged. 'They're interviewing anyone connected to Operation Hawthorn.'

'She didn't work on Operation Hawthorn.'

'She's back on the team now, clearing up the family liaison stuff, overseeing the file builders preparing everything for court. They'll be checking it's all in order.'

Beth looked back down the driveway. Something about the other woman's presence there unnerved her. The last thing she needed was for an aggrieved colleague to say something, a passing comment that might plant an element of doubt.

'Are you still operational?' Nick words pulled her back to the present.

'For the moment.' She tipped back her head, stared skyward a moment. 'What are you doing here, Nick?'

'I'm taking you for a drink.'

'I'm not sure that's a good idea.'

His mouth twitched. 'I'm still your sergeant. It's called supporting my team. Now get into the car, Beth.'

She eyed him a moment, then crossed to his Spider and climbed in. 'One drink couldn't hurt, could it?'

Acknowledgements

I have been privileged to spend time with some incredible people while working on this novel.

First, I'd like to thank Garry Liburd for the afternoon in Costa Coffee, explaining the role of a Family Liaison Officer and helping so much with research for Beth's character. I hope you enjoy your much-deserved retirement!

Also, Rajeet Loibl and her lovely family for giving up their time to provide a wonderful insight into Sikh culture, and Agata Dunliniec for the amazing evening at The Castle in Brixworth discussing Polish culture. All so interesting and absorbing. We could truly have gone on and on.

Gratitude goes to the late DC John Thorogood for his unrelenting assistance with financial investigations. Your sense of fun and laughter will be sadly missed.

For Darren Paterson for explaining tax and company rules, and former firearms officer, Andrew Tuff for explaining the ins and outs of using a Glock handgun. As usual, any errors or inconsistencies within the book are entirely mine.

Also, my paramedic brother, Derek Archer, to whom the book is dedicated, for advice on accident and emergency department procedures, and championing my writing right from the very beginning of this extraordinary journey. And to the lovely wardens at St Luke's Church in Duston who opened up one wet Saturday morning for me to have a look around. I hope you'll forgive me for a few liberties I have taken with the interior!

To my early readers, Ian Patrick and Rebecca Bradley, both former detectives and now brilliant crime writers themselves, who kept me in line with police procedure - I really appreciate your continuing friendship and support.

To Rhea Kurien and all the team at Aria Fiction who've been lovely and supportive to work with on *The Other Woman*.

Thanks also to Debi Alper, Emma Mitchell, Helen Baggott and Yvonne Betancourt for their help with the original version of this novel, *After He's Gone*.

One of the great things about writing books is the online community. The writers who keep me sane – you know who you are! The wonderfully supportive book clubs including Anne Cater and all at Book

Connectors; Shell Baker and Llainy Swanson at Crime Book Club; Tracy Fenton, Helen Boyce, Teresa Nikolic and all at The Book Club (TBC), David Gilchrist at UK Crime Book Club and Wendy Clarke and the gang at The Fiction Café Book Club. Also, the amazing reviewers and book bloggers, far too many to mention individually, who work tirelessly to spread the word about new books. I'm truly honoured to be part of such a lovely world.

So many friends have listened to early storylines, helped with cover art, proof read, talked through characters and generally offered a shoulder to lean on, most notably David and Lynne Anderson, Colin Williams, Emma Thompson, Stephanie Daniels, Martin Sargeant, and Philip and Abi Bouch.

Finally, to David and Ella. Living with a writer is never easy. You spend time with my characters, my ideas and plotlines daily, and accompany me on endless research trips. I'm sure I never say thank you enough!

About the Author

Jane Isaac lives with her detective husband and daughter in rural Northamptonshire, UK where she can often be found trudging over the fields with her dogs. Her debut, *An Unfamiliar Murder*, was nominated in the Best Mystery category in the eFestival of Words Best of the Independent eBook Awards 2013. The follow up, *The Truth Will Out*, was selected as the 'Thriller of the Month' by E-Thriller. com in April 2014.

Jane is the author of eight novels. Her latest series is based in Northamptonshire and features Family Liaison Officer, DC Beth Chamberlain.

Hello from Aria

We hope you enjoyed this book! If you did let us know, we'd love to hear from you.

We are Aria, a dynamic digital-first fiction imprint from award-winning independent publishers Head of Zeus. At heart, we're committed to publishing fantastic commercial fiction – from romance and sagas to crime, thrillers and historical fiction. Visit us online and discover a community of like-minded fiction fans!

We're also on the look out for tomorrow's superstar authors. So, if you're a budding writer looking for a publisher, we'd love to hear from you. You can submit your book online at ariafiction.com/we-want-read-your-book

You can find us at:
Email: aria@headofzeus.com
Website: www.ariafiction.com
Submissions: www.ariafiction.com/we-want-read-your-book

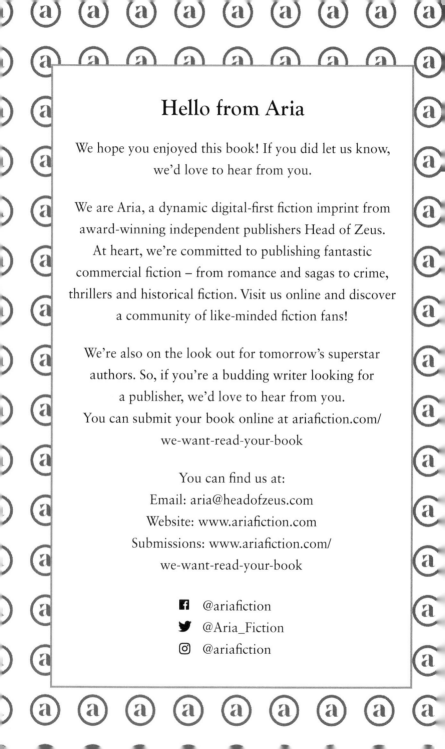

- ⓕ @ariafiction
- 𝕏 @Aria_Fiction
- ⓘ @ariafiction